# Rituals to Observe

# Rituals to Observe

STORIES ABOUT

*Holidays*

FROM THE
FLANNERY O'CONNOR AWARD
FOR SHORT FICTION

EDITED BY
ETHAN LAUGHMAN

THE UNIVERSITY OF GEORGIA PRESS
ATHENS

© 2019 by the University of Georgia Press
Athens, Georgia 30602
www.ugapress.org
All rights reserved
Designed by Kaelin Chappell Broaddus
Set in 9/13.5 Walbaum

Most University of Georgia Press titles are
available from popular e-book vendors.

Printed digitally

Library of Congress Control Number: 2019945880
ISBN: 9780820356594 (pbk.: alk. paper)
ISBN: 9780820356587 (ebook)

# CONTENTS

# ACKNOWLEDGMENTS

The stories in this volume are from the following award-winning collections published by the University of Georgia Press:

Sandra Thompson, *Close-Ups* (1984)

Molly Giles, *Rough Translations* (1985)

Gail Galloway Adams, *The Purchase of Order* (1988)

Carole L. Glickfeld, *Useful Gifts* (1989)

Dianne Nelson Oberhansly, *A Brief History of Male Nudes in America* (1993)

Alyce Miller, *The Nature of Longing* (1994); "Color Struck" first appeared in the *Los Angeles Times Magazine*

David Crouse, *Copy Cats* (2005); "Morte Infinita" first appeared in *Quarterly West*

Peter LaSalle, *Tell Borges If You See Him* (2007); "The Christmas Bus" first appeared in *Virginia Quarterly Review*

Peter Selgin, *Drowning Lessons* (2008); "My Search for Red and Gray Wide-Striped Pajamas" first appeared in *Glimmer Train Stories*

Hugh Sheehy, *The Invisibles* (2012); "The Invisibles" first appeared in *Kenyon Review* and then in *The Best American Mystery Stories* 2008

Jacquelin Gorman, *The Viewing Room* (2013)

Karin Lin-Greenberg, *Faulty Predictions* (2014)

Becky Mandelbaum, *Bad Kansas* (2017)

A thank you also goes to the University of Georgia Main Library staff for technical support in preparing the stories for publication.

# INTRODUCTION

The Flannery O'Connor Award for Short Fiction was established in 1981 by Paul Zimmer, then the director of the University of Georgia Press, and press acquisitions editor Charles East. East would serve as the first series editor, judging the competition and selecting two collections to publish each year. The inaugural volumes in the series, *Evening Out* by David Walton and *From the Bottom Up* by Leigh Allison Wilson, appeared in 1983 to critical acclaim. Nancy Zafris (herself a Flannery O'Connor Award–winner for the 1990 collection *The People I Know*) was the second series editor, serving in the role from 2008 to 2015. Zafris was succeeded by Lee K. Abbott in 2016, and Roxane Gay then assumed the role of choosing award winners beginning in 2019. Competition for the award has become an important proving ground for writers, and the press has published seventy-four volumes to date, helping to showcase talent and sustain interest in the short story form. These volumes together feature approximately eight hundred stories by authors who are based in all regions of the country and even internationally. It has been my pleasure to have read each and every one.

The idea of undertaking a project that could honor the diversity of the series' stories but also present them in a unified way had been hanging around the press for a few years. What occurred to us first, and what remained the most appealing approach, was to pull the hundreds of stories out of their current packages—volumes of collected stories by individual authors—and regroup them by common themes or subjects. After finishing my editorial internship at the press, I was brought on to the project and began to sort the stories into specific thematic categories. What followed was a deep dive into the award and its history and a gratifying acquaintance with the many authors whose works constitute the award's legacy.

Anthologies are not new to the series. A tenth-anniversary collection, published in 1993, showcased one story from each of the volumes published in the award's first decade. A similar collection appeared in 1998, the fifteenth year of the series. In 2013, the year of the series' thirtieth anniversary, the press published two volumes modeled after the tenth- and fifteenth-anniversary volumes. These anthologies together included one story from each of the fifty-five collections published up to that point. One of the 2013 volumes represented the series' early years, under the editorship of Charles East. The other showcased the editorship of Nancy Zafris. In a nod to the times, both thirtieth-anniversary anthologies appeared in e-book form only.

The present project is wholly different in both concept and scale. The press plans to republish more than five hundred stories in more than forty volumes, each focusing on a specific theme—from love to food to homecoming and homesickness. Each volume will aim to collect exemplary treatments of its theme, but with enough variety to give an overview of what the series is about. The stories inside paint a colorful picture that includes the varied perspectives multiple authors can have on a single theme.

Each volume, no matter its focus, includes the work of authors whose stories celebrate the variety of short fiction styles and subjects to be found across the history of the award. Just as Flannery O'Connor is more than just a southern writer, the University of Georgia Press, by any number of measures, has been more than a regional publisher for some time. As the first series editor, Charles East, happily reported in his anthology of the O'Connor Award stories, the award "managed to escape [the] pitfall" of becoming a regional stereotype. When Paul Zimmer established the award he named it after Flannery O'Connor as the writer who best embodied the possibilities of the short-story form. In addition, O'Connor, with her connections to the south and readership across the globe, spoke to the ambitions of the press at a time when it was poised to ramp up both the number and scope of its annual title output. The O'Connor name has always been a help in keeping the series a place where writers strive to be published and where readers and critics look for quality short fiction.

The award has indeed become an internationally recognized institution. The seventy-four (and counting) Flannery O'Connor Award authors come from all parts of the United States and abroad. They have lived in Arizona, Arkansas, California, Colorado, Georgia, Indiana, Maryland, Massachusetts, Texas, Utah, Washington, Canada, Iran, England, and elsewhere. Some have written novels. Most have published stories in a variety of literary quarterlies and popular magazines. They have been awarded numerous fellowships and prizes. They are world-travelers, lecturers, poets, columnists, editors, and screenwriters.

There are risks in the thematic approach we are taking with these anthologies, and we hope that readers will not take our editorial approach as an attempt to draw a circle around certain aspects of a story or in any way close off possibilities for interpretation. Great stories don't have to resolve anything, be set any particular time nor place, or be written in any one way. Great stories don't have to *be* anything. Still, when a story resonates with enough readers in a certain way, it is safe to say that it has spoken to us meaningfully about, for instance, love, death, and certain concerns, issues, pleasures, or life events.

We at the press had our own ideas about how the stories might be gathered, but we were careful to get author input on the process. The process of categorizing their work was not easy for any of them. Some truly agonized. Having their input was invaluable; having their trust was humbling. The goal of this project is to faithfully represent these stories despite the fact that they have been pulled from their original collections and are now bedmates with stories from a range of authors taken from diverse contexts. Also, just because a single story is included in a particular volume does not mean that that volume is the only place that story could have comfortably been placed. For example, "Sawtelle" from Dennis Hathaway's *The Consequences of Desire*, tells the story of a subcontractor in duress when he finds out his partner is the victim of an extramarital affair. We have included it in the volume of stories about love, but it could have been included in those on work, friends, and immigration without seeming out of place.

The stories in this volume all amount to something more than a celebration of the holidays that dot our calendars from month to month. Even though holidays represent a return to the familiar, these stories challenge our cultural understanding of holidays and lead us to question the traditional sentiment associated with them. However, the underlying rituals—which make us pause, feel, love, and act—remain in place. Not a single story in this anthology features a holiday as its main focus, yet the holiday provides vital scaffolding for each. Many of the stories display family tensions that heighten the unpredictability of an already fraught gathering. Some characters feel pressured to buy into a holiday's assigned emotion—fear on Halloween, gratitude on Thanksgiving—whereas experience leads them in another direction. Maybe it's a holiday's time of year, or the personal baggage with which it arrives. For whatever reasons, each holiday comes with its own distinct atmosphere. Each story complicates how we view the human observation of holidays and offers a nuanced understanding of related themes such as family and parenthood, travel, grief and mourning processes, and memory. More generally, holidays are days of observance, which provides us with opportunities for reflection and discovery.

Alyce Miller's "Color Struck" begins the volume's reflections on family by examining how the pressure of the observation of a holiday, in this case a family Thanksgiving dinner, changes a family dynamic and inspires thought about family obligations and identity. Its central character, Caldonia, a black woman, has recently given birth to an albino baby, and the Thanksgiving dinner is fraught with tension as the family leads her toward acceptance of her new child.

The other autumnal holiday, Halloween, also occasions reflection on family and identity, often through quasi-purgatorial experiences centered on fear. David Crouse's "Morte Infinita" explores how a daughter and her father, bound together by their mutual love for classic movie monsters, are emboldened by emulating the hideous strength of those very monsters. The young protagonist escapes Halloween's paralyzing horror by freeing herself from dependency on others. Hugh Sheehy uses the holiday to magnify the unease present in "The Invisibles," the story of a missing persons case. Sheehy taps into a raw fear that many teenagers—and many adults, for that matter—struggle against: being condemned to invisibility despite your best efforts to make yourself seen and understood. Karin Lin-Greenberg's "Faulty Predictions" follows two elderly roommates as they crash a nearby university's Halloween party on a hunch that a murder will soon take place. Before the night is through, connections form as one roommate makes discoveries about family and an unlikely friendship takes hold. In Jacquelin Gorman's "Permanent Makeup," nurse and multiple sclerosis patient Ellie leads a support group for women who have lost children. "Permanent Makeup" compels the reader to visualize Halloween, saturated with grotesquely cartoonish images of death, through the eyes of parents still reeling from the loss of a child.

The following two stories associate familial holiday gatherings with violence, vulnerability, and the ugly truths we would rather keep hidden. "Mother's Day," by Sandra Thompson, juxtaposes a Mother's Day dinner with memories of trauma, and Becky Mandelbaum's "Thousand-Dollar Decoy" begins with an accidental act of violence that disrupts a family Thanksgiving dinner and forces the protagonist to confront failings in his relationships.

In Peter Selgin's "My Search for Red and Gray Wide-Striped Pajamas," New York City becomes Steven's playground as he works through the grief of his father's passing by searching for a pair of pajamas similar to those his father had worn. The story ends during Christmastime in a mixture of both alienation and resolution. In Dianne Nelson Oberhansly's "The Uses of Memory," the wife and daughter of a dying man negotiate rituals associated with Halloween, Thanksgiving, and Christmas as they work through the memories evoked by the holidays.

Carole L. Glickfeld's "Useful Gifts" centers on the life of a young Jewish girl named Ruthie, the daughter of deaf parents, as she experiences Christmas at an affluent neighbor's home and gains new insight into her parents' frugality, as well as their deep love for her. Peter La Salle's "The Christmas Bus" examines family, attachment, and the vulnerabilities attendant upon holiday travel. "What Do You Say?," by Molly Giles, follows a woman's internal monologue about her ex-husband's father, grown thin and alone, after he unexpectedly arrives at a diner decorated with a flimsy background of Christmas trappings. Finally, Gail Galloway Adams's "The Christmas House" portrays a ritual—the children's annual construction of a gingerbread house—during Christmas, a holiday of "rejoicing or mourning" as the family collectively copes with their losses and cherishes continuity and those who remain.

In *Creating Flannery O'Connor*, Daniel Moran writes that O'Connor first mentioned her infatuation with peacocks in her essay "Living with a Peacock" (later republished as "King of the Birds"). Since the essay's appearance, O'Connor has been linked with imagery derived from the bird's distinctive feathers and silhouette by a proliferation of critics and admirers, and one can now hardly find an O'Connor publication that does not depict or refer to her "favorite fowl" and its association with immortality and layers of symbolic and personal meaning. As Moran notes, "Combining elements of her life on a farm, her religious themes, personal eccentricities, and outsider status, the peacock has proved the perfect icon for O'Connor's readers, critics, and biographers, a form of reputation-shorthand that has only grown more ubiquitous over time."

We are pleased to offer these anthologies as another way of continuing Flannery O'Connor's legacy. Since its conception, thirty-seven years' worth of enthralling, imaginative, and thought-provoking fiction has been published under the name of the Flannery O'Connor Award. The award is just one way that we hope to continue the conversation about O'Connor and her legacy while also circulating and sharing recent authors' work among readers throughout the world.

It is perhaps unprecedented for such a long-standing short fiction award series to republish its works in the manner we are going about it. The idea for the project may be unconventional, but it draws on an established institution—the horn-of-plenty that constitutes the Flannery O'Connor Award series backlist— that is still going strong at the threshold of its fortieth year. I am in equal parts intimidated and honored to present you with what I consider to be these exemplars of the Flannery O'Connor Award. Each story speaks to the theme uniquely. Some of these stories were chosen for their experimental nature, others for their unique take on the theme, and still others for exhibiting matchlessness in voice, character, place, time, plot, relevance, humor, timelessness, perspective, or any of the thousand other metrics by which one may measure a piece of literature.

But enough from me. Let the stories speak for themselves.

ETHAN LAUGHMAN

# Rituals to Observe

# Color Struck

ALYCE MILLER

From *The Nature of Longing* (1994)

They'd always gathered at Mother's for Thanksgiving. That was before Daddy died and the house on East 23rd was sold to a Chinese man, Lee Wong. Think of it! Ten of those Wongs crammed into the old stucco house that used to feel crowded with just five: Mother, Daddy, Caldonia, Vesta, and Clayton. It made Caldonia shake her head in disbelief. At the phone company she worked with several Chinese women who could barely get their mouths around English words. The words, when they spoke them, stuck like peanut butter in their throats.

Caldonia's latest obstetrician was Chinese, or was it Japanese? She never could keep it straight. A Chinese girl at work had recently corrected her and said, "I'm Filipina." Then she reached out and laid her narrow hand on Caldonia's rounded stomach, so unexpectedly that Caldonia felt she'd been intruded on. The girl, seeing her surprise, smiled and said, "For luck. For me. I want a baby too." Caldonia was troubled by the warmth of the girl's hand long after it had been withdrawn.

Up until a month ago, Caldonia's Chinese or Japanese or whatever-she-was obstetrician had been seeing her once a week for the last month of pregnancy. The doctor was a small, friendly woman with bright eyes who dressed in elegant suits, as if she were running off to business meetings instead of squatting on a chair to peer up between her patients' legs. She spoke proper English without any accent. "Everything looks good," she told Caldonia. "Everything looks just as it should."

This was Caldonia's third child, the conception so unexpected that at first she had not told Fred about the pregnancy. She waited over a week. Not that she would have ever considered not having the child, but she needed time alone to absorb the fact that, even with Iris and Nadia both in school, she was going to be the mother of a baby again, faced with diapers and sleepless nights.

Now, as she busied herself in the kitchen, she longed for the past Thanksgivings at the East 23rd Street house, when Mother had festooned the doorways with crepe paper and Daddy, in his matching slacks and sweater, carried out the holiday routine of washing and polishing every inch of his two black Cadillacs. Standing in that immaculate driveway, chamois in hand, he always greeted and chided them all as they arrived, his children, then his grandchildren, encouraging everyone to pause and admire the shine of fenders and hoods, and listen to him brag for the hundredth time, "Look at that, a hundred thousand miles and not a scratch, not a bump . . ."

Thanksgivings with Mother and Daddy had always been so perfect. There was plenty of room and more than enough food for anyone who happened along: neighbors, friends, extra relatives, dropping in for some of Mother's famous sweet potato pie. "Oh, and while you're at it, honey, try a little taste of turkey and a bit of oyster dressing, and just go on ahead and get you some of my bread pudding too."

But the last year had brought many changes. Daddy was dead and Mother had squeezed herself and her possessions into one of the cement-block Harriet Tubman Senior high rises in West Oakland. Her cramped fourth-floor apartment with its tiny kitchenette overlooking the freeway no longer accommodated the swell of family. She now boiled tea water on a two-burner stove and heated up frozen dinners in a microwave.

And Mother, gone stoop-shouldered and irritable, complained that the grandchildren made her nervous when they came to visit. She reproached them for being too loud in the elevators, always threatening to pull on the emergency buzzer, and she worried they'd tear up her furniture, so she'd covered everything in plastic, including runners along the beige pile carpet. She spoke more sharply to Caldonia, Vesta, and Clayton, her three grown children, as if they were still children themselves, wearing on her last good nerve.

Everyone agreed Mother wasn't herself these days, dependent on a cane after her hip operation in the spring, forgetful, eyes blurring from encroaching cataracts, balance uncertain. As Vesta took to saying, "Mother's just an old crab. I can't stand to listen to her."

What Mother announced to Caldonia about Thanksgiving this year was "I've retired from cooking and now it's somebody else's turn."

What she meant was "It's up to you, Caldonia. Clayton and Vesta are useless."

So Caldonia and Fred won by default, even though Caldonia was just a month past giving birth and still feeling sore and irritable. This child had come cesarian, a fact that dulled Caldonia's sense of accomplishment. It seemed the child had not really come out of her own body. Now here she was, barely recuperated, roasting the turkey and browning homemade bread crumbs, all because she knew better than to count on Vesta and Clayton.

"Y'all gonna have to pitch in, I'm not the Lone Ranger, you know," she told them by phone, with special emphasis in her voice just to make the point. She wondered if God was growing weary with her impatience. After all, He'd seen to it that Caldonia and Fred were blessed with so much.

That's how friends and family saw it too. She and Fred seemed to make good choices, beginning with each other. Fred was always getting promotions and raises on the police force. Caldonia had just made supervisor down at the phone company. They paid their bills on time, they attended church, and they'd saved enough money to put Nadia and Iris in a private Christian school.

Their good fortune wasn't lost on Vesta. "Y'all got all my luck," she was fond of saying. "I can't seem to win for losing."

But luck always has a limit. It started with the cesarian birth of this third child. Caldonia suspected Fred was a little disappointed the baby wouldn't be a boy, though he'd never say such a thing.

In her hospital bed, breathing hard and pushing, she recalled the Filipina woman's hand touching her. At the time, she had felt too startled to be annoyed, and then she realized the woman meant no harm. But it felt like a curse. And her labor was long and hard.

When the pains got worse, the doctor ordered a cesarian. It was a disappointment, but after a short sleep and the drowsy aftermath Caldonia found herself coming to in the bright light of her own excitement. She made out the shape and length of a perfect form—eyes, ears, fingers, and toes all there and accounted for. She cried out in happiness, a miracle even the third time, grasping the wrinkled little thing in her arms. But later, after her mind cleared, Caldonia got a good look. She began to suspect a blunder, a genetic contretemps. During her sleep something had happened. The child, made up of parts of her and Fred, did not seem to belong to either of them, and she wasn't sure where to lay the blame: on God (whom she fiercely loved) or Nature (whom she tried to respect) or the very chromosomes in the cells of her own body which had bleached the child the color of milk, tinted her eyes pink, stained the thin spread of hair an off-shade of lemon.

If Fred hadn't reassured her that the baby emerged from her body, she would have been certain there was a hospital mix-up and some white couple was going home with her child. Later she recalled an article she had seen once years before in *National Enquirer*: White Couple Gives Birth to Black Baby. The article went on the say that the woman, unbeknown to her, carried black genes. The husband accused his wife of infidelity and divorced her immediately. Caldonia though about the situation in reverse: Black Woman Gives Birth to White Baby. But it wouldn't work because a black woman's baby, no matter how light, would always be black.

Fred had to remind her that this was a gift from God, and that whatever God had in His plan they must accept with humility. Caldonia cried bitterly anyway. "It's our child," he kept telling her. "What is wrong with you?" But Caldonia prayed secretly and fervently that the child would darken.

From upstairs there came a soft cry. Caldonia set down the wooden spoon she'd been stirring the cranberry sauce with and turned down the flame under the pot. She was quicker to attend to the needs of this child than she'd been with Iris and Nadia. By the time she'd gotten upstairs and was peering into the crib, the baby was sleeping soundly again in her nest of quilts. Caldonia had taken to dressing her in blue; pink was so unflattering, causing her features to all but disappear in that little white face.

Often, while the baby slept, she sat close by and watched her. She wanted to understand exactly who this child was. She couldn't help comparing the luscious dark silk of her two older daughters' baby skins, how warm they were to the touch. This child seemed cold and foreign, a baby from some northern clime—Scandinavia, perhaps, a place inhabited by people with white skins and canary yellow hair, with eyes like frost. And yet Nature had played a trick, for the baby's small lips were full, her cheekbones high, and her nose broad like Fred's. And her hair, which was plentiful, was a thick cap of tight nappy curls. Daily, Caldonia checked the little crescents just below the child's tiny fingernails, but she found no indication that the skin there intended to darken.

Caldonia lingered by the sleeping baby, reassured by her soft breathing. From a certain angle, with the blinds drawn, the child might almost be considered pretty. There was a loud knock, followed by several more, at the front door. Caldonia pulled herself away from the child and hurried down the stairs, fastening her apron strings as she went. It was baby sister Vesta, the first to arrive. And barely noon, but since Vesta's tenth or so separation from Harold Sr. she was in the habit of showing up places early.

"You're going to take all of the skin off your knuckles pounding on my door like that," Caldonia scolded. Vesta was holding a large green salad in a wooden bowl, covered with Saran Wrap. Behind her, Rosie and Li'l Harold were still piling out of their dented and badly rusted red Toyota with the bad starter and moody brakes and the cockeyed windshield wipers. As usual, they were already fussing with each other.

Caldonia stepped back and let Vesta pass, bearing the salad bowl, which reminded her of a miniature terrarium.

"Now, why'd you go and dress the salad like that?" Caldonia was annoyed. "Dinner's not until two."

Vesta was unfazed. She was already peeping into the living room to inspect the new sectional furniture Caldonia and Fred had ordered from a catalog. "Oooooh, this musta costed y'all a fortune!" she exclaimed. "Mmmmmm, and light colored too. I'd never dare have something light colored with Rosie and Li'l Harold around."

Vesta had never been considered pretty (certainly not the way Caldonia was—high school homecoming queen and so on!), what with her lumpy potato shape, funny lopsided smile, and eyes set too close together like a moth's. She was the lightest of Mother's children, honey butterscotch, but her complexion was uneven in places, scarred dark by childhood acne. And Vesta had never learned to dress. "*Really*, Vesta!" Caldonia would exclaim as Vesta arrived in skin tight pants displaying all her bulges, teetering along in shoes so high she'd break her neck if she fell off. Today she was wearing yellow and black striped tights two sizes too small and an oversized yellow turtleneck with black pockets. Caldonia thought her sister looked like a misshapen bumblebee. And those red shoes, like Minnie Mouse! She had never seen anything so ugly and cheap-looking.

Rosie and Li'l Harold burst through the door and flung themselves on her. These wild children were the opposite of Iris and Nadia—careful, precise children who rarely made messes, and whom Vesta had referred to disparagingly one infamous Christmas as "those little prisses." It took two whole weeks for Caldonia to get over that slight.

"Where's the baby?" cried Rosie, and Harold echoed "Where's the baby?" They'd come clutching armloads of complicated toys with small and multiple loose parts that would soon be scattered. They continued to press themselves against Caldonia with wet kisses and sticky hands.

"Yes, where *is* the baby?" Vesta wanted to know, bending over to see if the plastic flowers in the vase were real.

"She's 'sleep, upstairs," said Caldonia gently.

"Y'all named her yet? Mother's fit to be tied about that poor child."

Caldonia made her voice firm. "*No*, we haven't decided on a name yet."

Vesta clucked her tongue like an old woman. "Scandalous," she said cheerfully. "You can't have a no-name child."

Before Caldonia could snap back, Vesta went on, eyeing Caldonia's new beige curtains at the window, "I can't wait to have me my own place. I'll tell you, girl, Clayton is driving me nuts. He's so damn picky, picky this, picky that. He blew up at the kids the other morning, I mean really lost it, because he said they'd eaten all his cold cereal. Can you believe that? Yelling at my kids. Over cold cereal!"

"Brother's doing you a favor," Caldonia reminded her. "What you need to do is get things straight with Harold."

Vesta blew big air from her mouth. "That man works my final nerve!" She turned so quickly on her red shoes that her heel left a scuff mark across Caldonia's polished hardwood floor.

"Harold *is* your husband . . ." said Caldonia.

Rosie and Li'l Harold started on a mess in the hallway.

Caldonia jumped in. "You kids set your toys over there and then you can go swing out back. Take turns. No fussing. I don't want to have to come out there."

When she turned around, Vesta was poking her face into the oven for a peek at the turkey. "This thing's big as a elephant!" she exclaimed, swallowed up in steam.

"Girl, get outa my oven. You're gonna make it cook uneven."

"I could baste it."

"It's self-basting," sighed Caldonia. "Close the door."

"Where *is* everybody?" Vesta asked.

"Fred's in the family room watching the game, but don't bother him, and the girls are down the street."

Vesta was wearing that awful wig again, the straight hair pageboy three shades too light for her complexion. It reminded Caldonia of one of the old Supremes. So what if Vesta's real hair was thinning, it was all that worry over Harold. If she'd just ditch him once and for all, her hair would thicken, her skin would clear, and her whole life would improve. She'd lose some weight, could afford decent clothes, and she'd get another man if that's what she wanted.

Caldonia didn't believe in divorce, but in this case she thought it was high time Vesta and Harold Sr. split up for good. How those two had managed to last all these years was a mystery! Everybody'd warned her from the start, that very first day Vesta dragged Harold home from high school. They'd succeeded in putting a stop to their eternal fussing long enough to produce two unruly children, but otherwise it was always hurricane weather at Vesta's.

Daddy'd had a fit. He had forbidden her to marry Harold, told her the boy was all flash and foolishness, barely one step up from a hoodlum. But Vesta was so hardheaded and downright silly (Caldonia frequently thought, a little simpleminded, if you wanted to know the truth), she just thumbed her nose at Daddy and forged ahead with a huge wedding, marrying Harold in an expensive ceremony at the Methodist church Mother attended. Daddy ended up bankrolling the whole business, including the expensive lace dress with train, though everyone knew Vesta had about as much business wearing white as the devil himself.

So it was that Vesta had spent these last fourteen years paying the piper. Over and over she'd packed up the children and left Big Harold lock, stock, and barrel. This time it was Clayton who relented and let her move in with him in his two-bedroom apartment down on Lake Merritt. It was supposed to be temporary, just until Vesta made other arrangements, but now six months had passed and Clayton had confided to Caldonia his patience was wearing thin.

Foolish Clayton! It wasn't as if Caldonia hadn't cautioned him. He was always getting suckered into things like this, and now he was whining to her. Said he was tired of coming home from the college where he taught accounting to find the living room floor littered with Rosie's black Barbie and her accessories, and the horse doll with the eyelashes and purple hair and all *her* accessories, and pieces of Little Harold's Lego set strewn around, and an oblivious Vesta curled up on the sofa with Clayton's plaid bathrobe over her legs watching *Jeopardy* and eating Cheez-Its out of a crumpled bag.

At first Caldonia tried to listen patiently, the way the Lord would want her to. But she finally had to tell Clayton straight out that he needed to "put the girl out." She spoke from experience.

Just a year ago she and Fred had hosted Vesta and the kids, and now here they were having to spend good money replacing their sectional furniture that Rosie and Li'l Harold had crayoned on.

Vesta leaned across the countertop to steal an olive from the cut-glass dish. "You know, Clayton's bringing a woman over today," she announced coyly.

Caldonia launched into making biscuits. "A woman? He didn't mention it to me."

"That's because he's afraid you won't approve." Vesta let that sink in. "Let's see, Jean or Jane. Shoot! I never can remember her name." Vesta headed over to the fridge for a diet soda. She found a can, popped the tab, and brushed a loose strand of wig hair from her face. "You ain't heard about her yet?"

Caldonia shook her head. "I can't keep up with Clayton's women. It's enough to keep up with three children."

"This one's *different*," said Vesta knowingly. "And he's crazy about her too." She paused, watching for Caldonia's reaction. "Now I don't want to say something I shouldn't . . . Mother said don't upset you . . ."

"Then don't," said Caldonia and rinsed her fingers off at the sink. From the basement family room came a whoop and a shout from Fred.

"Well," Vesta went on, "I haven't seen him like this with anybody for a while. She spends the night four, five times a week."

"What? With you and the kids there?"

Vesta nodded and swiped another olive.

"She's pretty and polite. Mother thinks so too."

"Pretty and polite!" murmured Caldonia. "You and Mother."

Vesta seemed especially pleased with herself. "There's something you won't like about her, but I'll let you find out on your own." And she let out a ladylike belch and squished the diet soda can in her right fist.

To herself, Caldonia murmured, "Lord, Lord, Lord," and then,

mercifully, the baby cried and she excused herself and went upstairs in search of her third child.

Clayton arrived shortly after one-thirty, sporting a new trim
haircut and supporting Mother's stout crooked body against his
skeletal frame. He reminded Caldonia of a marionette, arms and
legs dangling off the sides of his body as if held on by wires. Nervous energy seemed to eat up any pounds that might have settled
onto his frail frame.

Once Caldonia had asked Mother about Clayton's puniness
and his high voice, worried that Clayton was being denied en-
try to manhood, but Mother cut her short and asked her what on
earth had gotten into her? What could she possibly mean bringing up something like that, was she trying to say her baby brother
was *gay*? Mother's eyes had hardened like marbles. No, that
wasn't what Caldonia had meant at all, she'd only said he was
"frail," but by then it was too late because Mother'd already interpreted, in the narrowest terms available, what Caldonia meant
about Mother's favorite child. "He's a good son. He finished college. He's done well for himself and he does well by me. Don't you
talk about your brother that way."

Clayton kissed Caldonia on the cheek, and now he was kissing Vesta too. "Let's see, it's been a hour since I've seen *you*," he
teased.

"Ha ha ha," murmured Vesta, unaware her wig had slid an
inch off her forehead and a portion of her mashed-down real hair
was exposed. "You're still pissed off at the kids about that cold cereal, I know you."

Mother shot them both a look and said she needed to sit down
right away, she wasn't feeling right. They found her a comfortable spot on the new sectional sofa in front of the living room
television where she announced, "Now, I don't want to look at no
football." Clayton crouched on the floor and began to search the

channels. A quick perusal through the networks produced mostly oversized men tumbling around in helmets.

"How about a parade?" Clayton suggested.

"Don't want to see a parade either. Just find something pleasant for me to look at and turn down the sound."

Clayton settled on a PBS travelogue of pubs in Ireland and got Mother adjusted. Caldonia brought out glasses of juice for them both.

"Oh, goodness, you know I can't digest all that acid," said Mother.

Caldonia took the glass back to the sink and added water. There was just the slightest edge to her voice as she said, "Vesta, take this back out to Mother, please, and tell her it's good for her. Just a little cranberry juice and some mineral water."

Clayton hovered in the kitchen doorway, glass in hand. His eyes burst like raisins from his light-brown face.

"Jill call yet?" he asked in a voice meant to sound matter-of-fact, but which came out overeager and tinged with plaintiveness. He had a nervous habit of rocking on his heels, then rising onto his toes as if in preparation for ascension.

"No, nobody's called," said Caldonia primly, wiping her hands on a kitchen towel.

Vesta let out a shriek. "Ooooh, honey, and I called her Jane. Shoot, you know me, I'm just bad with names. Guess I been so nervous I'd call her Evelyn, I just don't call her by a name at all."

Clayton's complexion went gray for a moment. He leaned back hard onto his heels, suddenly grounded.

"Vesta, you are something else, bringing up Evelyn like that!" snapped Caldonia.

Evelyn had been Clayton's fiancée the year before. A beauty queen, Miss Black Something or Other, standing over six feet tall, with legs like a giraffe's, and eyes that had seen just a little too much of life for Caldonia's tastes. Evelyn Gilroy: the color of dark butterscotch, with flawless skin and a set of thick eyelashes that swept across her cheeks, blinking like a doll each time anyone asked her something. "I believe so," she'd say if something were true, or "I believe not," if it weren't. And she'd cold-shouldered Clayton's family, let them know they weren't really good enough.

But Clayton hadn't seen it coming, he never did. Evelyn kept him tied up in a knot so tight he wouldn't eat and he lost weight and took to having migraines. Like a fool he went ahead and spent all his money on the diamond ring he placed on her finger. He saw engagement, a lifetime of long, brown Evelyn, his forever; Evelyn saw only an expensive diamond. She had the gold melted down after the breakup and put the diamond in a pendant.

Caldonia had kept her mouth shut. "Six things the Lord hates . . . a false witness telling a pack of lies, and one who stirs up quarrels between brothers." She tried not to say anything bad about anybody.

Clayton looked at his watch. "Almost two o'clock. I better try calling Jill again."

"Turkey's about ready," said Caldonia. "And what did *you* bring for dinner, Mr. Clayton?"

Clayton's eyes shot over to Vesta. "Didn't Vesta bring my salad?"

Caldonia turned, hand on hip, eyebrows arched. "Well then, what did Miss Vesta bring?"

"Oh, shoot," Vesta moaned, without shame. "I thought the salad was from all of us. I mean, we live in one place, me and Clayton and the kids . . ."

"But there are four people living there," Caldonia pointed out, "and that means four big appetites."

"I'm sorry. I've got so much on my mind," sighed Vesta. "Harold called this morning wanting to know what me and the kids were doing today. He's wanting to come back . . ."

"I don't want to hear it," said Caldonia.

Fred was cheering again from the family room. Caldonia cast

her eyes ceilingward. "Now watch, the baby'll start crying any second."

"I'll get her!" said Clayton. "You named her yet?"

As predicted, the thin high siren of Caldonia's newest addition scored the air. "Oh, shoot," said Caldonia. "I knew this would happen. Vesta, would you set the table, please?"

From the living room Mother's voice rasped out, "The baby's crying. Aren't we going to eat sometime today?"

Then the children surged through the back door, all four of them, Iris announcing that she and Nadia were back and that Rosie had yanked the barrettes from her braids, Li'l Harold was spitting on ants, and what was Caldonia going to do about it?

Upstairs, Caldonia found relief from all of their demands, lifting the fussing child from the little crib. The blue watery eyes were squeezed into slits. The doctor had said sensitivity to light might lead to blindness. Keep her out of direct sunlight, protect her eyes and skin. He sounded like he was speaking of a household plant, to be tended in the dark. Caldonia held her until the cries turned to soft whimpers.

"There, there, sweetheart," she murmured. She carried the child down the back steps, avoiding the rest of the family, to where Fred sat on the edge of the family room sofa. She handed the baby to him. "There's my little girl," he said joyfully. His long-limbed dark body dwarfed the pale doll beside him. "There's my little sweetheart."

"Everyone's here," said Caldonia.

"Shoooooo, my little baby," he cooed into the child's ear and lay her against his thick, dark chest. "My little Angela, my little Monica, my little Bo-Peep."

Caldonia started out the door, then turned and paused a moment. She was trying to make sense out of Fred's long arms and the tiny wriggling shrimplike creature now being caressed, ever so gently, by his capable black hands.

I wonder, thought Caldonia, if I'll ever love her enough. It was an ugly secret thought, one that haunted her with all its awful possibilities.

Three o'clock, and Mother snored on the sofa. The turkey sat browned but untouched in its pan on top of the stove. The salad continued to wilt in the refrigerator.

The table, arrayed with Caldonia's wedding china, held an air of empty expectation. The kids were snacking on peanut butter and arguing over Chutes and Ladders on the dining room floor.

"I really think we should go ahead with dinner," Fred finally said, "meaning no offense to your lady friend, Clayton, but I don't want to hold things up any longer."

Caldonia saw her brother's face fall. "Maybe just a half hour more," she said sympathetically. "You sure she's got our number and the directions?"

Clayton nodded. He sat hunched on a hassock in the living room, clasping and unclasping his hands, looking himself like a scolded child. The phone rang. Both Vesta and Clayton practically leaped from their seats, but it was only a friend of Fred's from the police force.

The baby's tiny bright pink face nestled itself against Caldonia's bosom. She squeezed the nameless child to her. The funny little face called to mind a newborn kitten's. Caldonia knew the family was talking behind her back. Even Fred was running out of patience. She kept waiting for the name to announce itself, the way Iris's and Nadia's names had.

By four o'clock everyone was so bad-humored that Clayton finally gave in and agreed they should eat, but his voice was tight and hollow when he spoke. "Something must have happened to her," he said. "I really wanted us all to eat together."

Fred rounded up the kids. The girls danced their way to the table; the adults settled themselves around somewhat grimly. There was a scraping of chairs and the usual compliments about how good everything looked.

"I don't know *why* we had to wait so long," complained Mother. She surveyed the table with a critical eye. She focused in on Vesta, who was now holding the baby. "Oh, there's my sweet little grandbaby." She looked the child up and down. "When are they going to find you a name, hmmmmm? You've got to have a name. Such a shame, poor little thing!"

"I think my cousin's so pretty," said Rosie. "Pretty cousin!"

"My sister's going to be blonde!" Iris explained. "There's a girl at my school with really blonde hair." She added exploratorily, "The girl is white."

"Child needs a name," murmured Mother into her plate. "It's been a month now." She looked up hard at Fred. "I thought you were going to call her after your aunt."

"Iris, eat your food, Iris," said Fred warningly to his daughter. Mother maintained her sharp stare.

The doorbell rang. Almost a quarter to five. Clayton leaped up and disappeared into the hallway. Fred caught Caldonia's eye and winked as if to say everything was all right, she should ignore Mother, ignore them all. Caldonia could hear a woman's voice, hushed, then Clayton's apologetic.

A moment later Clayton reentered the dining room with false cheer. "Hey, hey, hey!" he announced. "Everyone, can I have your attention? I'd like you all to meet someone. This is Jill."

At first Caldonia couldn't see much more than a pair of brown boots and a long black coat, but when the woman stepped from the shadows she was startled by the fine, straight hair the color of corn silk and skin the color of eggwhite.

Caldonia immediately looked at Mother for an explanation, but Mother was placidly spooning more oyster dressing into her mouth.

"You know Vesta and my mother," said Clayton, "and this is my sister Caldonia and her husband Fred."

"Hi, Jill," called Vesta cheerfully, then turned to Caldonia with a sly smile. She was enjoying this moment thoroughly. "Isn't she

pretty? I *told* you she was so pretty," she observed for Jill's benefit.

Caldonia sat stunned. She felt betrayal, from Clayton, from
Vesta, but most of all from Mother, who went right on eating. Vesta's ignorance could almost be excused; the girl was color struck,
thought all white women were pretty, had been that way since
she was a child. When she watched old black-and-white movies,
she was always sighing over old pale-white, dead actresses.

Fred got up from the table and took Jill's coat. Clayton pulled
out the empty chair at the end of the table for her, and Jill set
about squeezing herself in between Nadia and Iris.

Still, Caldonia hadn't said a word.

"Let her see the baby!" cried Vesta. "Show Jill the baby!"

"Let her get settled first," Caldonia murmured. "She doesn't
need to be bothered with the baby." She felt suddenly proprietary
toward her child.

But Vesta was on a roll. "Ask Jill what she thinks about the
baby."

Anger rose in Caldonia. "I don't need to ask Jill anything" was
what came out of her mouth, and Mother's head shot up with the
speed of a bullet.

Vesta didn't seem to care. "Now that I think about it," she
grinned, "that could be Jill's baby."

Clayton was trying to change the subject, but Jill interrupted.
Her voice, when she spoke, had the sharp bell-like sound of so
many white women. "Clayton tells me you just had a baby. Con-
gratulations."

"Thank you," said Caldonia, surprised by her own relief.

Vesta wouldn't let up. "Jill, look at this pretty child my sister
has. She's got your coloring."

Clayton went to work fixing Jill a plate. "Turkey? Cranberry
sauce? Gravy?" He went down the list with an eagerness that
filled Caldonia with loathing. Jill murmured, "Clayton, not so
much, you know I've already eaten."

*Already eaten!* Caldonia thought. Well, knock me over with a feather. *Already eaten!* This, while everyone had waited so patiently, the kids getting fussier and hungrier. As if in sympathy, the baby on Caldonia's lap let out a long wail.

"Mama!" cried Iris and Nadia simultaneously. "The baby's crying." It felt like an accusation.

"Bring the poor little thing over to me," said Mother. "Let me hold her."

Caldonia snapped back, "Not now, she needs to be fed."

The baby began to howl full force. It was as if all the tension in the room had settled over her and drawn her little face up into tight red fury.

Jill asked Clayton to please sit down and not worry over her. Caldonia had a sudden, unexpected image of Jill emerging from her brother's bedroom and traipsing into the bathroom, dressed only in her panties and bra, in front of the children. Caldonia alternated between fury with Clayton and fury with the girl.

Fred turned to Caldonia. "Honey, want me to take the baby downstairs with me?"

"I'll keep her," said Caldonia. She got up from the table.

"Isn't she just the prettiest little thing?" Vesta prodded Jill. "I think she's so *cute*."

"She's sweet," Jill agreed, but she was staring hopelessly at the mounds of turkey and dressing Clayton had heaped on her plate.

"I told you the baby was cute, didn't I?" said Clayton, as if to leave no doubt as to what he might have said about the child. Then for Jill's benefit he launched into his version of how he'd been the one to get Caldonia to the hospital just in time.

"Don't be tellin' her that," said Mother, biting into a turkey wing. "Your sister was in labor for almost eighteen hours before that Chinese lady did something about it.

"MO-ther," warned Caldonia.

Jill tentatively reached out one pale hand and touched the baby's blanched skin. "I don't get to see newborns very often," she said.

"Let her hold the baby," insisted Vesta. Her eyes had gone round and bright. Without explanation, the baby stopped crying.

"Jill's eating," said Caldonia, pulling the baby back against her body. "The baby's too fussy."

"No, it's okay," said Jill. She was working hard at being polite.

Now Clayton was urging. "Come on, Caldonia, let Jill hold the baby."

Caldonia could see she had no choice without offending everyone. She leaned down and handed the baby to Jill. Jill gathered the child against her and rocked gently from side to side. "Mmmmm, she's so little."

Caldonia arranged the loose-knit blanket under the baby's body.

"Look at Jill holding the baby," commented Mother, her turkey leg held up in one hand. "Isn't that something?"

"The baby could be hers," said Vesta.

Caldonia caught Fred's eye and she saw a warning there.

"They sure look a lot alike," Mother went on, hope in her voice. She leaned across the table and studied first the baby's face, then Jill's. "They got that same pretty complexion, don't you think so Clayton? What do you think, Jill? Is that a pretty baby to you?"

Jill was trying to be polite for them all. "What's her name?" she asked. A moment of silence followed.

"She doesn't have one," Mother said bitterly. "It's been a month now and Caldonia can't decide what to call her."

The heat rose in Caldonia's face. She snapped back, "The baby's albino," as if that answered anything. She meant the word to sound bold, even cruel, despite the fact the Lord would be shaking His head at her.

Clayton jumped in. "What Sis means is that she's not sure if the baby's eyes will have sensitivity to light . . ."

"That's not what I meant at all," Caldonia said matter-of-factly. "I mean what I said, I'm upset my baby is white."

It was the first time she'd actually said it. Not to Fred, not even to herself. But now it seemed necessary. And truthful.

The room grew very still. Fred cleaned his throat. Mother murmured, "Hmmmmm mmmmmm!" disapprovingly under her breath. The children eyeballed one another with keen interest. But Jill didn't seem to mind. She looked straight back in Caldonia's face. "Isn't the albino trait inherited?" she asked.

Caldonia nodded. "It's from Fred's side."

"I still think she's pretty," defended Vesta. "Maybe she'll grow up and look like Jill."

"Being albino," said Caldonia, "is different from being . . ." She paused. She saw no point in offending Jill further. "A blonde nappy head just isn't pretty," Caldonia heard herself saying.

"That's called funny looking."

Everyone laughed uneasily except Mother, who pursed her lips and murmured, "Y'all some wrong folks!"

Caldonia bent down and retrieved the baby from Jill. "I'm afraid she'll spit up all over you," she said with false concern.

"Maybe everybody'll think the baby's mulatto," said Vesta, her mouth full of stuffing. "That's what they call a white and black mix. You know, like you and Clayton." She used her fork to gesture toward Jill, as if joining her with Clayton in midair.

"Clayton and Jill are not mulatto," Caldonia said stonily. She felt her anger giving her direction. "Clayton is black and Jill is white. Mulatto would be what they'd have if they had a child, Vesta. It's not the same thing."

"Hold on there, don't rush us now," said Clayton, but he said it only for Jill's sake. His smile had broadened, his eyes brightened. Caldonia could see he rather like the idea of having a child with Jill. And she could see by Jill's tense but civil expression that this would never happen.

"I don't mean nothin'," said Vesta cheerfully. She grinned at

Jill. "You know me, I'm just over here runnin' my mouth like I usually do. My best friend in grade school was white. 'Member her, Caldonia? Patty What's-her-face, that big old fat girl, pretty face though."

The baby began to fuss in Caldonia's arms. Quickly her bad humor escalated to rage and her face turned the color of Pepto-Bismol.

Caldonia excused herself.

"Feed the baby here," Clayton called after her.

But the truth was, Caldonia didn't want to nurse her baby near a stranger. She pulled shut the louvered doors that separated the kitchen and dining room. She sat down in one of the vinyl-backed kitchen chairs and arranged the baby's pink mouth at her brown breast.

The louvered doors opened ever so slightly and Fred squeezed through. If he was annoyed with Caldonia, he didn't show it. Instead, he bent down and kissed the nursing baby. "You know I love you," he whispered in her tiny shell-pink ear, "even if your mama's actin' crazy."

Caldonia had to smile in spite of herself. She hummed softly to the pink and yellow child. When Fred went out again, she caught a glimpse of Clayton's slender brown fingers caressing Jill's pale arm, and then the stiffening of that arm as Jill carefully and surreptitiously moved just out of reach. It was a simple gesture, designed not to embarrass Clayton in front of his family.

Caldonia looked down at her youngest daughter. She didn't know which was worse, going through life toward blindness or going through life white. In a way, it was kind of the same thing. How was her daughter going to feel, this little pale stalk in a dark field?

Iris and Nadia let themselves through the louvered door into the kitchen.

"Close the door!" Caldonia hissed.

"Mama, we love our sister," said Iris pointedly.

"Well, of course you do!" Caldonia hadn't meant to give the girls a wrong impression.

"We could put her in the sun," suggested Nadia helpfully. "She could get a tan and be like us."

The two girls ran their hands over the baby's little pink ones and cooed at her.

"She is like us," Caldonia corrected. "She *is* 'us.'"

"Excuse me . . ."

Caldonia's head shot up. The voice was clear and precise. It was Jill, first poking her head through the kitchen door and now standing in the doorway, small and white, not much taller than Nadia and Iris. Caldonia quickly covered her breast.

"I want to thank you for having me," Jill said softly. "And I'm sorry about all the inconvenience and the mix-up."

For a moment, before she was able to line up her thoughts, Caldonia actually thought the girl was apologizing for the absence of the baby's color. "The mix-up?" she said vaguely. She reached for the right words. "Clayton's friends are always welcome," she said. "Come back any time."

"I will." The girl smiled, and Caldonia knew they both were thinking how this would not happen. "Thank you," said the girl, relieved and forgiven, as if Caldonia had it in her power to do that.

That night, when the dishes had been washed and the kitchen swept, and the children put to bed, Caldonia asked Fred tentatively, "I've been thinking, do you think it would be foolish to name the baby Ebony?"

Fred burst out laughing. "Girl, what are you talking about?"

"I want to give my child a *real* name," said Caldonia.

"That's real all right," he chuckled. "What is wrong with you, Caldonia? You can't *make* her black, you know. Naming her Ebony would be as bad as naming a dark child Pearl, or Magnolia. We should call her Angela, after my grandmother."

"I just want her to know . . ." Caldonia began. "I just want her to feel . . ."

Fred looked at her long and hard. "She *is*, Caldonia" was all he said before he went upstairs and turned on the news.

Caldonia stood next to the sink under the framed "God Bless This Mess" sampler Mother had made for her last Christmas. God, she thought wistfully, in His infinite wisdom has given me this child without a name. She wasn't blaming God; she wasn't blaming anyone but herself for the pinch in her heart that prevented her from running right upstairs and calling the child by her rightful name.

# Morte Infinita

DAVID CROUSE

From *Copy Cats* (2005)

On the last Halloween Kristen spent with her father they dressed as vampires, and when he hefted the rock that would shatter the Eisensteins' bay window and send their dog yelping into the woods, he smiled a sad vicious smile, and his face became the face of a vampire too.

"There are two kinds of people in this world," he said. Then he side-armed the rock, and the street exploded in noise, and she was running and he was not. He just stood there in his cloak and black shirt and white Converse All-Stars, as if he were not afraid at all, as if he were not even visible to anyone but her. As the rock left his hand and arced over the neat lawn she suddenly re-membered what he had told her a few days before when picking her up from detention. "We all have to suffer the consequences of our actions," he had said as he opened the passenger door for her. "And sometimes we have to suffer the consequences of other people's actions too."

That was Saturday, five days before Halloween and two days after her mother had left for Florida. There was a horror movie festival playing downtown, so that's where they headed, and as they pulled away from the school, Kristen gave the gray build-ing a single-finger salute. The principal was deep inside, his head bowed over paperwork, and her dad was saying something about the forces of social control. She wondered if he even knew the specifics of her crime. "I spit at him," she explained after a while. "I didn't hit him though. He sidestepped it like a matador."

"Who?"

"Mr. MacEllan," she said. "The principal."

"Your principal is your pal," he said with a laugh, pulling into a space near the theater. Even lately with her dad's eyes grown bloodshot, they loved to watch horror movies together. In the dark of the movie theater Kristen could feel him next to her vibrating with emotions some people would never, ever feel in their entire white-bread lives, and she felt herself vibrate too, because she carried 50 percent of his biology in her blood.

She knew what would happen. The screen would go dark, and her father would lean over and whisper something funny about the titles or the music or the fatheaded guy in front of them, and then they would be quiet except when they gasped with joy as the villain made his first appearance. Whether it was Vincent Price staring into the eyes of a skittish dinner guest or some skin-masked, ax wielding psychopath chasing down a girl in cutoff shorts, Kristen was on the side of the devils. In horror movies freaks and ghouls were the clever ones, the fascinating ones. "The heroes are boring," she told him once as the screen glimmered with violence. "The monsters are the only ones who do anything interesting with their lives."

She liked to change his words around a little and speak them back to him so that she could watch him smile and nod at their wisdom.

"I can't go in," he said, looking into the rearview mirror at the theater marquee. He smiled tightly without taking his hands off the wheel, as if they were still driving down the road. "I can't go in there with those people. I just can't." He was crying. He leaned back his head, let out a deep breath, and said, "Oh boy."

She pictured the inside of his head as a labyrinth where he

would sometimes get lost. The houses he designed were smooth and made with lots of glass, beautiful and transparent and cold and not at all the kind of place most people would want to live. She wondered if his brain was too full of these beautiful buildings, variations of shape and form and function and strange angles like a whole other neighborhood that existed and did not exist. That was where he spent most of his time lately.

Her mother—she resided in sunnier climes.

When little Edward Eisenstein introduced Kristen to *Morte Infinita* that Halloween—the Halloween her father lifted the rock and smiled as if he were the daddy of all vampires—well, it was a revelation, what her father would have called the opening of the mind to new frontiers. On the 29th of October her mother had called from Florida, and for two days Kristen had searched for meaning in each one of her father's pinched expressions. But then on Halloween afternoon in the Eisensteins' furnished basement the haze lifted, and it was like, oh yeah, man. It was like before and after pictures in the back of comic books.

"This is the kind of movie even *your* dad wouldn't let you watch," Eisenstein explained before hitting the play button on the VCR. He didn't know that her dad wasn't up to watching movies these days, not since the aborted horror festival. Her father just sort of stumbled around at night, wandering like he was a ghost in his own house, while her mother sexed it up in Key West with her new boyfriend. "He's got this dark tan," her father had told her on Saturday as they sat outside the theater. "It's the kind of tan a certain kind of person likes."

Kristen had never met Stephanos, but she could imagine him through her father's eyes as a man blessed with looks and decisiveness and not enough goodness or evil to get him into much trouble. "I bet he does sit-ups in the morning," her father had told her. "He seems like that kind of person. I bet your mother wakes up to the sound of him grunting from the floor." This alone was reason enough to dislike him and his stupid ponytail and rubber flip-flops and the numberless cigarettes he smoked on the bow of the boat and then dropped into the sea. He did not own a boat himself but worked sailing the boats of the rich and lazy. Did these lawyers and doctors know what kind of man they were trusting with their most prized possessions?

Her mother had never sailed in her life, but when Kristen thought of her, she imagined her on a boat, white sail taut in the wind. She had been gone for five days when she called on Tuesday, and she wore new clothes in the three pictures she had e-mailed. None of them featured Stephanos, who must have been the person holding the camera. There was a conservative hint of a smile on her face—a hesitant, shameful smile—but her skin was darkening in the sunshine, and she looked healthy. She was changing, blending into her new environment like a chameleon. Kristen was changing too. Everything was.

Well, not everything. Her father wasn't getting worse, not really, and that's what Kristen told her mom when she asked her about him. She said, "He's doing great. We're having an amazing time. We saw a movie festival." She laughed nonchalantly like they were in Paris. And by saying that, it was like they *were* in Paris or at least someplace as exotic as Florida. Neither of them brought up Stephanos. Her father had said Kristen wasn't supposed to know, that he had figured it out himself only a few weeks ago. So Kristen said, "What are you doing?" and her mom said, "Just hanging out with Aunt Clair. We're heading on a little road trip tomorrow. I'll be home on Thursday next week. Can the laundry wait until then?" They talked about Mickey Mouse and Donald Duck and Goofy—losers, every last one of them—and Kristen said yes and no and maybe and then handed the phone over to her dad like it was something smelly. He lifted the receiver to his ear, put on his best, calmest voice, and said, "Hello, dear." He nodded and then turned to Kristen and said, "Would you mind going upstairs for a little while? Your mother seems to think that we need to keep secrets from you."

Upstairs Kristen lay flat on her bed and listened. Her dad was meek as he pleaded with her mother—for what exactly Kristen didn't know—and then loud again in a rushed jumble of sentences, and Kristen stopped her own breathing to listen harder. "I just told you what I want," he said, and for a second Kristen imagined him gripping her mother by the shoulders and shaking her, although she was hundreds of miles away. Then something metallic hit the wall and clattered to the floor.

"Sometimes people feel guilty because they *should* feel guilty," he yelled into the phone. "We're only a little club because you left. That's why we're a little club." His voice became mock childish and keening, and he said, "She loves me more than she loves you." Kristen pushed her face into the pillow and tried to brainnap because tomorrow she had tests in two subjects. But she couldn't close her eyes for more than a minute, and when she came downstairs her father grinned at her from the sink. "Hey, kid," he said. "Just tidying up a little."

"Looks good," she said. Sometimes she wanted to kiss his forehead softly. She had seen her mother do that once when her father was in bed, still wearing his coat and tie.

He said, "Let's do something fun. I'll make it up to you for the festival thing. I still feel bad about that." She looked at him. He knew what she was thinking, boom, like telepathy. "I promise to forget about work if you promise to forget about school," he said.

They drove through town slowly, past the large sprinkler-soaked lawns, and he talked more about Stephanos, although he did not mention his name, just that there was someone else and that this person did something exotic and manly like sail boats or run a hot dog stand. Had her dad forgotten that she knew the man's name, his profession, the way his hair curled around his ears? Kristen felt like she could pick him out of a lineup.

She said, "Don't worry. It's okay. It'll be all right."

As he headed over to the south side of town, where Kristen was not allowed to ride her bike, he talked about the pressures of his job and the responsibilities of marriage. "In sickness and in health," he said. "That's a very important part of those vows." She wondered what they would be learning or not learning in her second-period history class. It seemed like her mother would never come back, although everybody was still using the word *vacation*.

"Watch out for that cat," Kristen said.

"I'm difficult to live with," he said. "I know that. Times have been rough lately. The last few years. But I thought we could work it out."

"What did she say?" she asked. "Tell me."

They passed people raking leaves and putting up Halloween decorations in the fading afternoon. Occasionally he waved or beeped the horn in greeting, but he was close to tears and his voice was breaking. Kristen wondered if *she* should be driving. She said, "Let's go home, Dad. We don't have to do this," but they continued their tour, heading east now toward the abandoned factories along the river, where bar bands rehearsed heavy metal songs and kids shattered beer bottles on the sidewalk. They drove by buildings the opposite of the kind her father designed, squat and old and tired.

Then her father glanced over at her and grinned like someone was going to snap his picture. "You know, I can take the rest of the week off. You don't want to live in Florida, do you?" And then, "No. No. Of course you don't. It's the land of make-believe. I went there once, with your mother when we first married, to visit your aunt. It's full of crocodiles and the elderly. Did you know that crocodiles were around in the Jurassic age? They're pretty much dinosaurs."

Kristen looked out the window at the restaurants sliding by and said, "I'm so hungry I could eat a dinosaur. I could eat a rock. I could eat a minivan." She laughed and put both sneakers on the dash. If her mother had been here no way would she have been able to get away with that.

Her father pulled into the parking lot of the Great American Pancake House, and she smiled because she loved this place most of all. They often came here together after going to a movie, and in the vinyl-seated booth he tried to explain that the films were like society's subconscious and that the seamless narrative arc of body-body-body-body-end was beautiful in its own naturalistic way and that she should brush her teeth twice a day and none of this waving the toothbrush around in her mouth like it was a magic wand. By just putting on his turn signal her father had made today like those other days. By the time he stopped the car and opened the door, Kristen decided that her mother was at home reading the *New York Times* on the couch.

Kristen told the waitress she wanted pancakes and waffles both, two each, and a big glass of milk, and sausage on a separate plate, and a side of mashed potatoes with gravy. The waitress smiled at her like she was the source of all cute in the world, like her existence made having a suck-ass job a wonderful experience. "You have a darling daughter," she said as she filled his coffee mug. It was like they were driving cross-country or something. The car was packed with camping equipment and a cooler full of 7-Up. That was the kind of thing fathers did with their daughters, right?

"Thanks," her dad said. "We're very close."

"I can tell," the waitress said.

He gave Kristen's hand a conspiratorial squeeze. "We're practically family," he said, and the waitress laughed. So did her father. If there were people at the next table they would have joined in. It was a comedy routine.

"You're happy, right? You're content?" he asked her when the waitress had gone. He smiled and sniffed at something bad in the air and his expression hardened. "That's the chief aim of everybody around here, isn't it? To be content? The Thorstons are content. The Eisensteins are content. Your mother is doing everything she can to be content."

They sat in silence for a while, looking out the dirty window at an elderly man shuffling across the parking lot. It looked like the poor guy couldn't find his car. He stopped and turned around in the twilight, turned around again, and then his hand moved slowly to his unshaven cheek.

"So you think Mom is happy?" she asked.

The food arrived with a nervous clatter. When the waitress headed back to the kitchen, Kristen asked the question again and felt like she was jabbing him with something small and sharp— her fork, her sticky knife. "Do you think Mom is happy?" He didn't answer. He was still watching the man in the parking lot, where the streetlights were finally coming on. "What about you?" Kristen asked. "Are you happy?"

He was smoothing his mashed potatoes down with the curved back of his fork like he was petting a kitten. "It's all very primal, what's happening right now. Very, very primal. But the people around here wouldn't understand that. I mean, look around. Just have a conversation with somebody. Try to get past *oh, what a nice day* and *nice weather we're having.*" His voice trailed off. She swore she could hear the people at the other tables chewing, but maybe it was just him. Her mother said he was always in a hurry, that he chewed his food like a shark.

The guy in the parking lot still hadn't found his car. He looked feeble and helpless, the kind of person who would get it between the fifth and sixth ribs in the first ten minutes of one of the movies they loved so much. She looked over at the next table where little kids were fidgeting in their seats and sucking on straws and giggling, and she realized it hadn't been long ago when she had been that ignorant. Her dad was talking about death and divorce and the depressing sound canned tomato soup makes as you plop it into the pan. "It's the little things that will bring you down," he said. "Happiness requires a certain—I don't know—indistinctness of vision. But that doesn't mean you shouldn't be careful. That's not what I'm saying. Remember what Kierkegaard said. 'The torment of despair is not to be able to die. To be sick unto death is not to be able to die.'"

That was the way he spoke to her, as if she were forty years old and four years old, making references to philosophers with names like curses and explaining that ice cream was really bad for her. It was like he couldn't get a bead on the place in the universe she was right now. He shot too long or too short—at various future and past selves—and he could never find his true target: a thirteen-year-old girl with braces who just a few days before had slapped a freckle-faced boy on the side of the head and then spit at the school principal when he tried to break it up. What had her mother asked her the night before she left? "Kristen, are you angry?"

Kristen had a new idea, and she tried the thought on for size the way she sometimes tried on ugly clothing at the mall—just to see how bad it looked. Her mother had died from a horrible illness. It was one of those devastating dark age kind of diseases, a dawn-of-time pestilence sort of thing. Her father sat across from her, simmering in his grief, which was natural, even kind of noble, and Kristen had to be strong, because his love had made him weak.

But halfway through the second waffle she felt the first waffle hardening in her tummy, and she pictured her mother embraced by brawny sailor's arms—the arms of the hero—as if this were the end of a Hollywood movie and the credits were about to roll. But it was not the end. It was the beginning, right?

"The name of the movie is *Morte Infinita*," Eisenstein said two days later on Halloween afternoon as they moved around the side of his house to the cellar. They let themselves in—the backdoor was unlocked—and he popped the tape in and clicked on the TV. Kristen pushed a square of cardboard against the nearest window to block the sunshine. Children and parents would be roaming the darkened streets in a couple of hours, and then they would return to their houses and take off their costumes and be in bed by ten o'clock. The next morning it would be sunshine and morning newspapers and kisses on the cheek, but right then the ground was beginning to break open like something ripe. Zombies. Foreign zombies. The TV was full of them. "Is that Spanish?" Kristen asked.

"It's Italian," Eisenstein said, and then he pronounced the words with relish, *Morte Infinita*, as if he were pronouncing the name of a complicated Italian dish. She reached into the bag on the cushion between them. The cheese snacks left orange dust on her fingers. She sucked them clean, one at a time, as she leaned forward. The zombies scrambled over shattered bricks and along the banks of dried-up rivers. Without people to kill they were sad and lost and innocent as babies. She was reminded of her mother's voice on the phone a couple of days before. At the time it had seemed normal. But after the fact, in her memory, it sounded desperately hopeful, like the voice of a person on a game show trying to figure out the right answer. "I needed to get away for a little while," she had said. "I hope you understand. Your father will take care of you. He will. Is he taking good care of you? He's not good at much, I guess, but he's good at taking care of you. Sometimes, I think, better than me. But I'm sure you don't think that. Is he there?"

When the prettiest woman in the cast was killed twenty minutes in, Kristen knew she was in for something special. When the sliver of wood penetrated the eye of the local doctor and the camera zoomed in and held the shot and the music swelled as if something romantic had just happened, Kristen felt her heart beating strong and fast. When a zombie in a tattered priest's robe took a chunk from the hero's neck and he was lost in a sea of rotting corpses, well, God bless Anthony Fentana, the director of the movie and writer of the screenplay, a man who was probably dead himself in an Italian cemetery. The disjointed plot, the graininess of the film, the detail of the gore, all of it confirmed something. "That was *amazing*," she said as the screen turned black and then sky blue.

Eisenstein said, "What did I tell you? There's nothing like the Europeans when it comes to zombie movies." He took off his black-framed glasses—he wore them only when watching television—and Kristen could see from his tentative toad-lipped expression that she had been called here for other purposes. The week before, he had tried to put his arm around her while they were watching *The Angry Red Planet*, and she had bent forward and laughed. It wasn't like he was a jerk or anything, or that repulsive even, although he had a weak chin and greasy, feathered hair. But there was something about him that would probably make girls laugh until he was middle-aged, and Kristen guessed he knew this too. "Kristen?" he said.

"Yes?"

"Do you love me?"

"Of course not," she said. It was enough to make her smack him. Jesus Christ.

"I know," he said, and they listened to the video rewind.

"Kristen?" he said after a while.

"What?"

"I'm sorry," he said.

"Don't worry about it." She reached out and touched him on the shoulder and thought about how young he seemed in his spindly puberty. She saw him as a different species altogether, something slow moving and amphibious and sensitive to light. His father was a big man with a truck driver's body, but he worked as a consultant for insurance companies, making spreadsheets and graphs and giving presentations about the statistical likelihood of people dying from this or that or the other thing. Little Eisenstein would probably end up doing something similar.

"I wish there was something I could do to help," Eisenstein said.

"Help with what?"

"Everything," he said, and the crack in his voice made her want to wrap her arms around him and squeeze. He said, "My dad was talking about having you stay at our place until your mother comes back."

The window shades were down day and night, but their lives were still on display as if they lived in one of her dad's glass buildings. She said, "Your father also said that the Red Sox were going to win a pennant last year. I remember him telling us that. Do you remember that?"

"Yeah," he said.

She said, "Did your dad mention anything about Stephanos? Is he coming back with her?"

"Who?" he asked, and she told him never mind, and then she made her hands into fists and played drums on her knees, and they were quiet except for the music she made on her body.

"I'm just trying to help," he said finally.

"If you want to help then just sit quietly." She sounded like his mother or teacher or some stupid thing. The idea of her needing Eisenstein's help made her feel small, like he could lift her up in his hands. Her father was not a big man, but he was bigger on the inside than the outside, as if he followed some extradimensional logic. She was the same way. They could handle this together. They always had, right down the line.

"But Kristen," Eisenstein said. His voice was whiny with love and goodwill. She cut him off with a shush, and then they were quiet. It was a perfect moment.

Then she said, "Let's watch the movie again." He found the remote and the opening music began to play, plodding piano chords like something shambling and aimless. She watched Eisenstein's face, poor lonely Eisenstein with the 125 IQ and nervous stutter. She turned back to the TV and said, "The blood looks real."

The night her father threw a cloak around his shoulders and told her that they were going trick-or-treating, Kristen had raced against time to be with him. She had taken the short cut from Eisenstein's house. Her bike crashed through the woods, and as she peddled faster she gave out a yelping howl of delight and rage that she hoped people might confuse for something other than a girl of thirteen. It had been a week since her mother left for the airport, and yes, maybe her dad wasn't doing so great, maybe he was in pain, but who gave a shit if he mowed the lawn? And it was wolf pain anyway, the kind of wound that made you smarter and sharper and keener and hungrier and just plain better when everything was done and you were on the other side of it. Leaves and branches snapped against Kristen's face as she sped down-hill, and she imagined herself as something dark and mysterious, a one-of-a-kind animal that occupied a solitary ecological niche and was only now deciding to enter the foolish world of mankind.

Her father was in the hall sitting at the desk, writing with the long black feather pen he kept there. "I'm trying to cultivate as many affectations as possible," he sometimes said when using it. She remembered her mother laughing at that joke, the way she threw her head back. Her head was back now too, in bed, Steph-anos grunting between her spread legs, his mouth against her shoulder like it was an apple. Kristen had seen her father and mother locked in that pose a couple of years ago through the crack in the door.

"Hey," he said, straightening up and looking through her as if she were invisible. "Who goes there? Is that my faithful servant?" That joke again. She knew what was required.

"No," she said.

"It's not my faithful servant?" Mock panic rose in his voice.

"Oh, dear. Who then can it be?" He was an effeminate character in a story by Edgar Allan Poe, and she was some deceased relative returning for revenge, dripping water from the pond where she had drowned. She smiled in the dark, and her love became a kind of light by which she could see him clearly.

"No, it's me," she half yelled, and she was suddenly outrageously happy. She wanted to tell him about the movie and the sick, wonderful mind behind it and the blood that looked real and the burning church and the endless body count. She wanted to relive it through his senses. He could show it to her in new ways, open it for her like a book.

He said, "And who are you?"

She said, "You know who I am." She looked at the desk and said, "What are you doing?"

"Writing out a check to the credit card company. It's amazing how expensive your mother's tastes are." With a flourish of his pen he was finished. He cleared his throat and said, "Well, you ready?" She did not know what he meant until he stood up, and she realized he was dressed in the black cloak. "Trick-or-treat," he said. Then they walked downstairs together.

Ghouls and freaks and superheroes smiled at them as they emerged from the house and made their way through the neighborhood. Two Batmans walked side by side toward them. "Neither of them wanted to compromise," their mother explained, and Kristen's father nodded as if he understood. The kids frowned back at Kristen, clutching tightly at their bags of candy. This was serious business. They knew that. Monsters moved in solemn processions of three or four. There was something mournful in the way they walked, as if they were all lost and searching for their homes.

"Here, take these," her father said. He handed her something. Plastic fangs. She was dressed in a black T-shirt and shit kickers. She put the teeth in her mouth, and abracadabra, she was a vampire. "Your mother never enjoyed this kind of thing," Kristen's father said as they walked across the street holding hands. "She was always so afraid that someone was going to get hit by a car."

He was talking as if her mother was dead. For a ridiculous split second Kristen wondered if he had read her mind in the diner when she had considered the same thing. "Dad?" she asked.

"Yes?"

"How did Mom meet what's-his-face?"

His lips pursed slightly. He was thinking.

"Dad?" she asked.

"Yes?" he said.

"You're in a lot of trouble, aren't you?"

"That's a hard question to answer," he said. "I'm not sure." He squeezed her hand a little more tightly. They walked past a brightly colored spaceman holding a plastic Kmart bag. Her dad made a sound like he was eating candy, a soft sucking noise, but he didn't say anything else until they reached the sidewalk on the other side of the street. Then he stopped and bent down and looked in her eyes the way a softball coach might before a batter goes to the plate. He said in the most steady and reasonable-sounding voice she had heard from him all week, "Your mother and I met sixteen years ago. I was thirty-three, and she was twenty-two. That's a big difference. That's almost your whole life, kiddo. You don't just throw that away because someone's hit a rough patch." He put his fist to his mouth, as if he was about to clear his throat. "Let's just say there was no other guy involved in this mess. Just me and you and your mother. That still wouldn't be an excuse. Especially in this day and age. There are medications. There's all sorts of crap. Analysis and stuff. Aromatherapy, for Christ's sake." He began to laugh, and he rubbed the top of her head with two knuckles. "We live in an enlightened age, after all."

She did not want this. She wanted an answer. She would keep

looking into his eyes until he gave her one. She said, "Dad, are you getting better?"

He looked at her as if she had just said something super cute and amusing. He said, "You wouldn't remember, but she did this a couple of times when you were this big." He held his thumb and finger apart an inch, as if he was holding a bug or a screw or some small thing that could be lost if you let it go. "I wouldn't be surprised if things were back to normal by next week," he said.

She remembered again her mother's craned neck through the crack in the door, head tilted back as if posing for a painting, her eyes shut tight. She thought of their conversation a few days before, her father's pleading voice. How many things like this had Kristen missed—moments when the door was closed or the words were exchanged late at night when she was sleeping? For each she had seen there must have been a hundred that had slipped past her. "What about Stephanos?" she asked, and there was a sharp edge to her words. Her own voice startled her.

Her father scowled as if he had forgotten this important part of the equation, and then he said, "Don't worry about him. He's just a fling. That's all he is." Then he straightened up, smoothed out his cloak, and headed up the steps to the front door of their destination. He knocked three times and stepped back, raising both arms in the air ready to strike.

Mrs. Van Dyke seemed surprised to see them, but she opened the screen door and smiled. "We're supposed to be vampires," Kristen said quietly, and she opened her mouth to show off the teeth. She was too old for this.

"Oh, yes," Mrs. Van Dyke said, and she handed her an apple and a Snickers bar. They thanked her and walked away, back down the steps, Kristen feeling the woman's farsighted eyes on her back.

A few houses were dark, and Kristen wondered what was inside them, behind the window shades, down their cellars. Most, though, were lit up with orange light, or decorated with paper witches and ghosts. A few played eerie music from open doors or recordings of people screaming and evil laughter. Two big beefy kids passed by wearing hockey masks as costumes, and although Kristen vaguely recognized them, their real faces were hard to remember. The same with the skinny Darth Vader who ran up Mrs. Van Dyke's stairs as they were heading down. Was he from her homeroom?

"Don't eat the apple," her dad said as they walked away from the house. "I don't trust that Mrs. Van Dyke. She could snap any minute." He took the apple and bit into it with a little growl. "How is school going these days?" he asked between chews. "That hillbilly kid, is he still picking on you?"

"A little," she said.

"He only does that because he likes you."

"No, he hates me," Kristen said. "He wants to stomp me into mulch. I can see it in his eyes." She didn't mention that he had also insulted her dad, calling him a mental patient. That's what had made her rain punches on his gross freckled face and then spit at the principal when he had interfered with what was really a question of honor.

"That's just his way of showing you that he has a crush on you," her dad explained.

She stopped and spit her teeth into her hand so she could speak more easily. "The costumes suck this year," she said. "Maybe it's just that I'm getting older."

Nobody came to the door of the next house, although the porch light was on and she had seen other eager people receiving candy there. Her dad tapped on the window with his knuckles, threw his coat around his shoulder in a gesture of exaggerated indignation, and walked down the steps. She followed him to the Eisensteins' house, where she knew sad little Eisenstein was watching *Morte Infinita* for the third time. She popped the teeth back in her mouth and nudged them into position with her tongue.

"We're vampires, Charlie," Kristen's father said to Eisenstein's dad when he opened the door. "Don't invite us in, for God's sake. Put garlic in your windows and get a cross. We've come for you and your wife and son, but especially for your wife."

"Very funny," Mr. Eisenstein said. "Do you want to come in, or do you just want some candy?" He was holding a bag of mini 3 Musketeers in his hand. Kristen could hear the television playing in the living room, some voice talking about a helicopter disaster. She didn't know where or who or how, just that it had happened. She looked at her father, who was smiling tightly, the way he had that day outside the movie festival.

Mr. Eisenstein said, "Do you want a beer?" and moved back from the door.

"No, thanks," her dad said, "but I bet Kristen wants some of those delicious 3 Musketeers." They stepped into the house.

"I bet I don't," she said. She was looking around for Eisenstein himself peeking around a corner or something, but he was probably in the cellar. She saw evidence of him, though, in the little black sneakers in the entranceway. She hadn't realized his feet were so small.

"I'm surprised to see you here," Eisenstein's dad said to her father.

Kristen's dad smiled and looked around the room, at the photographs of their dog and brothers and grandparents and great-aunts—their entire history on display. "Yeah, well, that's the way it is with vampires. We rely heavily on the element of surprise."

Eisenstein's dad made a sound like he had something stuck in his throat, and for a second Kristen thought candy was lodged down there somewhere, but then he said, "Are you treating her well?" He didn't look in her direction, but Kristen knew he was talking about her, and she had the momentary feeling that her body was back home and only her spirit was here as an observer. She wondered what part of the movie Eisenstein was watching and what he meant when he said he loved her. Her mother had used that word many times and so had her father. Kristen loved her father and loved *Morte Infinita*, and she wanted to be alone with one or the other, not standing here listening to Mr. Eisenstein. "She looks skinny," he said. "She looks like she's getting thinner."

"Vampires are thin," her dad said and then, "Have you talked to my wife lately, Charlie? Does she deign to call you from paradise?"

"Paradise?" Mr. Eisenstein said.

"Just a little joke."

"I don't get it."

"Does she call you?"

"She called me once, a few days ago. She was concerned about you. She said you sounded funny." There was something apologetic in his voice. "I'm sorry. You're putting me in a difficult position here."

"My wife knows a lot about difficult positions," her dad said. "And she's still my wife, you know. And Kristen is still my daughter." Then he laughed as if something funny had been said on the television, but the announcers were still going on about the helicopter accident. She wondered if someone famous had been killed.

"Come on," Mr. Eisenstein said. "Let's not start."

Kristen's father was looking at a magazine on the coffee table. The cover of the magazine showed a smiling young woman dressed in a bright sweatshirt and little yellow shorts. She was touching her toes and smiling. From the expression on his face, Kristen's dad looked as if he had suddenly recognized this woman and was now remembering something awful she had done to him once. He went to the table and picked up the magazine. Leafing through it he said, "Don't pretend you know what's good for her. That's all I'm saying."

Closing the door Mr. Eisenstein came and looked at the magazine as if he wanted to read it next.

"I thought you were doing okay," he said. "I wanted to give you the benefit of the doubt. I really did."

"I wanted to give you the benefit of the doubt too," her dad said, his voice high and mocking, "but I'm pretty curious why you're protecting her. I've seen the way you two flirt. Don't pretend you don't."

Eisenstein's dad laughed then, arms folded across his chest. He looked down at the floor, at his shoelaces, at the zigzag pattern in the carpet. "This is ridiculous," he said.

"Are you fucking her?" Kristin's dad said. "Or do you just *want* to fuck her?"

Kristen thought of her mother walking hand in hand with her new boyfriend on some stoneless beach and wanted to believe it because it was what her father had told her. She looked at him turning the pages of the magazine, his body draped in black, and loved him so fiercely that she wanted to tear at his clothes and dig down into those hidden places and find the darkness there and grab it like a tumor. Mr. Eisenstein said, "You're going through some tough times. I understand that. But turning it into a performance piece is only going to make it worse."

"I don't think you understand," her dad said. "I didn't make it into theater. You made it into theater. Cheryl made it into theater. You're the ones who put me on stage. Do you think I wanted that?"

Kristen knew she had left his mind, his imagination. She was invisible, but there was no power in that.

"She was worried," Mr. Eisenstein said, "so she made a goddamned phone call."

Her dad dropped the magazine to the table and looked at Mr. Eisenstein in the same way he had been looking at the girl on the cover. "She's worried about herself. That's who she's worried about."

"About you too. And Kristen."

"Which is why she left."

"You were wearing her down. You know that. She needed a break. Jesus, you're wearing me down, and we've only been talking for five minutes."

"It's my problem," he said. "Not yours. Not hers."

"That's just stupid," Mr. Eisenstein said. "You think you could keep it private? It's like you're living in a fantasy world."

"Well, I'm sorry about that," her dad said, "but I like it here," and he laughed again. Kristen moved over to the window and looked out at the street, where a few more mermaids and Tinkerbells and cardboard robots were coming up the sidewalk. Why did they all look mad?

Mr. Eisenstein said, "You may be unwell, and that's fine, but you're also a prick. Get out of my house."

Her father smiled and took a step toward Mr. Eisenstein, and Mr. Eisenstein flinched the way his son sometimes did in the schoolyard. Even though he was bigger than her dad, even though it was his house they were standing in, he was the one who was afraid.

Kristen wanted to tell him to cut it out, that it was just her dad, her dad who dreamed about buildings and never hurt anybody.

The doorbell was ringing. One time. Twice. Three and then four times. Her father laughed and pulled his cloak in front of himself in the manner of Bela Lugosi and took another step forward, but his movements were exaggerated. They were funny. It was Dracula as played by Groucho Marx. It was definitely not *Morte Infinita* or even *Nosferatu*. "You see, you see, you see," Kristen wanted to say. There was no danger in him.

The two men looked at each other and then turned away.

"Mom doesn't *have* a boyfriend, does she?" she asked as they were walking down the steps back to the street.

He turned his back to her, hunching his shoulders, and she thought of the first horror film she had ever seen, years before on late-night cable. At the end of the movie the villain had spun away from the crowd and staggered off into the shadows, trying to hide his acid-scarred face from the stares of his loved ones. But her father didn't move.

She listened to him make muffled baby sounds, and after a few moments she took him by the hand, and they walked across the lawn. Mr. Eisenstein was watching them from the window. Then the curtains closed, and the porch light blinked off, and she thought of Eisenstein down in the basement and then of Stephanos, the imaginary man who had been so vivid to her. Her father had hexed him into existence with some sleight of hand—a bunch of words was all it took.

And if he did not exist, then in a strange way her father did not exist—at least not the person she thought she had known. She looked at him, one hand rubbing his reddened eyes, the other gripping her hand, and was surprised that she loved him even more. She gripped him back, but he stepped away from her and picked up the rock. "There are two kinds of people in this world," he said, and he grinned his Dracula grin. And he was right. She wanted him to be right.

Two kinds of people in the world. You were either a vampire or a zombie, and just like in the movies, the zombies were many, many, and the vampires were few and far between. And although the zombies had the numbers, the vampires had class and skill. They lived on the margins, peeking in from time to time when it suited them or pretending they were not vampires at all. She wanted so much to believe.

Kristen was a vampire—she knew that now more surely than ever before—and as she ran down the street, the faces of ghouls and Raggedy Anns and blue-skinned Smurfs and superheroes all turned in her direction. Faces of parents too, holding hands with transformed daughters and sons and suddenly shocked alert by the breaking of glass and the yapping of the Eisensteins' Labrador retriever. They were all zombies really, and she despised each and every one of them almost as much as she hated her mother and her imaginary boyfriend. She hated them for not being what her father called on them to be. She hated them the way she hated the victims in horror movies, and herself, for running so quickly without thinking about whom she had left behind.

Remembering the movie. That's what brought her around the house to the bulkhead, where she rattled the double doors. She could hear yelling from the front of the house. Eisenstein said, "Who is it?"

"It's me," she said, but the doors did not open. She tried to picture herself as a vampire and Eisenstein as the innocent victim struggling to resist her. She wanted to hold him and bury her face in his pale neck and swallow and swallow until she felt better—until his innocent blood mixed with her own. "Open up," she said in her most confident singsong voice, but it came out wrong. It sounded afraid and frail and as human as human can be, and for a second she did not recognize it.

People were running up the street toward the window her father had just shattered, and Kristen tried to think of her mother on her sailboat, but all she could see in her mind's eye was the rock on the Eisensteins' shag rug. She banged on the door until her hand hurt. She tried to make her clatter a match for the noise on the other side of the house, where her father must have been doing something else to make people yell. She spit her teeth into the grass. She gave the door a kick. "It's me!" she hollered.

"Who?" Eisenstein said.

"It's Kristen," she said. "Just Kristen," and the door opened and she stepped inside.

# The Invisibles

HUGH SHEEHY

From *The Invisibles* (2012)

The end of my fifth summer singled it out forever in the stream of my childhood. Many days my mother and I cooked canned soup on a toy stovetop in our basement, pretending bombs had ruined the upstairs world. And one afternoon at the zoo, surrounded by wild animals in cages and tamer ones in trees, my mother confiscated my snow cone and yanked me behind a hedge. She crouched down and directed my attention to a small, gray-haired woman standing in front of the lions. Her face was wrinkling, rendered sexless by neglect. Families passed without the faintest interest in her.

"Cynthia, see her. She's more or less invisible, except to the lion, who sees lunch. She's not really invisible, but she might as well be. Wipe away that smile, little girl. We're exactly like her."

My fascinated mother drank from the snow cone until her lips were stained purple. She scowled and jerked her head toward the woman—the invisible, a person who is unnoticeable, hence unmemorable. Mother knew all about invisibles and kept her eyes open in public. She brought home reports: a woman licking stamps at the post office, an anguished old man in line at the bank, a girl crying by a painting in the museum. The library crawling with them.

"Remember, Cynthia, you're an invisible, too," she said. "Just like me. We're in it together. Forever."

That summer I collected her sayings and built a personality with them. I mastered my bicycle and braved the creeks and abandoned barns that lay within an hour's journey of home, never doubting that if a bad guy appeared, he wouldn't see me and, if he happened to be an invisible, that I moved in the aura of my all-knowing mother. Then, one August day when the corn crop was blowing, giving glimpses of sweet ears ripe for the picking, she disappeared from our house.

Over a decade after she vanished, a strange van appeared in the old parking lot at the Great Skate Arena. At once I knew an invisible drove the thing. Around the corner, in the main lot, honking cars inched forward. The grouchy cop waved his ticket book at drivers seeking a place to release excited children. No one had noticed this van, faded maroon with a custom heart-shaped bubble window on the passenger side near the back. Scabs of rust clung to the lower body, over new tires. It wasn't the sort of car you liked to see outside a skating rink or anyplace where the typical patron was twelve years old.

"First of all it should go without saying that a guy drives that thing. But mainly I wonder how he it got into the lot." Randall was our tall, brainy boy. He lived for logical problems like this one; the old parking lot where we smoked was separated from the new parking lot by a row of massive iron blocks with thick cable handles that only a crane could have lifted. The back of the old parking lot was closed in by a tangle of vines and meager trees. Beyond this dark thicket, from below, came the sounds of the highway.

"He must have come from down there." Brianna squinted at the wall of vegetation. I'd put the purplish paint around her eyes. "There must be a bare patch we can't see."

"I would bet that a pervert drives that baby," Randall observed of the van.

"Vans are too obvious for pervs these days." Brianna took a stance in her vintage black and white stockings. She was little, hot, and adept at finding killer vintage clothes in thrift stores. "He's probably some poor escapee from the psycho ward."

They turned to me to decide, these two kids who didn't know what invisibles were, even though they were in the club. They bore the symptoms of invisibles in denial, dying their hair black, punching steel through their lips and nostrils, wearing shirts that pictured corpses. They hung out with me. We hung out at a skating rink with junior high schoolers. No one ever caught us smoking. The list went on. Rather than try to explain our metaphysical plight—I'd never been comfortable talking about my mother—I shrugged, faked a smile, and ignored the sickening presence I sensed in the van's heart-shaped window. The mind I detected in that window was that of an all-knowing bully waiting for you to contradict him. "I don't know, but he's probably sleeping in there, and either way we don't want to wake him up. Can we go inside now and skate?"

I puffed at my cigarette between breaths, trying to hurry things along, confident that under the dome of the skating rink I'd shake my fear that a knife-swinging but otherwise unremarkable oddball lurked behind one of the dormant air-conditioning units lined up behind the skating rink.

Randall absentmindedly played with his recent nose piercing. "Look at that creepy window. If he's in there he's probably watching us right now."

Through the dusty window we could see the surface of an opaque space. In our own ways we acknowledged the disadvantage of the unknowing souls we'd spied on from behind unlighted glass. Our spines all twitched a little.

"You think he's in there?" Brianna pinched a cigarette above the filter, breaking it as she sometimes did when she was nervous. She let it fall on the cracked lot. Her voice grew quiet. "Why would someone want to sleep here?"

Randall walked over to the van and knocked three times on the heart-shaped window. Against the thick, curved glass, his knuckles made a hollow sound that echoed in my chest. Doing a good job of looking unafraid, he stood looking up at it, then smiled at us. Brianna and I watched the window for a terrible face.

Randall threw back his head and laughed like a cartoon villain who has just tied a woman to train tracks. Even at his most raucous he couldn't draw attention from the main parking lot. He cackled until Brianna snapped another cigarette in her shaking hand, and I put my arm around her tiny shoulders. She looked so helpless, her lip shaking, her stick palm dotted with tobacco.

"You're such an asshole," she blurted. "I'm not going to couplesskate with you if you don't come back right now."

"Okay, okay." Randall returned to the little field of safety we seemed to occupy between the brown steel door and the dormant air-conditioning unit. Above our heads, a light snapped on, and I could see how pale my friends looked, how afraid, and knew they could see it in my face, too. Randall squeezed between our bodies, with an arm for each of us. "Shall we?"

As if he could make us forget the unknown behind the dark window in the maroon travel van, he ushered Brianna and me toward the entrance around the corner, where, if she recognized us each Thursday night, the obese woman in the ticket booth would give no sign.

My mother had bad habits which arose as a result of being an invisible. She stared at strangers. She burst into laughter. These were marks of her frustration. She liked to tell cashiers that she'd already paid and make them admit that they hadn't been totally attentive. Then she'd give the money back.

One day my father and I came home from the farmers market to a house that bore all the signs of her presence. The garage door was open, revealing the backside of her blue sedan. In the oven, cooked blueberries pushed through the flaky crust of an unwatched pie. Suspecting she was hiding in one of her usual places, I parted the dresses in her closet and looked under my parents' tightly made bed. Outside my father walked the rows of the well-tended vegetable garden, and I balanced myself on the patio rail and stood, searching for her face in the field of swaying cornstalks that enclosed our house. Hiding was a game we played together, and with each shift of my eyes I expected to find her grinning among the rows.

When we grew tired of shouting for her, we went into the house, set the pie out to cool, and waited for her to emerge. I was excited to learn what new hiding spot my mother had found, but my father was upset over her absence. He slumped beside me on the couch and pinched the bridge of his nose. A fidgety, bald-headed man who knew numbers and tax laws, he was always forcing himself to keep his mouth shut around his wife.

The detective we spoke to offered no answer.

"Sometimes people disappear out of their lives," he said. He kept a neat steel desk with a rectangular wire basket on one corner beside his computer monitor. Beneath a glass reading lamp he'd arranged a scene with cast-iron miniatures, an eyeless, large-chinned policeman interrogating a tied criminal who glared up with red eyes. "They just vanish, you know what I mean."

"Not like this," said my father. The very suggestion she'd left infuriated him. "That's on the highway, on long road trips. Hitchhikers disappear." He didn't quite look at the policeman, directed his ire internally. His entire forehead seemed to throb. He held my hand with incredible gentleness.

The detective tried to disguise his pity with a perplexed smile. He looked at me as if reading my thoughts, then reached for a Rolodex. "I can direct you to someone who's good at talking about this sort of thing."

My father flinched away from these words, said no, thank you.

Early that winter my father told me not to expect her to come home. I stopped asking him about it but continued to watch milk cartons and mail flyers for her face. I'd just begun kindergarten and wanted to tell her she had been right all along. I was an invisible. My new teacher couldn't bring herself to remember my name. Other children never looked at me and seemed to avoid the spaces where I played at recess. I was stuck wearing my name written on a construction paper label strung around my neck with yarn, long after the teacher had memorized my classmates. For weeks I felt like a unit of space in which a sign floated: "Cynthia invisible here."

My mother would have laughed. But by then it was just me and my noninvisible father and the noninvisible woman who had begun to hang around, in a restored farmhouse out in the cornfields that ran to forgettable stretches outside the city.

After the rink let us out with a drove of children to waiting parents, Brianna and Randall left in his car to go screw in their latest secluded spot. With a mild case of virgin's blues, I drove off alone, with a scentless, yellow, leaf-shaped air freshener swinging above my head. My drive toured the well-lighted streets of suburbs, and no headlights followed long enough to make me more than a little cold. For a few years now my fear of the dark had been completely relocated to a fear of people and especially to the signs of them in the dark, like the headlights of solitary cars and the sound of footsteps on a sidewalk. The full, rustling fields of corn I drove among on the road to my township had long been reassuring company. Though I'd seen enough horror films to envision the travel van pulling out of the vegetables, I'd ceased to think much about it.

Before leaving the rink I'd checked the old parking lot and

seen only weeds bent to the gravel by new autumn winds. I'd asked the police officer who oversaw Great Skate's traffic if the van had been towed. A tall, sour-mouthed man with a crab-red face, he considered me as if I'd claimed to have seen a UFO.

"What van?" he said. "I've been here all night, and there hasn't been any van. Believe me, I would have noticed a van like that."

"Never mind," I told him. "I must have it mixed up with a creepy van in another abandoned parking lot."

The memory of this snappy comeback kept me happy while I drank a chocolate malt in a booth beside a tinted diner window and watched drunk older kids come blaring in to devour large sandwiches and plates of chili cheese fries. They spilled food on their faces, shirts, and arms while getting most of it into their mouths. It was disappointing that the boy my imagination blessed with charm and intelligence stood up to belch with greater force than he could muster sitting down. Completely unseen, I made my careful exit through a fray of shouting and reckless gestures. It was after three by then, and I felt snug in my sleepiness and invisibility.

At home the lights were on, the ceiling fans spinning, but the rooms were empty, the doors that should have been closed, open. The air felt charged with a panic that made me run around the ground level, looking for someone.

On the patio I found my stepmother, an impressive work of self-made beauty with big pale hair, smoking in her black robe. She stood beneath the moon and gazed out over a mile of dark, shining corn. She'd been asleep and since getting up had poured herself a glass of wine. When I came up to the rail near her, she gasped and took a step back.

"Just me," I said. "No psycho killer."

She squinted down and took a step in my direction. "Your father's looking for you."

I laughed, imagining my father exploring warehouses, deserted docks, shouting my name. He never worried about me and never made me come home by a certain time. "Where is he look-ing?"

"He just needs to feel like he's doing something." When she was sleepy, speech did not come easily to her, and I took her strange look for effort. "I've been watching him drive around the block for an hour." By "block" she referred to the square mile of cornfield fringed every few hundred yards with houses like ours. Across the field, where the highway joined back road after back road, the twin twinkles of headlights turned in the direc-tion of our road, and disappeared into the dark mass of the crops. "That's him now."

As I looked for his headlights she grabbed hold of my wrist with her cold, hard hand. Something like profound relief came over her. Her grip was strong, and she gazed resolutely into the darkness of the field that lay between us and the sight of my fa-ther's headlights. When I tried to pull away she said, "Stay right here with me until he gets here, please." I'd never heard her voice so grim.

I let her hold my hand and stepped closer to her. We were still getting to know each other and, being the girlier of us, she looked almost afraid that I would touch her. Then she hugged me against her and sighed.

"What's happening?"

"Your little friends. Your poor little friends." She could never remember their names, but she could still feel sorry for them. She repeated herself twice and wouldn't say anything more.

The police had discovered Randall's car in a new subdivision where no houses had yet been built, a street making a wide figure eight among undeveloped plots of land. Through the summer the grass had grown tall and seedy, hiding the view of the new street from the country road that led to it, and it was no shocker that Randall and Brianna had been going back there to get it on. They were connoisseurs of discreet sex nooks, the way some couples criticize movies and people they know. Until then I'd believed that doing it in seclusion was an appropriate pastime for a pair of invisible teenagers, but now I felt ashamed of my joke.

The police had been called about teenagers screaming in the subdivision. When they arrived they found only the car and no sign of Randall or Brianna, who evidently still had her purse. People agreed that this was a good sign, though maybe just to agree there was a good sign. Both windows on the driver's side of Randall's car were shattered. But there was no blood in the car or on the street, no further signs of struggle, and so the police were hopeful.

Because the detective considered time was an important factor, he questioned me that night in my living room. Eager to help, I rehearsed describing the van while watching our front window for headlights. When they arrived my father and stepmother left me alone with a youngish, good-looking detective and a couple of policemen. This wasn't the same detective who'd looked for my mother, but his personality made up for the dissimilarity.

Detective Volmar had a scar on his lip and spoke courteously. He sat with his legs crossed and listened as I explained the awful prognostications I'd experienced at Great Skate when I'd seen the van.

"But afterward you let your friends go home," he said at one point. "Why did you do that?"

"I guess I wasn't scared anymore. I should have trusted my instinct. I knew he was an invisible."

The detective had a mean-spirited, doubtful smirk. "An invisible?"

"It's someone who doesn't get noticed, who for one reason or another isn't memorable. I think maybe some of them go bad, become things like kidnappers, or serial killers."

"That's interesting. How do you know this van driver was an invisible?"

I explained how invisibles stand out to one another, how the traffic cop at Great Skate hadn't even seen the strange van, even though it was parked so conspicuously in the seemingly inaccessible old parking lot. Therefore, I reasoned, the van driver was an invisible.

Detective Volmar told one of the cops standing by to find out who this traffic policeman was and to get him on a cell phone or radio. "How did you notice him, then? If he was an invisible."

"Because I'm an invisible," I said. "And my friends are, too. That's how he saw us."

After asking a few more questions Detective Volmar thanked me and said he'd appreciate it if he could question me at a later date, should his investigation require it. I told him I only wanted my friends to turn up.

He laughed, I suppose at my eagerness. "Gosh you're a nice kid, um . . ." He glanced at his report for my name, then admitted with a wince that he'd forgotten it. "Sorry."

"Don't worry. Happens all the time."

The suburb was in an uproar for days. The police department issued a temporary sunset curfew, and in every class at school I sat within earshot of some boy or girl who complained about getting taken into the station or sent home by stern police officers. There were as many stories about sightings of the maroon travel van, near the trailer park, in the oceanic parking lot of the old supermarket, all of them obviously derivative of urban legend. In the halls you saw the usual theater created around a local tragedy. Outwardly my peers showed sympathy for Randall and Brianna. Many joined hands and wept at the assembly where the principal reminded us that we were one community. Girls who never spoke to me invited me to sit with them at lunch.

I declined, sat in the bleachers by the baseball diamond, as usual, though the absence of my best friends made it impossible to eat anything. The weather was getting colder and windier, the sky higher up, and it was even a little frightening to sit near the empty dugout, so far from the school building that no one would have heard me shouting if I'd needed help. But mostly I felt sad, hoped my friends would turn up, and doubted they would. This struck me as the kind of situation where hoping is something you do to allay dread. Our farming region was small, its people interconnected in a way that made secrets short-lived, and I feared that the driver of the maroon travel van and my friends were long gone.

Once my mother explained that invisibility could be an advantage. "I don't want to fill your head with too many possibilities, little girl." We were sitting on swings at the metropark, her shoes mired in wood chips while mine dangled above them, and she was talking on and on while I adored her—our usual rapprochement. "I don't want other people's inventions to get in the way of your imagination. Who knows what you could come up with? I talk too much to have a good idea, so I sure as hell don't know. You seem like a good apple to me. Am I right? Are you a good apple?"

"I'm a good apple," I insisted.

"I know it, little girl. You don't have to tell me. I don't have to worry about you going off the map and doing something crazy."

Going off the map, she'd said. The idea intrigued me, though at the same time it was a disappointment. Hadn't I been off the map my whole childhood? Wasn't I still off the map, a seventeen-year-old whose idea of a good time on a Friday night was roller-skating in giant circles in a crowd of twelve-year-olds?

No one knew what I thought, and I was little more than a statistic in attendance- and grade-books. English teachers wrote little congratulatory notes on my essays, but I only wrote back to them what they'd said in class. And anyway they were invisibles, too. My father had to work all the time. His parenting style consisted of giving me money and trusting me.

The first time I dreamed of Brianna and Randall after they disappeared, my bed was in the middle of the floor at Great Skate. The rink must have been closed, because the music was off and only a few lights were on. We appeared to be the only people in the place. I had awoken there, still wearing baggy pajamas, to find them skating circles around me. My friends had changed. They spoke and skated like Randall and Brianna but looked older, sickly, their eyes sunk in their faces.

"Hi, Cynthia," said Brianna, whizzing past.

"Hey, Cynth," said Randall, over her shoulder.

"Where have you two been? Everyone's been so afraid for you."

"They shouldn't be," said Brianna.

"No reason to worry about us. None at all."

"You shouldn't keep secrets from your friends," said Brianna, circling again.

"You should have told us we were invisibles, Cynthia," said Randall.

"You knew."

"I didn't think you'd believe me," I said.

"You should have trusted us," said Randall.

"We're your friends."

"We could have gone off the map a long time ago," said Randall. He frowned, shaking his head. "A long time ago. That would have been best for everyone."

"What did you say?"

"Have you ever thought about going off the map?" asked Brianna.

"I definitely prefer life off the map," Randall said. "It's everything I dreamed it would be."

"Or would have, if someone had told us about it."

"Have you seen my mother?"

Brianna's grinning face glided close to mine. There were frown lines around her little mouth. "You want to know where we heard that?"

Randall moved up next to her. His teeth looked gray in the low light. He was pointing off to the side of the rink, to the shadows around the concessions counter. "We heard it from him."

The moment I became aware of the silhouette of a man standing at the edge of the rink, I was possessed by such a desire to scream that I woke up in my bed, back in my bedroom. It was early morning, before seven, and in a few minutes my alarm would go off. Outside, rain fell from a dark sky into the acres of dispirited corn plants.

Though the wait tortured me, I let two weeks pass before investigating the site where Randall and Brianna had vanished. Each night my friends met me in the dark skating rink and cautioned me to wait for the police to leave the crime scene alone. Their faces were getting older. For a few days I stayed home from school and flipped through yearbooks, reexamining pored-over panoramic photos for our faces. In all three yearbooks there were only the standard shots of each of us and, the one year I missed picture day, they hadn't even listed me under *Not Pictured*. Afraid of police by day, afraid of the maroon van by night, I drove around, often taking the road that led past the subdivision where they were heard screaming. I couldn't see over the tall grass that blocked the street inside. I attended unsolicited conferences with the pamphlet-bearing guidance counselor at school and watched television in an empty house.

One morning, just before I woke for school, Brianna and Randall told me the crime scene would be deserted.

"It's safe to go now," said Brianna.

"If you're still interested, that is," said Randall.

The subdivision-to-be was north of the next township, on a farm road with a few old houses perched jauntily along a deep irrigation ditch. The autumn rain had begun to break down the high grasses in the undeveloped lots, but I still had enough cover back there that I didn't mind getting out of my car to walk around. The weather had knocked down the police tape. Clean light poured out of the sky, drying the few leaves that the brisk wind picked up and flew around the new-paved street.

There was evidence of my friends all over the ground, though the police probably couldn't see that. Dried wads of Brianna's green bubble gum lay like moldy little brains all over the pavement. Cigarettes only she could have broken. There were the wrappers from the tacos that Randall ordered in what he deemed practical boxes of six. Walking along the concave gutter, passing out of the crime scene, I came to a kind of midden of used condoms and wrappers, blown dry and brittle through the warrens of tall grass. I wondered how many were scattered through the undergrowth, and was overcome with the sense that this was all that remained of my friends.

"I seen you come in here."

When I looked up I didn't see the old man who had come from across the street to talk to me—I saw the maroon van, idling in front of me, with a tall man beside it. Long, muscley arms hung out of his shirt, and he wore faded, tight jeans. His blonde hair was long and filthy, his skin a burned red, his black eyes bright and dense. Only a few times in my life had my imagination brought something into this world—usually it took me elsewhere. The vision lasted a second, and then I was looking at an old man in bib overalls, standing a few feet away from me. Seeing he'd scared me, he lowered his shoulders and turned slightly. He'd parted his hair on the right, presumably with the comb in his breast pocket.

"Hi," I said.

"You should go home. The police still come around sometimes, and they wouldn't be happy to run into you back here."

"My friends were the ones who . . . were here." I didn't know how to describe what had happened to them to this stranger.

"The ones got taken." The old man nodded. "I called the cops about it."

It was only then that I noticed the blandness in his face, the lights-out quality that rises in a person's eyes after years of being overlooked. "You saw the van, too?"

From the way he puckered his lips as he nodded, it was obvious he felt responsible for my friends' disappearance. "I used to think, 'Let them have their fun back there.' I know things are different now, but I got married when I was about their age. I always thought any kids who had the nerve to go off like that deserved a little time alone." He looked at me hard and said, "Not all of us find somebody who's exactly like us, if you catch my drift."

"I know," I said, remembering how my mother pitied my father for failing to understand her.

"Then I seen him follow them back in here, and I knew I made a mistake letting them have the place." He stood with his hands in the deep pockets of his overalls, staring at the taped-off crime scene, which the wind had broken down into an awkward triangle. "I knew I couldn't help them then. Still I came running back here, and that van almost ran me down."

"Do you think the police will find them?" It was stupid to ask this, because asking him to answer hurt him, more than it did me, watching him struggle to lie.

He gave up and said, "I don't know if I can in good conscience tell you to hope too much."

"I keep dreaming about them," I said.

"I do, too," he said.

Detective Volmar telephoned a few days after I'd visited the subdivision where the driver of the maroon van apprehended my friends. He wanted to know if I was opposed to the idea of a free breakfast. He even offered to come out and pick me up.

"I hate to impose on people in their own homes," he explained a second time, as he drove me through the fields of yellowing cornstalks to the nearby diner where, he couldn't have known, I sometimes ate alone at night. "They get nervous to have a policeman in the house. I guess they're afraid I'll notice the infraction of a tiny law while I'm there, one they don't even know they're breaking. People break laws all the time. Sometimes I think we have so many just so I can arrest someone if I know I need to."

In daylight the restaurant was cleaner and full of shadows, staffed with new cooks and waitresses, strangers to me. We sat down at a booth whose window gave out to a view of the township's main street, the storefronts of old lawyers' offices and a realtor. Detective Volmar said he found all this very quaint. Then he ordered the largest breakfast platter on the menu and requested extra bacon. He drank black coffee in large gulps and knew where his mug was without looking at it.

I ordered a cup of yogurt with granola, something I could crunch on and finish without really trying to eat. Between the weird dreams and missing my friends, my appetite still hadn't returned. The detective may have thought I was a dainty eater, though maybe I flattered myself to think he noticed. He listened to me with interest, but his eyes were a critical compound of belief and disbelief applied to my every statement. He must have been thinking things he didn't say.

"The first time we talked, you didn't mention that your mother went missing a long time ago."

"Sorry," I said.

"Not at all. I'm surprised your dad didn't say anything. The case is still officially open, but nobody's working on it anymore. Whoever had it figured her for a deserter." With one skeptical shrug he won my gratitude and trust. "There's no evidence for that, though."

"Do you think the disappearances are connected?"

Detective Volmar smiled with what compassion he could muster. "There's no reason to think so. But I've been thinking about what you told me the night I interviewed you in your living room.

I'm curious about the connection you made between invisibles and serial killers."

"You really believed me about invisibles?"

He drained half his water glass and shrugged. "We'll see. You obviously believe in them."

"It's because I mentioned the van, and the old man did, too. Isn't it?"

He turned his head away slightly. "I'd appreciate it if you didn't talk to a lot of people about the details of the case. The public already knows too much. As it happens, we don't know much more than the guy who called us, and apparently, you know as much as he does." He paused and let the waitress refill his coffee mug, then continued solemnly, with his fingers playing together on the paper placemat. "But I cannot afford not to be open-minded about this. Two kids have disappeared."

"What do you want to know?"

"Well, you say you're invisible. Plainly, you're not. So what exactly do you mean?"

"It's hard to explain," I said. "I'm not sure I fully understand it either. My mother was never that clear about it. But think of it this way. How did you find out about me?"

Detective Volmar looked from the streaked window to me. "Your father called the station and said you were missing. I guess he'd heard about your friends and thought you were with them. Then you got home, and he called to say you were there."

"So the whole time you were coming to my house, you were expecting to question a seventeen-year-old girl, right?"

"Right."

"So maybe that helped you to see me a little more clearly. Maybe, if you knew nothing about me, I could sit right next to you, and you would never have known it. Not because I'm literally invisible, but because I don't connect to other people. Some people just fall through the cracks. But most of us want to be seen, so we make an effort. I'm somebody's daughter, and until a while ago I was somebody's friend. My mother was somebody's daughter, somebody's friend, somebody's wife, and somebody's mother, in that order."

"What does this have to do with murderers?"

"I think some people get themselves noticed by taking revenge."

"Why not get noticed in a more subtle way?" Detective Volmar's toast arrived, and he proceeded to question me as he scooped grape jelly from a plastic tub. "Why not become somebody's husband or wife?"

I thought of my friends and my mother, how much it enraged me to see the sunset curfew lifted the week before and to see life return to normal at the high school. "Because it hurts a lot when someone forgets you," I said. "Taking revenge is one way to make sure no one ever does it again."

There I was, in the dream that had become nightly. I sat up in bed in the middle of the skating rink, watching Brianna and Randall skate around me like a pair of professionals. They'd improved quite a bit, skating so much in my dreams, and they could do things like double axels and land rolling on four wheels. That said about their skating, their bodies looked considerably worse, older, more starved. One of Randall's ears seemed to be coming off, and a sore I hadn't immediately noticed on Brianna's cheek was growing. What fingernails remained were black, and the skin where the others had been was dry, red, and wrinkled.

Their moods grew nastier with their appearances. I didn't say much, mostly just listened to them describe what it was like to drive around in the van with the man who stood at the edge of the rink. He never moved. I'd begun to doubt that he knew we were there.

Sometimes Brianna or Randall would make a teasing reference to my mother, and I would beg them to tell me where she was, what had happened to her. However, my pleading could only last for so long, as I knew a game when it was being played at my expense, and then I would just sit there, my feelings hurt, as they laughed.

"So why didn't you tell your *boyfriend* where we are?" asked Randall.

"She's afraid he'll like me better. Even like this, I'm prettier."

"What's the use?" I asked. "He can't come into my dream and put you in handcuffs. He wouldn't be interested in that stuff. Besides, he knows where you are."

"And where's that?" said Randall, as Brianna turned about to skate backward, with her arms crossed over her small breasts.

"You're in the maroon van. With that guy. Isn't it obvious?"

Brianna smiled knowingly at Randall. "Do you want to know what we see?"

"Forests, mountains, lakes, eagles, coyotes, a comet," Randall counted off his list on the fingers of one hand, starting over whenever he reached his thumb. "A nautilus shell, sharks feeding in a school of silver fish, the White House, rattlesnakes, tarantula eggs, the Grand Canyon, your mother, cottonmouths, a panther."

"Your mother," said Brianna. "We saw your mother."

"When?"

"When!" Randall shouted.

"Where did you see her?" I asked.

"Where!"

Brianna shook her head at me. "Is that really what you want to know? Or would you rather know if she asked about you?"

Her insight left me speechless; yes, this was exactly what I wanted to know. Whether she missed me, thought of me, regretted leaving. Did she plan to come back?

"No, no, no, and no," said Randall, laughing in the villainous way he had beneath the heart-shaped window of the van behind Great Skate the night of his disappearance.

"Stop, Randall," said Brianna, putting her hands on her sides. I couldn't tell if she was serious; as her face deteriorated it conveyed fewer and fewer variations on a lurid scowl. "You don't know when to quit kidding. Honestly, you'll hurt a girl's feelings that way." She looked at me, the gleaming in her dry eyes limitless. "You can see for yourself. If you meet us. Come to Great Skate this weekend," she said. "You'll know where to find us. But don't tell your boyfriend. We'll know about it, and so will he." She nodded at the silhouetted man at the edge of the rink. The lights in the rink came up then, so I could see the line of his mouth, enough to know that he watched us and disapproved.

Sometimes I thought about what I would have been like if I still had a mother, if I'd look, sound, dress, and think like her. If I would love cruelty like she had.

We would play this joke on my father, when he got home from work.

The joke was only good on certain days. I wanted to play it all the time, but my mother knew better. She would stop in my bedroom doorway, interrupting whatever fantasy I had going on. Her toothy smile made me feel like she'd caught me doing something wrong. "Cynthia, should we hide from your father?"

Nodding yes, I would gather up my dolls, as they were necessary props.

"Where should we hide, so he can't see us?"

The pantry worked best. We could watch through a crack in the door as my father walked around the house, his loafers clacking on the wooden floors, his shoulders trying to shrug off his suit jacket. When he shouted our names my mother would hold me against her, covering my mouth with her hand. If I needed to laugh, tell me, I was to bite her.

After a while my father would grew so frustrated that his patience failed, and he would make himself a sandwich. This amused us because he'd never learned to snack properly. After watching him mutter miserably over his approximation of the perfect sandwich my mother had prepared and hidden in the pantry with us, we'd wait until he took a beer out onto the patio. Then, very quietly, we would emerge from hiding, she to make him a plate and fill the sink with sudsy dishwater, I to sit on the tiles at her feet with my dolls. Once we were in our respective swings of wash and play, she would open the window and call to him to come in.

"Where were you?" my father would ask, moving to dump his poor sandwich in the garbage, now that my mother's handiwork awaited him. "I was just in here looking for you."

My mother would wrinkle her eyebrows, and she'd send me a wink when my father wasn't looking. "Why, we were right here the whole time. You walked right past. I don't know why you didn't see us. Sometimes I think you just don't appreciate us."

Night was falling earlier now, and though the maroon van was not in the old parking lot when I arrived at the skating rink, I wasn't completely filled with doubt. If my friends were indeed alive, on the run with the driver of the maroon van, they would need to make an inconspicuous entrance. They were simply waiting for the right moment to appear and send me a signal to join them. I wondered what it would be like, to feel the road passing beneath me, what the van smelled like inside, all the things I would see from the heart-shaped window.

Every Friday in October was Halloween at Great Skate, and that night I waited in a line of fifth- and sixth-grade vampires, witches, he-devils, she-devils, and various other monsters. I had dressed up like the invisible man from the black-and-white movie by wrapping my face in white bandages and wearing sunglasses. I put my hair up in a bun, under a black fedora, and since I was neither a tall nor a large-chested girl, I blended with the younger children.

The heavyset woman in the little ticket booth charged me for a child's admission, an unforeseen bonus that under other circumstances would have thrilled me but now only disoriented me a little. I entered the booming atmosphere of the crowded skating dome, got a locker and put on my skates, then glided around the polished wooden floor to sounds of campy eighties hits. On the white walls of the rink, echelons of colored light spots slowly rotated against the flow of disguised skaters. The deep voice of the deejay, hidden away in his booth, announced specially themed skates. All around me boys and girls coasted together, five and six years younger than me, already oblivious to me. It was fine, that had been my childhood, and for a while I had fun being nobody, soaring along to the music. I could do and think anything, be anyone, the only catch being that I had no one to share it with. That's when I noticed the man watching me from the rail of the rink floor, back behind the bathrooms, near the fire exit.

He was tall and strong-looking, leaning over the rail on his elbows, staring directly at me once I'd noticed him. He'd brushed his long blonde hair behind his ears, revealing his ruddy face. He lifted one hand and waved at me. His attempt to smile only seemed to worsen his mood. A person like that you could never touch, only brush against, and never truly speak with, only at. At this moment I became sure that my friends were dead. I bent my knees and somehow avoided wiping out on the hard, hot floor. I neither waved back nor turned my head abruptly away, but he continued to watch me as I passed him. He would move his face over, as if to push it into my line of vision, and wink at me.

I tried to think of some way I might slip off the rink floor and telephone Detective Volmar without chasing off the man at the rail. I wanted not only to escape him but to see him hauled off by the police. Nothing short of a complete victory would be acceptable. Under my mask I wanted to cry but knew I had to keep moving. As long as I kept skating, I could find a way out, call for help, and do what I could. I skated until the man relaxed and let his hands hang limp over the rink floor, as if to say he would wait on me. Then I skated through a large group of angels and, with that blockade behind me, coasted off the floor at the far end of the rink. I skated out into the lobby, where I found the crabby traffic cop eating a soft pretzel as he peered into a vending machine that flattened pennies and stamped them with winged roller skates.

Once I'd pulled away the bandages and sunglasses he remembered me. Because I was so upset, he hardly needed to hear my story to come running with me around to the back of the rink. It was difficult to run on my skates, but I was afraid of being left behind, isolated in a space where no one could see me, the only kind of space where I'd be vulnerable to the man I'd seen next to the rink. The traffic cop barked into his radio as he ran ahead of me around the corner into the empty back lot. I nearly lost my balance when I saw there was no maroon van waiting for us.

The officer didn't need to think twice. "We've been looking for that van. He's probably driving something else." He pulled open the emergency exit door of the rink and ushered me inside. "Come on. Show me where you saw him."

We hurried into the red light that filled the domed room, and from the rail along the rink scanned a hundred masked faces for the one I'd seen watching me all night. I looked out on the floor, along the tables by the concessions area, among the few arcade games on the far wall. There was no place where the man could have been hiding, not really. The traffic cop dashed into the men's room and then the ladies' room. A group of little girls came running out, then the cop, looking frustrated.

A minute of confusion passed before the rest of the police came running in. The music was stopped and the children were herded off the floor so the cops could search the premises. The situation quickly became humiliating and inexplicable, with a lot of adults scowling, tweeners complaining. The man who'd been watching me was gone. None of the twelve-year-olds questioned remembered seeing him at the rail. A few said they might have seen somebody, but their voices were too eager. Their descriptions contradicted each other.

In all there were eight police cruisers in the parking lot, their lights flashing in the pungent autumn night. Some of the twelve or so officers complained while looking at me, to let me know I'd wasted their time. Detective Volmar showed up in an unmarked white car and was very kind to me. He told a few other cops that they couldn't understand what I'd been through, though I had the feeling that he, too, was irritated. He put me in the back of his car with the door open and told me to put my shoes back on. Then he telephoned my father.

About a year later, the man who became known as the Lake Erie killer was arrested in a small town in southern Michigan, a short drive from our suburb in the cornfields. The police discovered the bones of an estimated thirty-one people in the crawl space beneath his house. Brianna and Randall's clothes were some of the first pieces of evidence found, and a detective said it was only a matter of time before their skulls were identified. Also found in one of three garages built on the killer's sprawling property was the maroon travel van my friends and I had seen outside Great Skate the night they'd disappeared. I saw this after school in a news flash I watched in my living room and saw part of an interview with the killer's mother and then a segment where a serial killer expert compared this killer to others. When the station broadcast footage of the police arresting the man who had murdered my friends, he wasn't anyone I recognized. He was older, around average height, with neat brown hair and glasses. He had soft cheeks, the sort of face I would never imagine hid plans to kill somebody.

My father and stepmother were there with me, waiting for me to speak, to say that this was the guy I'd seen in the rink that night the police had tried to come to my rescue. They wanted to see my fear vanish forever. I only shook my head. What if my mother was one of the bodies they'd found, one of those so decayed it would never be identified? The more I thought about it the more possible it seemed and the more I understood I might still be sick. My face must have betrayed my fear, because my father and stepmother suddenly grew ashamed of themselves.

"Let's get out of here," I said. Soon, I knew, the telephone would be ringing. Randall's parents and Brianna's mother would be calling to speak to me. There was weeping to do, relief to share, and bitterness to acknowledge, and now there was a figure to blame it on. Out the window behind my father and stepmother, the sun rippled in the golden light above the drying, broken stalks of last summer's corn. It was getting cold again, the days shortening. Soon the outdoor businesses would close for the winter.

"How about ice cream?" I said.

By then I'd stopped dreaming about Brianna and Randall in the skating rink. They appeared in my dreams, but in the usual nonsensical places, their faces no longer marbled with decay, but fresh and young, as I had known them. They didn't seem to remember what had happened to them, even when, during a dream set in my front yard, I saw the maroon van drive slowly past us. In the dream it was sunny, there were birds hunting worms in the grass, and I felt no fear after the van had gone. "I've been wanting to ask you two," I said to my friends. "Is the driver of the van the killer or not? Or is he someone else?"

"What driver?" Randall said.

"I don't know any van driver," Brianna said.

On the day the police caught the Lake Erie killer, my father, my stepmother, and I came back from the ice cream stand having licked our fingers clean. The burnt flavor of sugar cones lingered in our mouths, and rather than accept the grim circumstances awaiting us, my father suggested we use the remaining daylight to build a scarecrow in the front yard. He dug a flannel shirt and a pair of brown corduroys from a trunk of old clothes, and I found a pillowcase we could use for a head. In the yard we stuffed these things full of leaves. We posted an old shovel handle in the hard ground and hung the great grotesque doll on it. I'd painted ferocious blue eyes and a stitched red frown for a face, and my father fastened on a gray fedora with safety pins. My stepmother sat on the porch swing, bundled up in a blanket, watching as she sipped hot peppermint tea.

The day turned dark over the bare trees, faster than we'd expected, and by the time we joined my stepmother on the porch swing, with leaf scraps clinging to our hair and sweatshirts, the sun was setting, and a wild wind had sprung up. The trees swayed, noisily rattling their branches together. We sat in a tight row on the wooden seat and watched the scarecrow flail its arms in the dusk, casting dead leaves up at the shuddering boughs of our maples, like a wizard trying to rebuild the summer. Inside the house, the telephone rang and rang. The answering machine kept switching on, and we laughed to hear my father gloomily repeating that we weren't home. Maybe that was a little cruel, hiding just then, but we would make up for it later. We would call those people back, and shout, laugh, cry—produce the sounds that people make when they're together. We owed them that much, out of the empathy we felt, listening to them speak slowly, faithfully putting words into the void of our answering machine, against the chill that grows when a name is said and silence answers.

# Faulty Predictions

KARIN LIN-GREENBERG

From *Faulty Predictions* (2014)

Hazel Stump and I were not friends. I moved in with her for practical reasons. The summer people who came to the High Country to escape the humidity and mosquitos in Florida had driven up real estate prices too much for either of us to afford living on our own. I found my room in her house through the classifieds in the *Mountain Times* three years ago. Both of our husbands were dead, and both of us had spent enough years in Boone that leaving and starting over elsewhere would be stupid. You didn't just start over at our age. Well, maybe that's not completely true. Most of my friends had moved away. Even though there was an influx of Floridians here, there was also an outflux of older folks who could no longer take the icy, wind-whipped winters in the mountains. But I stayed, dealt with the winters and dealt with Hazel. Hazel irritated me in many ways, but she had ideas, and sometimes those ideas translated into something to do. And I was always looking for something to fill my days.

On Halloween, Hazel and I shuffled to her battered Ford Focus, nearly tripping over the flat sheets from our beds. We drove down the mountain dressed as ghosts—Hazel draped in a pale pink sheet, I in one with faded daises. Hazel was certain a murder would occur that night at Mecklen College, and she wanted to prevent it. She had told me to make costumes so we could blend into the party we'd infiltrate that evening. She'd given me only half an hour to create the costumes, and in my rush, all I could produce were the ghost costumes, eyeholes hastily cut.

Hazel drove erratically down 321. An enormous black SUV with Florida plates zipped past us, and the driver honked when Hazel swerved. Hazel rolled down her window and shouted, "Floridiot!" I worried we'd get pulled over. And what would the police think looking at the two of us, short, round women in our seventies wearing bed-sheets with eyeholes cut out like we were characters in *A Charlie Brown Halloween*?

"Maybe you should take the costume off for driving," I told Hazel as she skidded around a corner. "I think it's affecting your peripheral vision."

"I got the bow perfect," she said. "I'm not untying it and retying it again."

She'd knotted one of her husband Walter's old ties around her neck so the sheet wouldn't slip off. She'd tied the tie like a bow, with two big red loops that hung down limply. The whole thing looked ridiculous, but at least she'd found a use for one of Walter's ties. He'd been dead for five years, but she still had all his things stuffed in the hallway closet.

The eyeholes on my sheet migrated toward my right ear, and I had trouble breathing. I should have cut holes for our nostrils and mouths. I pulled my sheet off.

"We need to hurry when we get there. Better to keep your costume on," Hazel said.

"It's two hours to Charlotte," I said. "I'll have time to get recostumed." I folded the sheet and held it on my lap. I looked over at Hazel; she wasn't wearing glasses under her costume. "Are you wearing your contacts?" I asked.

"I got one in," she said.

"Where's the other one?"

"On the bathroom floor somewhere. Or maybe Millicent ate it."

Millicent was Hazel's cat, a fat tan number who had never liked me, even though in all my life I'd never had a cat not like me. Small things—pennies, hard candy, buttons—disappeared in our house all the time, and I was certain most of these items had taken up residence in Millicent's enormous, swaying belly.

"You lose depth perception if you don't have two eyes," I said. "You have no depth perception and no peripheral vision. What if a deer jumps out?"

"I'll sense it," she said. Then, as maybe a gesture of kindness to me, she slowed down. I watched the needle on the speedometer drop from 75 to 60.

Hazel believed she could sense a deer because she was psychic. Sometimes she called herself a medium. She said she started getting psychic messages after Walter died. She heard voices from beyond the grave, but they were random people, people she did not know. She got a book from the library about being a psychic and read it again and again. Then she got more books. Then she went to Chapel Hill and met with a group of women who claimed to be psychics, and they told her she had "the gift." The only reason she worked so hard at being a psychic was because she hoped to talk to Walter again. After a year of building up her psychic skills, she opened a shop downtown near the university and did readings for ten dollars. It was a big change from her job as the bookkeeper for the dermatology clinic, which she'd retired from a handful of years before. Most of her psychic shop clients were college girls who stumbled in drunk and giggling and asked about their love lives.

Hazel had a little success with her psychic predictions the second year we lived together. She correctly predicted the exact dates when we'd have snowfall that winter, predicted the final score of the Duke-UNC basketball game in January, and predicted that Timmy Bender, a senior at Appalachian State, would win a seat on the city council. In February, she predicted there would be a fire at the general store on King Street, but no one listened to her. She went to the police, and they nodded and said they'd look into it. She went to the newspaper. They told her they could only write about things that had actually happened, not things someone suspected would happen in the future. One week later, lightning crackled onto the building and burned a charred hole right through the roof. Then people started to take notice of Hazel.

After an article about her appeared in the *Mountain Times*, some communications students decided to interview her for the school's radio station. Some mountain folk came from nearby towns, hopeful, with ten-dollar bills crumpled and warm, wanting to know whether they'd make good money that year. People seemed to believe in Hazel's abilities, although I did not because Hazel was just flat-out wrong so much of the time. I didn't know if it was possible for someone to be wrong about pretty much everything in life and still be right with psychic predictions.

Take for instance our neighbors, Darius and Antoine, two perfectly nice young men. It started with their cat. They moved into the neighborhood a few months after I did, and after they arrived, Hazel no longer let Millicent outside since she said the boys had a serval, not a cat, and she worried the serval would eat Millicent. So all day Millicent sat by the front door and whined to be let out, howling as if someone had stepped on her paw. I told Hazel that Millicent likely had ten pounds on Darius and Antoine's cat, but Hazel ignored me. "I saw on my news that rappers have been keeping servals as pets and some neighborhoods have had problems with the servals eating house pets."

When she said *her* news, she meant Fox News, which she had buzzing on the TV all day. When I'd first moved in, I tried to explain that those people were fearmongers. Hazel said I was too influenced by the liberal media and Fox News was good, truthful news. I learned then that it was useless to argue with Hazel. And if Hazel was a right-wing nutcase, that wasn't really my concern. I'd just let her believe what she believed and would continue to sweep the floor on Fridays and take out the trash on Sundays and wash the sinks on Tuesdays and life could go on smoothly. We didn't have to be friends. We were just housemates, that's all. Usually I ignored her ludicrous statements, let them hang in the air with no response, but this time I demanded to know why she thought Darius and Antoine were rappers.

"Why else would they have a serval?" she said.

"They don't have a serval. They have a spotted cat," I said.

"Servals are from Africa," Hazel said.

"Are you saying that Darius and Antoine are from Africa? Because they're black? They're from Greensboro."

"Well, you know," she said, but I wasn't going to let her off that easy.

"They graduated from App State last spring. Darius works in the Housing Office there. Antoine is a cook at Ruby Tuesday. I doubt they earn enough money at those jobs to purchase exotic animals."

"Well," said Hazel. "There are other ways to earn money that certain types of young men engage in." Then she left the room because I was certain she knew I was about to give her a lecture. I wanted to tell her that just because she'd spent so many years isolated in this town where nearly everyone was white—the students, the tourists, the locals—it didn't excuse that kind of backwards thinking.

But they were nice boys, and Hazel knew it, even if she didn't want to admit it. For a few months, my heart medication had been mistakenly delivered to Darius and Antoine's mailbox, and one of the boys always brought it over when we were home. They could have just left the medication on the stoop so they wouldn't have to speak to us, but they were decent enough to knock on the door and stand on the porch and talk for a few minutes. And I liked that, liked talking to young people, even if it was just a short chat. I missed that from when I worked in the nurse's office at the high school. So often the kids who came to the office weren't really sick, at least not in the bodily way. Some were lovelorn and some had shattered dreams when they hadn't gotten into the colleges they'd wanted, and I knew the stomachaches and headaches they complained of were really symptoms of heartaches. I liked talking to these kids and was happy to write them notes excusing them from class for the hour or two they spent in the office. Talking with Darius and Antoine reminded me of those times when I felt most useful.

The business with Darius and Antoine and rappers and servals wasn't the only unpleasantness between Hazel and me. Right around Thanksgiving of the first year I lived with her, I heard music and stomping in the living room late one night. I poked my head out of my bedroom. Hazel must have thought I was already asleep, because she was dancing. Her eyes were closed, and she waved her arms up and down, as if she were a big bird about to land in a swamp. An egret or something. Then she lifted her legs one at a time, like a dog that needed to pee. But the strangest part was what she was dancing to. It was a commercial jingle, and the lyrics went like this: "Winterzing gum makes you sing! Sing, sing, sing! Your teeth so white you glow at night! Sing, sing, sing!" It was a stupid song, but somehow Hazel had gotten this gum commercial on a loop on a tape and was singing along and dancing her weird bird/peeing dog dance, and I just couldn't stop staring. And then maybe Hazel sensed something, because she opened her eyes and stopped moving, but the tape kept going, "Sing, sing, sing!"

"I wasn't doing anything," Hazel said. She turned the tape off.

"I didn't think you were," I said. "I just wanted a glass of water."

"You should really knock when you come out of your room," she said. "We need to establish some ground rules."

"I'm not knocking when I leave my own room. It's not something a sane person does."

"Well, then," she said. "You should work on not sneaking up on people. It's not decent."

"You're not decent," I said, and trudged to the kitchen to get a glass of water I didn't even want.

About a month later I found a Christmas newsletter poking out of a Lands' End catalog in the pile of magazines and catalogs I planned to take out for recycling. I read the newsletter; it was from James Stump, his wife Yvonne, and their daughter Kelly. A small image at the top depicted a dark-haired teenager in a red dress posing in front of a Christmas tree. They lived near New York City and James worked in advertising. The letter mentioned the successful campaign he'd led for Winterzing gum. Yvonne volunteered at the town library and organized the women's book club. Kelly was waiting to hear back from the colleges she'd applied to and had just finished a winning season as the captain of the field hockey team at her school. They seemed like an ordinary family, nice, and the only possible connection to Hazel was the last name. Was James her son? She'd never mentioned a son. And she'd never mentioned a granddaughter. Was James Stump the reason Hazel had danced to the Winterzing commercial? I didn't know. I also didn't know whether Hazel had meant to save the Christmas newsletter or whether she was hiding it, even from herself. I reread that newsletter, committed it nearly to memory, slipped it back into the Lands' End catalog, then left the catalogs in their pile. If Hazel wanted to read the newsletter, it was waiting for her.

"Tell me again what you saw," I said to Hazel as we drove into Charlotte. It had turned dark during our drive, but it was a clear, star-filled night. We were only a few miles from the college. I was thankful we hadn't gotten into a crash, since Hazel had driven the whole way with only the one contact lens.

"It's not like a movie in my mind. How many times do I have to tell you?"

"But what do you know?" I didn't really believe a murderer was loose on Mecklen College's campus. I wasn't particularly worried or scared, but I knew that we'd stick out in our pathetic costumes. No one dressed as ghosts for Halloween anymore, especially not college students. When I saw the students from Appalachian State wandering King Street on Halloween, most of the girls were dressed as tramps.

"All I know is that there will be costumes. And a knife. That's it."

"And how will we stop things?"

"We'll figure it out when we see it."

I doubted we'd be able to stop anything, but I wasn't going to argue with Hazel. Plus, I was having an OK time. At home, I'd just be waiting for trick-or-treaters who never showed up because we didn't live in the nice neighborhood. By this time of night I would have eaten half the candy I'd bought.

We arrived at the college, and I wished we'd gotten here in the daylight so I could better admire it all. The campus was covered in trees, and there was a pond surrounded by weeping willows, and the dormitories looked like small castles. Ducks floated in the pond, and their quacks echoed through the quiet night. I thought about how much Larry would have loved this place. We had made it a habit to walk through college campuses wherever we traveled because they seemed like safe, beautiful small worlds full of knowledge and potential. When we'd first gotten married, Larry had harbored fantasies of one day becoming a college professor. He'd always been interested in learning as much as he could about World War II because his older brother, Hank, had died at Normandy. Larry kept an old black-and-white framed photograph of Hank on his nightstand in all the bedrooms we'd lived in. Hank was so young, permanently captured as that handsome, strong-jawed twenty-three-year-old. After I moved into Hazel's house, I slid that photo of Hank into the bottom drawer of my dresser. It seemed even sadder now, even more of a tragedy, that he'd gone so young. I couldn't let myself be haunted by two deaths—one so long ago and one recent—and looking at that old photograph of Hank in his uniform just reminded me of too much history.

Larry always said he wanted to better understand wars, understand why they had to happen and how they changed the course of things. He taught high school history but said if he worked at a college, he could teach classes that were focused on World War II instead of only spending the two weeks every December that were allotted for it in the high school curriculum. He could spend his summers traveling and researching and writing articles and books and maybe all of that would help him understand what had happened to Hank because, after all this time, he still couldn't make sense of it. In the years after our wedding, Larry slowly earned his master's degree at night, one class at a time, paid for by the school district. He kept saying that one day he'd go back for his doctorate. But then years passed and he kept teaching at the high school and I kept working as a school nurse and then, before we knew it, we were retired, all those years behind us. I'd had dreams myself, of going somewhere far away, helping on overseas medical trips, the kind where doctors perform surgeries on kids with cleft palates. I thought also about flying to foreign countries and bringing medicine and mosquito netting to combat malaria. But I never did go; Larry and I only left America twice, once when we went to the Bahamas and another time to London, but never to any of those countries where I could do something that would help someone.

Hazel pulled her car into an empty faculty lot and yanked up the parking brake. She got out of the car and barked, "Get your costume back on."

I pulled the sheet back on and held on to the sides so it wouldn't slip off. Hazel walked quickly, and I did my best to keep up, but it was difficult because of the arthritis in my knees. Hazel walked toward the music, a loud bass beat pumping out of a stone building at the center of campus. Dozens of students congregated outside. Just like at home in Boone, many of the girls were dressed in revealing costumes. There were scantily dressed cats, princesses, and what looked like a group of butterflies with sparkly wings. Boys were dressed as pirates and cowboys and skeletons and vampires. There were a few aliens in green masks who were of indeterminate gender. Many of the students held red plastic cups, and the air smelled like beer.

"Come on," Hazel said, flipping up the edge of her costume until a hand emerged. She grabbed onto my sheet and pulled me toward the door. She pushed past the students congregated outside, and I kept saying "sorry" and "excuse me" from under my sheet as we shoved through the crowd. At the door, a tall man with thick, muscled arms stood in front of Hazel. He wore a black T-shirt with the word SECURITY printed on it. "College ID?" he said. "Mecklen students only. You two students?"

Even with the sheets on, could we somehow pass for twenty-year-olds? It seemed impossible.

Hazel shook her head, and the man crossed his arms and seemed to grow bigger right in front of us. "Can't let you in without an ID," he said.

I wondered what Hazel's next move would be. Would she argue with him? Would she try to push past him? Would she unveil herself and hope he believed we were harmless enough to enter the room with thrumming music and flashing red and blue and green lights? But Hazel didn't argue or fight; instead, she turned and dragged me away.

When we were on the lawn, under a grove of trees and away from the crowd of students, I yanked off my sheet and said, "We came all the way out here and you give up like that?"

Hazel draped the sheet back on me. "This isn't the right place."

"We're supposed to be at another college?"

"We're supposed to be here. Just not at that party. I'm seeing a building that's shaped like the letter H. This isn't it."

"If I were a killer, I'd go to this party. Look how easy it would be," I said, sweeping a hand toward the campus center. "Most of them are already drunk."

"It's not the right place," Hazel said again. "Don't argue. Let's go."

"Where?" I said.

"Just follow me."

We walked on a paved path that cut across the middle of campus past a row of dormitories, one named Anderson, the next Harris, the next Wilson. "No, no, no," said Hazel as we walked past each one. I wished I could see her face so I could tell whether she was nervous or angry, whether she thought our mission was urgent. We passed the Gorton Science Building, and Hazel shook her head. "No," she said again.

"I have to use the facilities," I said. Hazel spun in a circle and pointed to a gray building across the lawn. A square sign outside the building said "Lancaster Hall." Above the door, the word "History" was carved in the stone. "The door's open," she said, and I followed her across the lawn. I half hoped the door would be locked, because I delighted in Hazel's faulty predictions. But I also half hoped she was correct because of the pressure on my bladder. We walked up the stairs of the history building, I pulled the handle, and the door swung open. "Hurry up," Hazel said. "The bathroom's down the hall and to the left."

Once again she was right. Maybe Hazel was just observant; maybe with her one good eye she'd noticed someone going into the building earlier and knew it was still unlocked. And maybe there were signs somewhere directing people to the women's room. I didn't want to believe Hazel had any sort of psychic powers, but sometimes she just seemed to know too much.

After I'd finished in the bathroom, I walked down a hallway filled with professors' offices, and I thought of how Larry would have loved to work here in an office with books lining the walls and a small chalkboard affixed outside the door for students to write messages. In the foyer, Hazel stood in front of a large bulletin board.

"Look," she said, a finger on a pink flyer. I stepped closer. The flyer advertised an art exhibition that would be held on campus in November in the Polk Art Building featuring the work of sophomore art majors. On the bottom of the flyer was a sketch of the art building. It was shaped like the letter H.

"Have you been to this campus before?" I asked.

"I've never been here," she said. "I've wanted to visit for a few years now. But that's not what this is about. We're going to the art building." She walked toward the exit.

I followed her out the door. "If there's truly a murderer on the loose, don't you think we should call the police?"

Hazel stopped walking and turned to me. "Remember what happened when I tried to tell people about the lightning? No one believed me. They thought I was crazy."

As we walked farther from the main quad, an eerie quietness settled over the campus. I could no longer hear the music throbbing out of the campus center, and I saw no students anywhere. I wondered why the college had decided to construct the art facilities so far out of the way. I didn't want to be in the cold, dark night anymore, my knees aching, charging toward an art building that might house a murderer. I longed for the dullness of Halloween at home, wanted to be sitting in my comfortable chair by the front door, a hand plunged deep into a plastic pumpkin filled with Reese's Peanut Butter Cups.

"Here," Hazel said, reaching out and taking my arm as if I were a blind person. "Don't trip." She led me over a wooden bridge covered in chipping red paint, and there was the Polk Art Building, a large concrete structure with light bleeding out from a side window. "Come on," she said, pulling me toward the lighted window. We walked through underbrush to the side of the building. The illuminated window was large, and we could see into the entire room. It was a studio, and only one person, a girl wearing paint-splattered overalls, was in it, painting. Her back was to us. "Keep your mouth shut," Hazel said, and led me right up to the window. When we got close, I could hear music playing in the room, something upbeat and cheerful. The girl dipped a paintbrush into a glass jar and cleaned it off.

"Is she in danger?" I whispered.

"What did I just tell you?" said Hazel. "Be quiet."

"If she's in danger, we might be in danger too," I said.

Hazel rubbed her temples, or what I assumed were her temples, through her ghost costume. "I might have been wrong," she whispered.

"Wrong?" I said. "What do you mean by 'wrong'?"

"I don't think there's a killer here."

"Then why are we here?"

"Just please, be quiet. Watch. Something is going to happen."

"Something bad?" I said.

"Just something."

"I'm taking my costume off," I said, and Hazel reached out and said, "No, please don't. I don't want to be the only ghost here."

We crouched, and my knees hurt. The girl moved her painting and the easel it rested on so it was under a bright lightbulb that hung out of a silver lamp strung from the ceiling. Now the painting faced us. It appeared to be a self-portrait. The girl in the painting had long brown hair and dark eyes and tan skin. I could see her features better on the painting than on her actual face. The painting was good, one of those pieces that's so realistic it looks almost like a photograph. The girl reminded me of the women I'd see on commercials and on the covers of brochures at the doctor's office; it was impossible to tell her ethnicity. I thought they used these actors and models in the commercials and brochures so everyone might see some of themselves in the women, might think they had some sort of connection. The girl could have any mixture of Spanish or Filipino or Eskimo or Hawaiian or Native American or Japanese or Chinese or Venezuelan or maybe even something Middle Eastern. She looked like everything at the same time and nothing specific; she looked like the face on the cover of my *Time* magazine when it had the headline "This Is What America Looks Like Now."

A new song came on inside, and the girl put down her paintbrush, looked around quickly, and when she confirmed that she was the only one in the room, began to dance. At first she was hesitant, but she got more and more bold, and her arms came out into the air, flapping like wings. She ducked and squatted and flapped. I'd seen this dance before.

"Kelly," I said. Even almost three years later, I remembered the name in the Christmas newsletter.

Hazel turned to me. "What?" she said.

"That's your granddaughter."

"Don't be foolish. I've never told you about a granddaughter."

"I'm turning psychic too," I said. "I know things." I tapped the side of my head.

"You know nothing," Hazel said, but she sounded puzzled.

"Let's go talk to her," I said.

"I don't know that girl," she said.

"And yet your intuition led you to her."

"Stop talking," Hazel hissed.

I tried to picture the Christmas newsletter I'd found tucked into the Lands' End catalog. I remembered the image of a dark-haired girl standing in front of a Christmas tree. "Why don't you ever talk about your son?" I said. "It's like he doesn't exist."

Hazel sighed. "We haven't talked in twenty-three years. And that's all you need to know."

"Is it because he married someone who wasn't white? Yvonne?" I felt like a detective attempting to solve the mystery of Hazel Stump. There was enough about the girl that reminded me of Hazel but there was also clearly something else mixed into the DNA.

"I'm not a bigot," Hazel said. She breathed in hard, and I saw the sheet over her nose pull in by her nostrils.

"Then why do you hate Darius and Antoine? They're nice boys."

"I just think they might be trouble," she said. "And I don't like that they brought a wild animal into the neighborhood."

If anything, Millicent was the wildest animal in the neighborhood, her yellow eyes glowing as she hissed and gurgled and howled for treats she did not deserve. The boys' spotted cat often came up to me when I walked to the mailbox and wound around my ankles, purring, begging me to pet it.

I didn't know what brought us here, whether Hazel had known Kelly attended Mecklen College, whether she'd known Kelly would be in the art studio instead of partying with her classmates. I didn't know whether at any point that night Hazel had actually believed there was a murderer on the loose, but now that we were here, there was something to be done. I thought about Larry and all those years he'd wished he could have become a history professor, about the books about the War he thought he'd write one day. I thought about my own desire to go overseas and help those who had little access to medical care. Now I could never do it; with my heart problems, it wouldn't be safe to attempt such a trip. But here was Kelly, and Hazel could easily go speak to her.

"Go," I said. "Take off the costume and go talk to her."

"What would I say?" she said.

"Just say hello. She's your family." Larry and I had never had children, and we'd both come from small families. Now that he was gone, I had no one. If I'd had a granddaughter just a few feet away, I would have marched right up to her no matter what had happened in the past.

Hazel straightened. It looked like her mind was made up. I expected her to unknot Walter's tie, pull off the sheet, and walk inside. But I saw that the areas under the eyeholes of her costume were wet. Was she crying? "I have no idea what you're talking about," she said. "I don't know who this girl is."

"Of course you do. She's your granddaughter. She dances that ridiculous egret dance just like you. It must be genetic. No one else dances like that."

"I don't know what you're talking about. Maybe you have dementia," she said. Her voice cracked, and I could tell she was trying to be cruel so I would give up. "Let's go," she said. "I was wrong. No one is getting murdered here tonight. I just got a mixed-up signal."

"No," I said, and I stood behind her and wrapped my arms around her waist. I pushed her away from the window and toward the front of the building. "You're going to talk to her."

"Get your hands off me," Hazel said.

"I read a Christmas newsletter the first winter after I moved in. You'd left it in the living room. That's how I know about James and Kelly and Yvonne."

"I knew you weren't psychic! I knew you only knew things because you'd snooped." Hazel wiggled hard, her elbows poking at my arms, trying to escape. I linked my fingers together and held on as tightly as I could.

"Does he send you a newsletter every year?" I said. "Why would he send them if you don't speak to him?"

"He wants me to know that everything turned out OK. He wants me to know I was wrong."

"Maybe it's his way of reaching out to you. Maybe you should call him."

Hazel snorted and attempted another escape. I tried to push her forward, but she made herself heavy, spread her legs wide so she was firmly planted to the earth. Then she suddenly slipped from my grasp, whipped around, and pushed me to the ground. I landed on fallen leaves and small rocks, and I could feel the rocks scraping my back. Hazel's hands were on my shoulders, and she pushed me hard into the ground, and it occurred to me that this was the first time in my life that I had been in a fight. I wondered if she would punch me. I tried to move my arms, but Hazel's grip moved down to my biceps, and I was pinned.

A window slid open, and the girl inside the studio stuck her head out. "Who's there?" she said.

"Kelly?" I shouted.

Hazel moved one hand to cover my mouth, but she was still straddling me, the other arm across my upper chest now so I couldn't budge. I could barely breathe with her hand pushing the cloth of my costume onto my face. She leaned in close and whispered, "My boy, Jimmy, was a wrestler in high school. We were close then. I went to all his meets. He taught me moves."

"Who's out there?" Kelly yelled. "I already pressed the emergency call button in here, so security will be here in a minute."

Hazel and I scuffled, but I was pinned and Hazel's hand was still over my mouth.

"I can hear you. I have a knife," Kelly shouted. Her arm popped out of the window, and she held a large X-Acto knife in her fist. "I'll use it if I have to."

I wanted to tell Kelly not to be scared, that we were just two old ladies, one of us frail and pinned to the ground, the other related to her by blood. How wonderful it would be if Kelly could speak to Hazel, and then Hazel could see that this girl was pretty and talented and it was no matter at all that Kelly's skin and hair were dark because she was Hazel's granddaughter and what a waste it was for them to have never gotten to know each other. I stared up at Hazel and tried to see her eyes, but I could only see the holes cut into the sheet. I'd never really believed in Hazel's psychic abilities, but now I tried to wordlessly communicate with her, thinking, *Please, please say something to Kelly.*

Footsteps crunched over the dried leaves behind us. "All right, you two, get up." A campus security guard stood over us, his flashlight's beam shining down. He looked almost as young as Kelly, with unlined skin and a high and tight military-style haircut. Kelly slid the window open all the way, then stepped through it and jumped to the ground. She still held the X-Acto knife. I thought of Hazel's prediction about a knife and someone in costume and realized it had come true. "I said stand up, ghosties," the security guard barked. He held his walkie-talkie up and said, "10-20 Polk Art Building. Some drunk kids looking for private time in the woods."

Hazel let go of her grip on me and stood up. I tried to move, but my back hurt and my heart pounded and my knees felt locked. I needed help. I reached a hand up toward the security guard, but he said, "Haul your own ass up. Now!" I still had the sheet over me, and I realized he didn't know my age and thought I was a hooligan. Hazel reached over and took one hand and then the other and slowly pulled me up. When I stood, I hurt all over.

"Take those pathetic costumes off," the security guard said. Neither Hazel nor I moved, and the guard stepped toward us. "You want to take the costumes off yourselves, or you want me to do it for you?"

I took my sheet off and dropped it to the ground. "Oh," said the guard, staring at me.

"Oh," said Kelly. She stepped closer to us, her face revealing that she was more intrigued than afraid now.

"Now you," the guard said to Hazel, but his voice was gentler.

"I don't want to," said Hazel. But she reached up and unknotted Walter's tie and took the sheet off. She let it drop to the leaves and twigs by her feet and held only the tie. Her eyes were red, her hair mussed and sweaty. She draped the tie around her neck.

"What in the world?" said the security guard. "What were you two doing here?"

"Fighting," I said.

"Fighting?" said the guard. "You live in town? You need a ride home?" Now he was speaking to us as if we were deranged, as if we'd escaped from a mental institution. "Do you remember where you live?" he asked.

"We know where we live," I said. "We drove here."

Hazel stared at Kelly, who still stood holding the knife out.

"You know these two?" the guard said to Kelly.

Kelly shook her head. "I've never seen them before in my life."

I wanted Hazel to say something to Kelly, to tell her that she was her grandmother. I wanted her to give Kelly our phone number and to tell her that once she'd processed it all she should give us a call and maybe when she had a break from school she could come visit us. I wanted Hazel to clean out Walter's clothing from the closet in the hallway so Kelly could leave her things there, so she could stay a while when she visited.

The walkie-talkie crackled. "10-22 duck pond, Don. Skinny dippers," a voice on the other end said.

The young man sighed. He lifted the walkie-talkie and said, "10-4. Be there in a few. Need to escort two people off the premises first." He turned to the girl. "You should bring a friend with you when you work in the studio late." She nodded. "And you two, I'll drive you back to your car if you tell me where it is."

"You want to say anything?" I said to Hazel. She shook her head.

"I'm sorry we scared you," I said to the girl. "We didn't mean to. You're a really talented artist."

The girl didn't say anything, just looked at me like I was the strangest person in the world.

"How did you know my name?" she said. "You're the one who called out my name, right?"

"No," said Hazel. "We saw some girls walk by. They were dressed like cats. They called out to you. You're Kelly?"

The girl nodded. "It was probably my roommates. They wanted me to go to the party, but I still have a lot of work to do before the art exhibition."

"You're very industrious," I said. "An excellent trait in a young lady. I bet you're a good kid. A good, smart, hardworking young lady anyone would be proud to know."

"We need to go," Hazel said. Her eyes were still fixed on Kelly, who looked at me. I was certain Kelly was now convinced I was crazy.

"All right, into the back," said the security guard, and he led us to his car that looked like a cop car but said Mecklen College Security on the side. Hazel told the guard our car was parked in the faculty lot, and the guard asked if we were professors.

"Yes," I said. "We teach history."

Hazel looked at me as if I were insane, and I thought how much her expression looked like Kelly's.

"Actually," I said, "I left something in my office. Can you drop us off near Lancaster?"

Hazel shook her head, but she didn't say anything. She popped out of the car as soon as it stopped in front of Lancaster Hall.

"You want me to wait?" the security guard said. "I can drive you back to the faculty lot."

"We'll be fine," I said, and I got out of the car. I didn't hear the engine start, and when I turned back, I saw him watching us to make sure we'd get in the building OK, and I held my breath as I reached toward the door handle. If it was locked, our lie would be obvious. We didn't have keys. The door opened, though, and I let my breath out, and I turned and waved at the security guard, and he waved back and drove away.

"He was nice," I said to Hazel.

"You think everyone's nice. Him, that girl, Darius and Antoine. Everyone's your best friend."

We stood in the foyer, and right behind Hazel was the flyer for the art show. I wanted to take it, bring it home, hang it up on the refrigerator. Maybe Hazel would look at it each time she opened the refrigerator door, and maybe she'd somehow convince herself that it would be a good idea to go see Kelly's exhibition.

"Well, your granddaughter did seem like a nice girl."

"Did you see her?" Hazel said. "She was dark. She looked nothing like me. Or like Walter."

"She's your granddaughter. She danced just like you. You wanted to meet her. And then you chickened out."

"Stop," Hazel said. "Just stop talking."

"Why don't you speak to your son? Is it because he married Yvonne?"

"I don't have a son," Hazel said.

"Yes, you do. He taught you how to wrestle." I rubbed the back of my neck, which was still sore.

"I don't have a son. I have a house and a closet of Walter's clothes, and I have you. And that's all."

"Me?" I said. I thought I was nothing to her but an annoyance and someone who could be relied upon to write a rent check every month. But maybe Hazel was right about this one thing. We both carried ghosts with us—everyone our age did—but what was important in the day-to-day was who was there, who we shared a pot of coffee with each morning, who would make sure we didn't fall when we climbed on step stools to change lightbulbs, and who we said "good night" to every evening.

"Why'd you want to come back here?" Hazel said.

"I knew there was a bathroom here. It's a long trip home." I didn't tell her that I'd really wanted to come to pull the flyer about the art show off the bulletin board.

"You have a bladder the size of an acorn," Hazel said. "Well, go already," she said, pointing toward the bathroom.

When I emerged from the bathroom, Hazel was no longer in the hallway. I called out her name and heard only the echo of my voice. Beyond the foyer the halls were dark. I held my arms out in front of me, feeling for obstacles, and took tentative steps down the darkened hallway. Halloween cast its spell on the silent, empty building. This echoing hallway, probably so alive during the day, was exactly the type of place where ghosts might appear after the lights were shut off. I thought of how badly Hazel wanted to see Walter again, how all of this psychic business was so she could communicate with him, and although I would never admit it to her, I wanted the same thing. How nice if Larry could appear somehow in this darkened hallway. I imagined opening the door to one of the offices and seeing Larry behind a desk, his glasses slipping down the bridge of his nose as he read a thick book.

I heard a scratching sound and moved toward it, and when I got close enough, I saw that Hazel was at the end of the hallway. She held a piece of chalk and was writing on one of the chalkboards outside a professor's door. Then she moved to another chalkboard a few steps down the hall and wrote something else. I found the light switch on the wall and flipped it up, and the fluorescent lights flickered on. Hazel turned to me, blinked. She looked surprised to see me, as if she hadn't heard me moving toward her. Walter's tie was still draped around her neck.

I looked at the chalkboards outside the professors' offices. On three of the chalkboards, Hazel had written HS JS KS. "What are you doing?" I asked.

"Nothing," she said.

"What does HS JS KS stand for?" I said.

"Nothing," she said again.

I stared at the letters, as if they were one of those puzzles where all you had to do was rearrange the letters and then a word would emerge. "There are no vowels," I said.

"What're you talking about?" said Hazel.

"How can you form words with no vowels?" And then, as I kept staring, I understood what the letters were: they were initials. Hazel Stump. James Stump. Kelly Stump. Hazel couldn't allow herself to say anything to Kelly, but she could mark the chalkboards in a building at Kelly's school.

"Are you done with the bathroom? Are you ready to leave?" Hazel said. Her fingertips were covered in chalk dust.

"Finish up," I told her, and I watched as she put the initials on chalkboards outside of all the offices in Lancaster Hall. I stood in the quiet hallway and waited for Hazel as she spelled out the connections she could not bring herself to acknowledge in any other way.

# Mother's Day

SANDRA THOMPSON

From *Close-Ups* (1984)

I'm afraid to walk the dog alone at night, so I ask my husband to watch me from the window. I go out into the street with the dog and look up at our parlor window. It's dark there; it doesn't look like anyone is home. I yell to my husband from the street. Not as loud as I would yell if I were being attacked, but loud. There is no answer. No one comes to the window.

In the Village, on the same street where I lived, a girl was murdered. The stabs took less than ten seconds. From the description in the paper, the girl looked just like me. I wish there had been a picture so I could be certain it was not me.

I go back into the house with the dog on the leash. I call to my husband. I walk through the parlor, through the bedroom, and into my husband who is coming out of the bathroom.

"Where were you?" I ask him. "I called out."

"I had to take a leak."

"But you promised you'd watch me."

"I was watching you. I just—"

"I could have been murdered ten times while you were in the bathroom."

I go back into the street with the dog. I walk the dog in circles in front of the house. Every time I turn, he tugs at the leash. He wants to walk forward in a straight line. I walk him around in circles in front of the house. Above me, filling the parlor window, is my husband watching over me.

It is noon on Hudson Street. The girl is walking downtown. She is carrying a small brown bag from the deli. She has a quart of Tropicana orange juice and a package of four English muffins. She is wearing a loose-fitting turtle-neck sweater and corduroy jeans. Her long brown hair has not been combed yet today.

She passes some men who are stripping antique furniture on the sidewalk. She says hi. They nod and keep on working.

She is thinking about how good the muffin will taste with sweet butter and honey on it, how good the cold juice will feel down her throat. She presses the paper bag to her breast. She can feel the cold juice carton through her sweater. Her head is down. Her fingers grope in her purse for her key. Before she can look up to see the face of the man who will fix the rest of her life at this moment in time, she feels her legs turn to butter and a cold-hot stream down her spine. She follows her paper bag to the floor. She sees the smiling orange face of Tropic-Ana peek out from the bag, and then it is dark.

It's Mother's Day. The celebration is at the Country Club. It has been an hour, and the waiter has not yet brought the salad. The children have eaten all the rolls. Large beige crumbs litter the tablecloth. My three-year-old daughter sits in her cousin's lap while her cousin puts nail polish on her small fingernails.

My husband's cousin leans across my husband toward me. His head is cocked, his eyes narrowed, his mouth lazy. "How's Charlie treat you, hmmmn?"

It is an odd question, but I consider it. I try to answer as truthfully as I can. "Well," I say, "Charlie has quite a temper. He is very demanding—"

"What!" my husband says. "I'm not demanding at all. I make no demands on you." He leans close to me and whispers, "Tell him you don't get enough. That's what he wants to hear."

"I can't," I say.

"Why not?"

"Because I'm not a talking dog."

My best friend goes into her apartment building on Sheridan Square. She waves to the hairdresser on the ground floor whose door is open. Her slingbacks make a click clack on the stairs in the hall. In her head she is composing a tune with the click clack as backup rhythm. At her landing she puts her key into the lock of her door. She feels something cold at her temple. Inside her apartment he lays the gun and knife on her pillow. Like a director he tells her what to do. He will cut her face, he tells her, if she doesn't. So she does. But she gags on it. Ever since she was a child she has vomited too easily. She gags, but keeps her stomach muscles tight and breathes hard in and out, in and out, so she won't throw up. She isn't really *that* frightened, she tells me later, because even though he had a gun with a silencer and a knife, his face was kind.

My husband's ten-year-old daughter is drinking his vodka gimlet. Her face is yellow.

"I want chocolate milk," my daughter says.

"Here," her cousin says. She shoves towards her a cocktail glass with a pink bubbly liquid and a cherry and a thin striped cellophane cocktail straw. "Try this. It's a Shirley Temple."

"I don't want Temple," my daughter says. "I want chocolate milk."

"She doesn't know who Shirley Temple is," I say. She knows who Spiderman is. She knows the Hulk.

The waiter's collar is too tight. Above it his neck and face are raw red. "When you get a chance," I say, "please bring my daughter some chocolate milk."

He looks at me. His eyes pinch. There is panic in his voice. "I'll have to mix it myself," he says.

"Yes," I say tentatively.

"I don't know if we have chocolate syrup. If we don't have syrup, I can't make it."

"Yes. If you don't have syrup, you can't make it. Then bring her plain milk."

I push open the door to my apartment and feel his chest up against my back and his arm alongside my breast. "Goodnight," I say. I am polite. I slam the door, but its momentum is stopped. It doesn't reach the doorjamb. The lock doesn't click. The door makes a muffled thud against his body which stands halfway inside, between the door and the frame.

Inside he talks fast, and his words are disconnected. His eyes fly. He says some white women don't like black men and that makes him mad. I say, "Oh really? How awful! Oh really? Oh really?" I want to keep him talking. He comes close and I step away; he comes close and I step away. My stomach hurts. I am constipated. I was looking for a drugstore when he fell into step beside me in the empty street on the dark, rainy night. The skin on my belly is stretched too thin. My skirt hurts. If he touches me I will implode. I offer him cheese and juice. He shoves me on the bed and spreads himself on top of me. His mouth clamps onto mine, his face pressed so deep into mine I cannot breathe. I jerk my head back and forth like a gagged woman.

We are driving on the L.I.E. to the Five Towns for Mother's Day. The rain is heavy. The traffic is heavy. My husband's two daughters and our daughter are in the backseat.

My husband drives in the far right and far left lanes where the potholes are lakes. Great sheets of water slice up from the tires, slam onto the windshield. The windshield is water. I clutch the strap on my seatbelt that cuts across my chest. I work my foot from the ankle, flexing when I want my husband to brake the car. He brakes several seconds after I would have.

"Is my driving making you nervous?" he asks.

"Well—" I say.

"Christ. My ex-wife was just like you. My driving made her nervous, too. So what did I go through all this for—the same old thing?"

"Does that mean it's the same thing?" I inhale, but my breath snags somewhere in my throat.

"It's just like my shrink said. We marry the same people. When I picked up the kids, my ex-wife said, 'I'm worried about you driving in this weather with the kids.'"

"Why do you assume that because your driving makes your wives nervous it means your wives are nervous? Maybe it means your driving makes people nervous."

He turns his head to the backseat. "What about you," he asks his ten-year-old daughter. "Does my driving make you nervous?"

"Children have no sense of mortality," I say.

His daughter's voice is matter-of-fact. "No, your driving doesn't make me nervous. I happen to think you're a terrible driver—"

"You what?"

"I said I happen to think you're a terrible driver, but your driving doesn't make me nervous."

The dark street is empty. The baby has not been inside me for six weeks; tonight the baby is not riding in its pouch on my breast. Still, I am heavy and dark as the night. But for a moment I feel a glimmer, a flash, of light, of lightness: that one day my body will be my own again.

Behind my left shoulder there is a pungent smell; it is human; there is warm breath on my cheek. I hear words, muffled beyond meaning, and turn to see a dark face with ski cap pulled down to eyelids. He steps in front of me and blocks my path, pounces like a big puppy, and knocks me down to the sidewalk. I lie on my back on the sidewalk. His face is too dark and too close. I cannot see it. "Take my purse," I say.

"I don't want your purse. I just want to kiss you."

His lips are soft, unformed.

There are headlights on the street. He leaps up. I scream, "Help!" I am standing. The car passes. Then the light is gone.

I am lying on the sidewalk and he is on top of me. In my ears my screams sound like his hand is over my mouth, though it is not. "If you don't scream, I won't hurt you," he says. His voice is soft, his hand is light on my thigh, and it is of the end that I am frightened, when it has not been enough, and he takes my head between his hands and smashes it against the sidewalk as if he were cracking open a coconut to get to the sweet milk.

My husband's aunt calls to me across the table, "Your daughter looks just like you."

"Yes," my mother-in-law says, "she is the image of her mother. I have never seen a child look so much like her mother."

My daughter's hair gleams red-gold in the light. I'm grateful that I washed it this morning. Her plaid, smocked dress is perfect. My daughter had not wanted to wear it. "But you look so pretty," I said. "Don't you want to look pretty?" I said, as if she weren't enough without the dress.

The women at the table beam at the perfect child and at me.

Inside me, waves crash as against groins built into the sea that split the ocean's energy in two. I am concerned with the barest survival, completing this day alive. The piqué trim at the collar of my daughter's dark plaid dress is brilliantly white and stiff against her small neck.

The waiter brings a bottle of wine to the table.

My husband's brother, who is divorced, gives the toast. "To the mothers!"

"And to the fathers," says my husband's cousin, who is also divorced, "without whom there would be no mothers."

"To the waiter," I say, but no one hears me.

"To the waiter," my husband says, and everyone laughs. The waiter's hand shakes, splashing wine into glasses.

My daughter crooks her index finger at me. "Come here," she says. "I wanna tell you a secret."

I lean close to her. Her smell is soft and young and unbearable. Her voice is not a whisper but a breath. "I can't hear you," I tell her.

She puts her mouth right up to my ear. I still can't hear her. Her face implores, is deadly serious. "You have to whisper a secret just a little bit louder," I say. Her face clouds in conflict: if she whispers it soft I cannot hear; if she whispers it loud everyone will hear, and it will not be a secret.

She raises her voice only barely. I shut out everything so that I might hear her.

"Bubble gum," she whispers. "Pink."

"Pink bubble gum?" I whisper back.

"Yes."


On the road the flat heads of the streetlights give off a light that is too yellow. Within the beams the wind-slashed rain is illuminated, then lost in darkness. In the backseat, my husband's daughters are asleep with their heads on their sweaters. My daughter is lying on the backseat floor. Silently, she passes wrappers from bite-sized Nestle Crackles and Hershey's kisses. I crumple the wrappers and put them on the dashboard.

The road runs along the airport. The small lights on the runways blur in the rain. A plane wafts over the car, a huge dark shadow, then clears the high metal fence to land. The rain falls in one thick curtain across the windshield. There is a glimmer of wet red at an intersection. A truck heaves to a stop; my husband brakes. The brakes squish. The car slides to the right and to the left and stops. The rear of the truck is higher and wider than our windshield. We can see nothing but close gray metal.

"I didn't even see him," my husband says. He is stunned that with no forewarning something so big could stop him. His face is pale and strained. He is driving more carefully now. "It's crazy the way people drive, isn't it?" he says. "Look at all the cars that are passing me. They're driving too fast for conditions, aren't they?"

"They're stupid," I say. "People are stupid."

As far as I can see, there are cars filled with sleeping children, cars driven too fast by men, their wives silent beside them. The rain and the dark have dissolved the line between land and sky, and the streetlights and the headlights mingle with stars in one vast blackness.

My husband is driving slowly now. I want to pull off the road and wait for the rain and the night to be over. But there is no safe place, so this is enough. I will take my chances. I put my hand on my husband's knee. He pats my hand.

# Permanent Makeup

JACQUELIN GORMAN

From *The Viewing Room* (2013)

Ellie could see the Grim Reaper from the parking lot, but she was not going to give him the time of day. She lowered her head and trudged through the entryway of the Torrance Community Center, shoving the ghastly image, both hands pressing against his black torso, so she could get inside. Someone with considerable talent for three-dimensional art had painted the glass door with the classic hooded figure emerging from a gray background fog, the face its usual blank oval of darkness, one empty sleeve cupping the bloodred handle of his perpetually sharpened scythe, the axe end drawn in sparkling silver puff paint. Alarmingly, the other sleeve seemed to reach out of the glass when the door swung closed. Ellie shuddered as she realized the ominous effect this would have on her Mothers' Grief Group. They were meeting in this building in less than half an hour, and she did not have enough antibacterial wipes in her purse to clean off this hellish door. Yes, everyone has to die, but people like her—parents who have outlived a child—did not have to be reminded of the one thing they could never forget. Ellie had hated Halloween since her daughter Mandy died.

She despised everything about it—the iridescent plastic skeletons hanging from palm fronds swaying softly in the ocean breeze; the fake RIP tombstones rising out of eternally spring-green front lawns; stuffed bloody hands sliding out from the back trunks of bright-colored convertibles—all of it. Another lifetime ago, when Mandy was born, she had carefully decorated their rental on a walk street in Manhattan Beach with the few cheerful items she could find: twinkling pumpkin lights outlining the door and a life-sized stuffed fairy godmother figure that held a magic wand in one hand and a huge bowl of apples in the other.

The Manhattan Beach walk streets were considered the safest part of Los Angeles to trick-or-treat, attracting families from miles away because no cars were allowed on the wide concrete paths of the sand section between perfect rows of imitation New England seaside cottages that oddly faced one another rather than the ocean. The houses were incestuously close together due to the premium lot value, some only two feet apart, so that one could hand a tissue to the sneezing next-door neighbor window to window. The great advantage of this demographic at Halloween was to get the most treat for your trick.

It was possible to visit more than a hundred houses in the space of an hour if you could run as fast as your children.

In fact, she soon discovered that walk streets were no more about walking than strollers were about strolling. The walk streets were made for wheels, a constant stream of carless traffic, back and forth: plastic Cozy Coupes, bikes, skateboards, and homeless women with grocery carts full of junk. The relentless scraping of concrete became white noise snuffing out all the other sounds around it, including the laughter of children playing, the tinkling of wind chimes, the roar of the ocean waves only a few short blocks away.

Ellie had finally moved away from all those sounds, taking a job as the on-call nurse in an assisted living facility in exchange for free rent in a handicap-access apartment. She was about the same age as most of the tenants, seventy-seven. She had moved just in time because the heat wave over the past few days had caused her multiple sclerosis to relapse. Her vision blurred and her lower legs numbed out when she was overheated, and even the slightest exertion derailed her, making her unable to see or feel where her feet landed.

At this time of year, the Santa Ana winds reversed the offshore airflow patterns, so that on Halloween the usually divine coastal weather was also under a witch's spell, the beach disguised as desert, the stinging hot dry air filled with ashes from inland brush fires. Everyone looked grief-stricken in this weather, constantly blinking back tears, so her slow-moving clumsiness could be excused as a result of allergy medication. She had never actually told anyone in her bereavement groups that she had the disease because she was sure that it did not affect her ability to facilitate. But the truth was that she was slowing down, not just with her unsteady gait, but mentally as well; she could not seem to think or speak in clear sentences after sunset, as if her cognitive brain worked on solar power.

She glanced at her watch. She had wanted to get there early so that she could have a few minutes with the guest speaker, Henrietta Hooper, a hospital chaplain she had met, of all unlikely places, at the movie theater a few months ago. She started to shuffle so that she could save time. That's what she was now, an official shuffler, because she could no longer pick up her feet when she was in a hurry, could not take the time to watch each step. She could move much faster this way, gliding like an indoor cross-country skier on ballet flats. She had tried walkers, but she kept misjudging the stride, over-compensating, getting her feet caught under the wheels.

She had mastered the art of falling without breaking any bones years ago. She had learned how to land on the soft part of her upper back and lower shoulder, holding her arms close to her sides, always backward. Nobody liked to see an elderly woman fall. Strangers knelt around her, cell phones in hand, ready to dial 911, whispering to each other but shouting questions at her, as if she had fallen down a well and was too far away to hear. She shuffled around the last corner, trying to pick up speed. Maybe Henrietta had already gotten there and would start the meeting without her.

She had left a message for Henrietta to come help her tonight, but she was not sure that Henrietta would be able to come, since the hospital would need extra chaplains on the night call service for all those grisly ER admissions, children who would be hit by cars, choke on candy, and suffocate inside their costumes.

Then she heard someone coming behind her in the hallway, and she turned to look.

"I thought you might need this. You left it in my car the other day. This damn heat is knocking us all off our pins. I tried to use it to scrape that Grim Reaper's head off, but it didn't work. So, here."

Henrietta, dressed formally in a black silk pantsuit, was holding up a cane, light blue, with butterflies, and she slipped it under Ellie's right hand. Then she took her left arm and hooked it through Ellie's, in that charming way Europeans do when strolling down boulevards. It had taken some time for Ellie to get used to this habit of walking as if Henrietta were her own daughter, and now she could not imagine any other way of walking. Suddenly, Ellie felt dizzy and out of balance and she leaned into Henrietta.

"Are you all right, Ellie? Let's stop a minute and let you rest a bit."

Henrietta laid her coat down in the hallway and told Ellie to sit there. Then she went ahead to the conference room to get her some water. Henrietta seemed so much older than her years. She was in her early thirties, she'd told Ellie once, and Ellie did not ask the exact year. Mandy would have turned thirty-two this August.

"You can't possibly understand true suffering until you become a parent," Ellie's younger sister had told her, with a smug hoarseness in her voice that had deepened with the birth of each of her five children, as if she were leaking estrogen out of her throat. Runners must present a certificate of live birth at the registration table before officially entering the Human Race. And Ellie had barely made the qualifiers at forty-five years old, an AMA mother, as it was noted on her medical chart. Not AMA as in Against Medical Advice, because she had become pregnant with a great deal of medical advice, as well as considerable medical intervention. AMA in her case stood for Advanced Maternal Age. She had every prenatal test available at the time, but none of them detected the fatal malformation, the tiny ticking time bomb in the tiny heart. Her baby was already dying before she was born. Was it because the mother was already late before she entered the race?

It had always been hard to keep up with Mandy when they went out trick-or-treating, especially as the night wore on. By late evening, Ellie's body and mind could barely connect with each other. She would weave drunkenly, bumping into people and slurring her words together in a sloppy run-on apology. "So-so-sorry, didn't see you, so-so-sorry." All the other parents, young professionals with double incomes into seven figures, had no time to listen, rushing past her, chasing their little knights and princesses faster and faster, as if none of them could afford to turn down this great deal of first-come, first-served free candy.

She remembered the relief that flowed through her like pure oxygen the moment she waved her flashlight ahead and caught the saving sight of Mandy's orange glow-in-the-dark butterfly wings floating in clear view above the other children's heads. How old was she then? Five? It had been the year that Mandy had suddenly grown into her rich, dark looks.

Mandy had her father's Mediterranean complexion, a head of thick, glossy auburn hair. It fell in cascades of soft ringlet curls around her heart-shaped face, making her look like one of those pageant children whose mother had spent hours with hot rollers and round beauty-salon brushes. She had huge hazel eyes, lush lashes, and rosebud lips that curved upward even when she was not smiling. She woke up looking like a reincarnated silent film actress, her face flushed, full of secrets she could hardly wait to reveal. Mandy's butterfly costume year was also the year that strangers had started reaching out to stroke her head and then catching themselves and stopping, staring in surprise at their own hands in midair. It was disconcerting, her child's siren beauty, a matter of public domain, to be admired from a distance but never directly touched, like fine art in a museum.

What would she look like now? It was cruel timing to take a teenager—the meanest of all tricks from a Trickster God. They would never know how tall she was going to be, whether she would have her mother's compact petite build or her father's long-limbed loping stride or some kind of hybrid all her own. Mandy was frozen in time at her most awkward stage, her breasts swelling, her hips widening, nothing fitting properly, her true size right between the manufactured sizes of the largest girl and the smallest woman. A few days before Mandy died, only a week before her fourteenth birthday, Ellie had taken her shopping for a certain kind of designer jeans.

"I will never get this afternoon of my life back," a father sitting on the floor outside the changing room said to his daughter as she swept by him carrying a pile of denim that must have been worth thousands of dollars. He had set up a portable office there in a half-circle around him, file folder with the months of the year labeled; paper printing calculator; prestamped, preaddressed envelopes. He was paying his bills and shaking his head, defiantly. "I am not going to waste one more moment of it."

He looked ridiculous sitting there, trying to make time obey him even if his surly daughter would not. All of Ellie's friends who were parents had warned her about this time-shift phenomenon, that having a baby would reset her internal clock forever. But it had not happened the way she had imagined. It was Mandy's

death, not her birth, that stopped time entirely. None of the moments that happened afterward, even the divorce, registered as
moments worth remembering.

Ellie and Henrietta entered the conference room. There was a
woman slouching at the far end of the table, with her hands over
her eyes as if the light were painful. When she took her hands
away, Ellie recognized her immediately, although it had been at
least six months since she had come to this group. It was Rachel.
The last time she was here, she cheerfully announced that she
was done with all the crying, done with sadness, pronounced herself a "grief graduate." Her daughter, Ariel, had died of anorexia
a few months earlier. Rachel was dressed tonight in a black turtleneck and black slacks, but she was still shivering, her arms
wrapped around her large steel-studded black leather purse,
shaped like one of those old-fashioned doctor's bags.

"Hi, Rachel, it's good to see you here," Ellie said as she walked
forward, her arms open to enclose her.

"Goddamned Halloween night, I knew this was the one place
I could go," Rachel mumbled as she stood up. She was very thin,
and Ellie could feel her bones trembling when she hugged her.

Ellie asked Henrietta to light the candle of Hope. It flickered
in the draft of the air conditioner but did not go out. Rachel sat
down in a seat close to the candle and stretched her hands out
in front of it, as if it could warm them like a fire. Ellie looked
over her group roster and wondered how many would show up
tonight. They tended to arrive in groups, having banded together
during the week, going on sad little field trips together, like cemetery visits and run-walk fundraisers for research into childhood
diseases, sporting tombstone T-shirts of their dead children's
faces and life and death dates stamped across their hearts.

This was the pattern Ellie noticed, although there was not supposed to be a hierarchy of suffering and she discouraged making
comparisons about who hurt the most. But natural alliances al-

ways seem to form anyway, according to the circumstances of a child's death. There were three distinct subgroups: the mothers who lost children slowly after long illnesses, the mothers who lost children suddenly in accidents, and those who had lost older children to suicide. The mothers of suicide cases usually did not stick around for more than one session because Ellie referred them out to Survivors of Suicide support groups, which had a rolling admission policy and no shortage of applicants.

This is why Rachel was a solo arrival, because anorexia is a grab bag of all three, a slow suicide resulting from a long mental illness, statistically predictable but still shocking in its finality. Rachel was not a good fit for a generalized grief group. Members of the group often shunned mothers whose children had died of seemingly preventable events, like getting into the car with a drunk driver or overdosing on drugs. There was always the unspoken judgment in the air that mothers of anorexics had advance warning and more time to save their children. As if good mothers were supposed to keep their children from starving to death, as if all it took to keep them alive was finding and cooking them more appealing food.

But Rachel would be safe here. This was a more inclusive group, kind to one another, not given to sudden bursts of rage and accusation. Four women came in quietly and took their seats around the oblong conference table. Each one tilted her head solemnly at the flickering candle as if it were on an altar. It was a small gathering, which was just as well for all concerned, considering the timing. Everyone with dead children was spooked tonight.

Last week, they had talked about dreading the coming holidays, with the stores already decked with joy. Ellie confessed that she had sent out holiday cards for fourteen years after Mandy's death, a reverse-life review, so that the last picture sent was Baby's First Christmas, Mandy at four and a half months, toothlessly grinning in a miniature Santa suit. Years later her friends told her how much they dreaded opening her cards each year, and how they could not bear to put them out on display but also could not bear to throw them out. She regretted it now, regretted how so much of her rage was misdirected.

She looked around at the familiar faces, trying to remember details about each one. Then she got to Henrietta. She glowed in this group, with her caramel-colored shoulder length hair, wide-spaced dark blue eyes, and a radiant complexion. She was surrounded by women who had long ago stopped caring about how they looked, prickly thorns around a blooming rose. They came in looking like the people at the homeless shelter where she volunteered. They were wearing the same shapeless sweats they wore to bed, not even noticing the fast-food ketchup stains spattered on their chests and knees.

Rachel was talking now. She did not wait for Ellie to announce check-in.

"And those goddamn skulls everywhere. Reminding me of Ariel, her sunken face, cheekbones so huge and pointy, like they're about to poke through her skin—God—that was so fucked up, those last two years!"

Ellie was alarmed by the raw anger in Rachel's voice. It was as if Ariel had died more recently. What happened to the self-proclaimed grief graduate? Ellie needed to disarm her somehow or she would suck up every second of the two-hour airtime, leaving out all the others. As the group leader, she had to be hypervigilant to the signs of a mother arriving in the midst of immediate crisis. But she couldn't seem to get on top of her own scattershot thoughts tonight, much less follow anyone else's reasoning.

The windowless room had turned stifling hot because the building's air conditioners automatically shut off at six. The stale heat was setting off short circuits in her neurological system so that all her reflexes, mind and body, were moving in slower and slower motion. Clearly, she was on the verge of another major relapse. Profound exhaustion was the proper medical term, and it was the first symptom.

It sounded so romantic, "profound exhaustion," for such a soul-killing feeling. It was impossible to explain to anyone this kind of tired, although the closest analogy could be made to other mothers: the first-trimester overpowering desire to sleep all the time, anywhere, anyplace, as if heavily drugged. She dug her fingernails into her thighs, trying to stay alert. It took every cell in her body to fight the urge to curl up in the corner and go to sleep on the floor. She ground her nails in deeper, her own makeshift bed of nails. Was it time for her to stop doing these groups? Yes, of course it was. She hated herself for being so absorbed in her own needs in the midst of all this seeping, open-wound desperate neediness around her.

Rachel looked around the room, blinking rapidly, as if she were also coming out of a trance. Her eyes were a soft shade of gray, hypnotic, mesmerizing, making it impossible to resist returning the stare. Ellie remembered her story now. Years before Ariel was sick, Rachel had gotten this permanent makeup done, sharp black lines around the edges of her eyelids and lips, with brows dyed to match. Now, tears poured down her smudge-proof, grief-proof face. Her eyes searched the room as if seeing for the first time that other people were there. She collapsed back into her chair, crumpling in on herself.

Check-in began. Nancy, seventeen-year-old daughter killed in a car crash with her three closest friends when a drunk driver went the wrong way onto their exit ramp. Colleen, son drowned in the neighbor's backyard swimming pool while his parents were preoccupied getting the house ready for his fourth birthday party. Rosalie, six-year-old daughter crushed by a falling tree branch on the kindergarten school playground. Patricia, twelve-year-old son, anaphylactic shock, peanut allergy, ate the wrong candy bar on a sixth-grade field trip.

So the accident group must have carpooled together tonight,

escaping any risk of a ringing doorbell and being expected to
hand out treats to other people's children. All were single mothers now, as a death in the family almost always killed the marriage as well. This was Rachel's situation. Ellie took a deep breath
and pushed the tissue box in front of Rachel, the go-ahead signal
that it was her turn to share.

"Ariel's dog is dead. This morning. I should have been ready . . .
She's a Maltese mix. Seventeen is old for them. Oh, God, Ariel's
age when she . . . Shit."

Rachel reached down to grab her purse, which had fallen off of
her lap, and put it back on the table. She opened it and took out
a framed photograph of a plump and dimpled toddler holding a
fluffy white puppy so tiny it looked like it should come with bat-
teries.

"We got Snowball when Ariel was two," Rachel said. "But the
dear little thing was dying so horribly. She had to go. Poor little
thing—so sick, kidneys failing, back legs not working, all of it—
but . . ."

She spread her hands out on the table, looking down at them,
and stopped talking.

"Your last living link to Ariel's life," said Patricia, reaching for
the tissue box. "Nobody ever tells you how every other death just
keeps opening the door to this one and slamming you in the face
with it."

"No more. Not anymore," Rachel said, shaking her head.

She started to root around in her purse again. Patricia slid the
tissues back to her, but Rachel ignored the box, intent on finding
whatever she was looking for, apparently not tissues. Finally, she
pulled something carefully from her purse, bundled in red cloth,
and lifted it out with both hands. Ellie's heart lurched. Was it the
dead dog? Jesus. It would be small enough to fit in that oversized
black coffin of a purse. Calm down and breathe, Ellie told herself.
It's probably just another picture. God, she really couldn't do this

anymore. She closed her eyes and gripped the arms of her office chair to keep steady. Panic swept over her and she was hyperventilating. Oh, God, she was going to pass out right there in front of everybody.

"Put that down now, Rachel. Help is coming. Five minutes more," Henrietta said, her tone firm and authoritative, as if speaking to a child.

Ellie opened her eyes. Henrietta had dropped her cell phone in Ellie's lap. Ellie looked down at it, a miniature black television screen encased in bright orange plastic with oversize white buttons on the top. It looked like a giant candy corn. Then the screen suddenly lit up and the words CALLING PET scrolled across it, followed by an image of an alarm clock with its minute and hour hands spinning around.

This made no sense to Ellie. Was Henrietta trying to call the dead dog on her cell phone? If she could make that kind of connection then she might as well go the whole distance and call God directly. She was an ordained minister, wasn't she? No, that still didn't make sense. Everything was falling apart and she could not connect the pieces.

Ellie shook her head as if that could clear her view. Maybe it was her vision fading out. She looked down at the cell phone and read it again. CALLING PET. That was exactly what the screen said. And then the clock started to dance, with a smiling happy face where its spinning time hands used to be. Ellie tugged on Henrietta's arm to get her attention. Henrietta's sweater was soft like silk and she couldn't get a grip on it. Henrietta jerked her arm away, and then Ellie realized that it was her skin, not her sweater, she had been pulling on.

"I don't understand. Who is calling? Should I answer?"

But Henrietta was looking at Rachel intently, as if she were the only person in the world who mattered. And Rachel was looking at the swaddled crimson object in her hands. Then she started to unwrap it slowly, knowing everyone was watching her, and smiling to herself, as if this were a party and she were opening up a gift.

"Five minutes, Rachel." Henrietta said. "Look at me and promise me that you will put the gun down for five minutes."

Gun?

"Sure," Rachel said calmly, nodding her head.

She turned the gun over carefully in her hands. It was dull and scratched on the both sides. She did not put it down.

"As soon as I check how many bullets are left. I used one for Snowball this morning."

"No!" Ellie screamed, as she realized finally what was happening. Then she tried to stand up and make a run for the door. How quickly could she get there and get everyone out with her? But she was too slow, and it was so awfully hot, and her feet slid out from under her. The chair caught her as she fell backward, and she was rolling away in the wrong direction, farther and farther from saving herself or anybody else. And then she was being spun around and pushed back to where she started. Nancy had gotten behind her and was wheeling her back to the table, patting her shoulder, as if this happened all the time.

"Rachel. Listen to me. *Right now.*"

Henrietta was not asking anymore. She was demanding.

"Five minutes. Promise me that you won't touch that gun for five minutes."

"All right," Rachel said. She dropped the gun with a thud back on the table.

Nobody said a word as they looked up at the clock and watched the minute hand go around. Seven women. All sitting in a circle around a loaded gun. Nobody seemed to skip a beat. At one point, Nancy shifted her legs restlessly as she stood behind Ellie's chair and sighed. Sighed. Like she was bored. Like five measly minutes was too long to wait for a crazy person to keep a promise.

Like there must be more exciting ways to spend five minutes. As if there were nothing important at stake.

And of course, it was true. Even with that suffocating toxic air softening her brain, Ellie could still understand why these women could look at a clock and remain perfectly calm, no matter if there were seven bullets left in that gun, one for each of them. Worse things had already happened than their own deaths.

There were women there who had said so, in this very room over the last year in so many different ways. Some wished they had already died. Others felt as if they were dead already. And others said that they were hoping Heaven existed only so that they could die as soon as possible to see their children once again. At some point Ellie had asked each of these women if they had a particular plan, and they shrugged. One of them said (was it Patricia?) that she could not even make a plan to program the coffee maker, much less a plan to kill herself. It took too much energy. Yes. It took Rachel six months to get the strength to come up with the plan. And one dead dog.

There was a pounding at the door. And the sounds of male voices, and the squawking of police radios. The door burst open and four uniformed men, two in blue, two in white, walked in, and with them the most wonderfully cool breeze, washing over all of them. And Ellie's brain cloud cleared. Now she understood. PET. Psychological Emergency Team.

PET moved like a splendidly choreographed dance. The first man who came in went straight for the gun and disappeared with it. The second two men gently escorted Rachel, arm in arm, out the door, out of the room, and then out of the building into a waiting ambulance, not stopping or slowing down for one moment. The fourth man led the group outside so that they could take full deep gulps of the brisk night air.

That's when the PET medic told them that Rachel was being placed under a three-day hold in a locked ward of a nearby hospital. There was nothing more any of them could do right now. The group left without another word, some still holding tissues against their eyes, absorbing the hopelessness of the night's events.

Ellie and Henrietta stayed behind, sat down on the front steps, and huddled together. They talked briefly about when they had last spent time together in a parking lot with ambulances and police officers and waving good-bye to another lost soul.

"We should not make a habit of this kind of thing," Henrietta said, leaning back against the Grim Reaper's shadow.

# Thousand-Dollar Decoy

## BECKY MANDELBAUM

From *Bad Kansas* (2017)

In the dream, the mallard on Elliot's chest weighs a hundred pounds, if not a thousand. It is crushing his lungs. He cannot breathe. He tries to turn, but he cannot turn. He cannot even move—the mallard is too heavy. It smells of algae and cut grass and is not without a hint of cuteness, the curve of its yellow beak forming a timid smile. Its eyes are liquid black and in them Elliot's terror is reflected back to him. In time, he discovers that his hands are free. With great effort, he brings them to the mallard's green neck. The iridescent feathers are smooth as skin beneath his grip. Elliot squeezes as hard as he can. He knows his life depends on it.

When he wakes, he finds that he is strangling his girlfriend, Alice. A low gurgling noise bubbles up from her throat and fills their dark studio apartment. This is only their first night in the apartment. Most of their possessions are still in the cardboard boxes that line the wall opposite their bed. Before they went to sleep, Alice had listed off all the things she wanted to do in the morning: hang pictures, assemble the closet organizer, locate her mother's china to make sure nothing had broken. Then, they had made love. Elliot had felt light with happiness as he drifted into sleep, Alice in his arms. Everything was exactly as he wanted it to be, down to the placement of the bed, which was centered against a wall instead of pressed into a corner to economize space. He'd never lived with a woman before, but now he was with Alice—*living* with Alice—and the bed belonged to both of them, an equal possession that required equal access. They were adults, and they were in love. They were sharing a bed. They each had their own nightstand.

They'd chosen the apartment because it was located exactly between their two jobs. Alice was a nurse in an oncology ward and Elliot inspected children's toys. When he told people what he did, they imagined him wearing overalls and a hardhat, examining racecars and baby dolls as they passed by on a conveyor belt. In truth, he had a PhD and worked in a lab. The winter before, he'd detected a potentially lethal amount of lead in a popular play food set. Alice liked to see him dressed for work, in his white lab coat and plastic goggles.

They'd met at a wedding, a fact Alice hated. If she had it her way, they would have met somewhere more interesting, perhaps at a symposium on fireflies or a hostel in Cambodia—anything for a better story. The wedding was painfully average. Alice's friend Heather was marrying a cousin of Elliot's, and both bride and groom were known for being boring, to the point where it was a sort of joke among their friends. A few people had even gone in on a gift card to Applebee's. The wedding was nearly unbearable—the Catholic ceremony was an hour too long and filled with the steady weeping of a large woman who held a silk handkerchief to her face, as if it might contain the sound. When the guests finally gathered for the apology of dinner, a sigh of disappointment circled the room when it was discovered that it would be a dry reception. What a treat, then, to find Alice. She was seated beside Elliot, who could not help but smile as her knee occasionally knocked against his. She told joke after joke, glowing like a lantern in the otherwise dreary reception hall. One man—a ruddy, balding creature with thick glasses that magnified his eyes—laughed so hard at one of her stories that he coughed a mass of green food back onto his plate, as if he were a giant baby. After dinner, Elliot mustered the courage to ask Alice to dance.

That was more than two years ago. Now he struggles in the comfort of their bed—really her bed, brought over from her apartment upon the agreement that hers was more comfortable than his—his hands clasped around her perfect throat. When he lets go, she whimpers. He knows it is the sound of everything he loves coming to a close.

After a moment of paralysis, she scrambles from the bed and runs to the bathroom and shuts the door. In the dark, Elliot sees only the strip of light coming from the bottom of the door and the shadow of her feet moving on the other side. He pulls himself from bed and goes to the door. He knocks.

"Go away," she says.

"Alice. I was dreaming."

"I said go away."

"Please, Alice. There was a mallard—it was suffocating me." He realizes how ridiculous this sounds. Why mallard? Why not duck? "I would never hurt you."

There is only silence, and then the sound of running water. Unsure what to do, Elliot goes back to bed, where he pinches the skin on his arms over and over again. Without meaning to, he falls asleep.

In the morning, there is still the strip of light under the bathroom door. Alice has slept in the tub, using a balled up bath towel as a pillow. She tells him this as she sits across from him at the breakfast table. He has made her French toast, her favorite, but she refuses to eat. She is not hungry. There are purple bags beneath her eyes and she smells sour, like curdled milk. Still, Elliot wants to kiss her, to suck the bruise from her neck and into his own body, to have it settle into the muscle of his heart. He would endure this bruise forever if it meant the one on her neck would disappear.

"I can't be here today," she tells him.

He tries to stay calm. "Okay. But what about the apartment? They're delivering the couch today." This is a lie—the couch is not set to arrive for another couple of days, but for a moment he believes that the couch can save them. It is their most expensive purchase—a horrendous red sectional from Pottery Barn. It took them weeks to finally choose one. He'd wanted something dark and leather, but Alice said she would rather go back to living alone than have to look at leather every day. To prove her point, she started looking up studios on Craigslist. She went so far as to tour two apartments, one of which she rather liked, before Elliot finally gave in.

"I'm going out," she says. "I'll come home when I'm ready."

He has no choice but to watch as she gathers her things. He is not the type to beg or make a fuss, a characteristic Alice has always faulted him for. She herself is quick to argue with others— family, friends, baristas, and bank tellers—and expects Elliot to back her up, even if he doesn't agree with her point. Of course, it's never about defending her point, but about defending *her*. "You'd sit back in the trenches and watch me get shot up," Alice once told him, after a particularly bad argument she'd had with one of their mutual friends in which Elliot stood by, eating a plateful of miniature hotdogs. Elliot argued that he wouldn't even be on the battlefield to begin with. He'd be off somewhere else—in a neutral country, like Sweden, eating cream puffs or watching a peace parade. She then compared him to the Germans who ignored the smell of smoke from the crematoriums. "You'd let millions of people die to avoid being bothered," she'd said, emphasizing this last word—*bothered*.

Now, he follows her into their bedroom, where she packs a duffel bag with T-shirts and pajama pants and underwear. She then goes to the bathroom. He knows he is in trouble if she takes her shaving cream; she only shaves once a week, on Sunday nights. When she is finally packed and gone—out of the apartment without even a kiss good-bye—he inspects the bathroom. The shaving cream is gone, as is the shampoo and conditioner and the little contraption she uses to curl her eyelashes. Even the bath towel is missing.

Elliot has called Alice sixteen times since she left the day before. It is the weekend, and so he has nothing to do but wait for the phone to ring, for the door to open, for time to rewind so he can undream his dream. Why couldn't the mallard have been a butterfly? Or a kitten? Why, for that matter, had there been a mallard at all? The only mallard he can even think of is the wooden one his stepfather, Roy, keeps on the highest shelf of his home office. It was an expensive mallard, hand painted by a popular folk artist in Jackson Hole, where Roy and his first wife, Barbie, lived before she was diagnosed with leukemia. The artist had given them a discount, but even then it was pricey. A thousand dollars. Elliot's mother has always loved the mallard, which she often refers to as "the avian sculpture." She once asked Roy to put it on the dining room table so that they could enjoy it during meals. Roy refused, saying a thousand-dollar decoy had no place on a dining room table. Once, Elliot caught him whispering to the decoy, "Barbie Doll, I miss you."

Now that he has remembered Roy's wooden mallard, Elliot cannot stop thinking about it. He wants to see the mallard, to hold it in his hands and feel whether it is heavy or light, smooth or textured. What kind of person buys a thousand-dollar decoy?

Elliot wishes he had the distraction of work to look forward to, but it is the weekend before Thanksgiving and he's taken the whole week off. Alice and he made plans to spend the holiday with his parents in Wichita. He wonders if this little stint will last until Thursday morning, when they are due to drive out. He cannot believe that it will, and so he waits. He tells himself he is virtuous for being patient.

To pass the time, he arranges the apartment without her. He

goes through his own boxes first, organizing his books on the bookshelf and putting his dishes into their proper cabinets. He constructs two matching IKEA end tables and puts them on either side of where the couch will eventually go, once it is delivered. He can imagine the couch taking the place of the emptiness, just as he can imagine Alice returning, replacing the quiet apartment with the sound of her voice, her laughter. She is the kind of woman who sings when she is happy—any song that comes to her mind. "Pop Goes the Weasel." "Sometimes When We Touch." The jingle for the Starlight Drive-In. Sometimes her singing drives Elliot crazy, but he does not remember this now. Nor does he remember the time he put a hand over her mouth and told her to be silent. Or how she bit his finger in response.

This is not the first time something like the mallard dream has happened, but Alice does not know this. It happened once before, when Elliot was only a boy. He'd been taking a nap with his cousin, Olivia, on their grandmother's living room floor. He remembers the green shag carpet and his grandmother's shih tzu, Dolly, sniffing the perimeter of where he and Olivia lay belly-up on an old down comforter. His mother had turned out the lights and forced the adults from the living room so the children could rest. They had to sleep in the living room because Elliot was frightened of the bedrooms. His father had died in one of them when Elliot was only a baby—which room, he was never told, but he knew it had happened in this house, in one of the beds, while his father was sleeping. And so it was on the floor of his grandmother's living room that Elliot had woken to find that he was pummeling Olivia's face with the palms of his hands. The adults had come in screaming—they pulled him off his cousin and made him sit alone in the master bedroom, perhaps the most haunted of all the rooms. Alone, he was forced to recall the dream. There had been a man sitting on his chest, his head bloated to the size of a pumpkin. The man had a skinny white tongue that he kept running across his lips, as if he were thirsty. He was wearing the same plaid button-down Elliot's father wore in the picture his mother kept above the fireplace.

And now there was this, the mallard. How could he ever trust himself again? He wonders what else he might do in his sleep, what other crimes he might commit. Of course, Alice must be thinking the same thing. And so he is not entirely surprised when she does not come home that day, or the next. She does not answer his calls. Desperate, he calls her sister, who picks up and says, "Hello?" only to then hang up when a male voice in the background shouts, "She explicitly told us not to talk to him, Marta. Can't you do anything right?"

He has loved Alice thoroughly since he met her, and the idea of living without her is almost too difficult a thought to bear. Outside of this, her absence also poses several logistical problems. The most immediate of these is Thanksgiving with his parents. The second is how he will pay rent, which is affordable if split between the two of them but which will drain him if he has to carry the burden alone.

And so he goes to the only place he thinks she could be hiding.

Alice's ex-girlfriend's name is Ramona, and she is the kind of woman who makes Elliot want to join a gym. She is not a beautiful woman—her face is acne scarred and dominated by a large, crooked nose—but she danced for the Kansas City ballet before settling into a career as a physical therapist. When she answers the door, she does so wearing sweatpants rolled down to reveal the blades of her hipbones. There in the background, sitting on the couch in her favorite pair of flannel pajamas, is Alice. Her hair is done up in a messy ponytail and she is wearing her glasses, the ones he spent hours helping her pick out at the optometrist's office. She'd been a pain that day, making absurd claims about her appearance. *My face is too small. I just don't have the same eyebrows I used to.*

He knows Ramona's address because Alice commented on the

building every time they drove by. She had made a point not to look at apartments near it, claiming she'd rather pay higher rent than see Ramona every time she went for a jog.

Elliot does not know exactly how or why Alice and Ramona's relationship ended. From what he's gathered, they were deeply in love until one day, while they were walking downtown, Alice saw Ramona kick an empty soda can toward a homeless man who was sitting on the corner. Perhaps it had been an accident—Alice never did ask Ramona about it—but Alice couldn't shake the feeling that Ramona had kicked the can on purpose. Was it possible she'd spent years of her life loving a woman who was capable of such a simple cruelty? Eventually, Alice asked for a break. She needed space, some time to think and unremember the sound of the can skipping across concrete. It was during this break that she met Elliot.

"Let me talk to her," he says to Ramona, who is trying to block Elliot's view into the apartment.

"She doesn't want to talk to you. If she did, she would have called you. Or answered one of your thousands of calls."

"Alice," Elliot calls from the doorway. "Alice, just give me five minutes. I think you at least owe me five minutes."

Ramona begins to close the door, but Alice finally appears behind her. "What do you want?" she asks.

Ramona gives up and retreats into the apartment. Now it is just him and Alice in the doorway. He wants to grab her, to kiss her and reclaim her as his own. But deep down, he knows that it is too late for this. He knows without knowing that his time with Alice is over.

"I want you to come to Thanksgiving," he says. "My parents are still expecting you."

She looks down to her bare feet. "I'm not coming anymore," she says. "I'm sorry."

"Will you at least come home so we can talk about it? I understand if you don't want to sleep with me for a while, but we can go slow, step by step. I want you to come home. You don't have to come to Thanksgiving, but I want you to come home. Please. All of our stuff—they've delivered the couch. It's a good couch. You should at least come back to see it. I only got it because of you, you know. I wanted the other one. The leather. But I did it for you. Because I love you."

Alice looks back into the apartment, where Ramona has taken her place on the couch, which is shabby and a horrendous shade of green. Her bare feet are up on the coffee table and she's drinking a cup of coffee, watching the two of them at her door. In the corner is an armchair. Tan leather.

"I'm sorry," Alice says.

"But your stuff."

"I don't even want to think about it. Not yet."

"But everything was fine," he manages to say. "Everything was so good—you didn't even give it a chance. The apartment is still ours. And the couch—"

She reaches up and rubs her neck, which is bruised a faint purple. "I just can't," she says. "I'm sorry. I really am, even if you don't believe me."

"But it was only a dream," he says.

"I know," she says. "But I was there. I was really there."

"What about the apartment?" he says. It is all he can find to say. "I'm sorry," she says, and then gently shuts the door.

Back at the apartment, he unpacks the rest of her things. He hangs her blouses in the closet and puts her shoes on the shoe rack, allowing each item to fill his head with a different memory. Her perfumes go on a little mirrored tray she inherited from her grandmother the spring before. He cannot help but spray some of her favorite scent onto his wrist, which he brings to his nose for the remainder of the day. Soon, the apartment belongs to the both of them again. Her favorite coffee mug sits on the end table, arguing for her imminent return. Her notebooks are stacked on the kitchen table. Her mother's china is in the display cabinet.

Thursday arrives too soon. When he leaves the apartment, he does so reluctantly. He has grown fond of the space, of seeing his and Alice's things comingling on the shelves and in the cabinets and the drawers. He's sprayed the couch cushions with her perfume, and every afternoon he takes a long, dreamless nap.

When he arrives at his parents' house, they are alarmed to find that Alice is not with him; he has not told them about the dream, about Ramona. He is, in turn, alarmed to find that his parents have both grown younger since he last saw them. His mother has dyed her hair the color of a rose and found a new kind of makeup that makes her skin look dewy and soft. Roy has lost fifteen pounds by eliminating desserts—a fact that this mother brings up at random intervals, chanting, *Fifteen pounds! Fifteen pounds! Can you believe it?* as she pats Roy's stomach. Roy is back in the clothes he wore when Elliot was in high school, the plaid shirts tucked into tight blue jeans, a kind of urban cowboy look that Elliot tried and failed to mimic as an adult, opting instead for an endless combination of earth-tone T-shirts and khakis, wool sweaters, and boat shoes.

"So is Alice coming later in the weekend?" his mother eventually asks. She has never liked Alice, whom she once caught checking the price tag on a bottle of wine Roy bought for dinner. Elliot tried to convince her that Alice had merely liked the wine and was checking to see if it was something they could afford for themselves, but of course his mother didn't buy this. If there was one thing his mother believed in, it was her ability to read other people. As the story went, she'd known his father was sick before he'd even felt symptoms; she was the one who told him to go to the doctor, to get the scans. She had also known that Roy, one of Elliot's father's best friends, would wait exactly a year before confessing his love to her.

"No, she's not coming," Elliot says, and something in his tone must tell her not to ask any more questions, because Alice is not brought up again until after the Thanksgiving meal. He and his parents have eaten nearly an entire turkey between the three of them, along with most of a large porcelain bowl full of sweet potatoes that Elliot notices are not actually sweet this year but instead taste like earth with a hint of nutmeg. Still, he eats two servings, along with three buttered rolls, a mountain of green bean casserole, and a portion of glazed ham that would have satisfied an entire table of children. He is sleepy and morose and uncomfortably full when his mother directs him to the living room couch and sits down beside him. "Okay," she says. "Where's Alice?"

Caught off guard, Elliot cannot help but begin to cry. It is the first time he's shared his grief with anyone, and the fact that it is his mother makes him return to his boyhood, when something as small as a splinter would send him running into her arms. "I had a dream," he begins, and then explains the rest. As he talks, he wonders if his stepfather is somewhere nearby, listening. While his mother and Roy were setting the table, he'd snuck into Roy's study to confront the mallard. He hadn't intended to do anything—he just wanted to look at it—but the sight of the mallard enraged him. He'd grabbed the mallard and gone to the yard, where he'd hurled it over the fence. There was a satisfying plop as it landed in the McBrides' swimming pool. His mother had found him just moments after, standing by the fence. When she asked what he was doing he told her he was checking to see if a carving he'd done as a boy was still in the fence. "Well, is it?" she'd asked. He'd frozen, unsure of how to answer. "No," he'd said. "It's gone."

When he finishes explaining about Alice—about the dream and the mallard and Ramona—his mother begins to laugh. "I'm sorry," she says, still laughing. "I just can't help it. You blame Roy? And his avian sculpture?"

"Yes," he says, only now realizing that it's the truth. "I do."

"All right," his mother says, and pats his knee as if he is once again just a young boy with a boo-boo. "All right. I won't take that from you."

"You're making it sound like there's something I'm not accepting."

"You were dreaming," she says, her tone suddenly serious. "You were asleep, Elliot. Who could blame you for something you did while you were sleeping?"

"I left bruises on her neck. She's terrified of me."

"Love isn't a china doll," she says. "It's a monster. If it was that easy to get out of it, we'd all be alone."

"You're saying she never loved me."

"Not that she never loved you, but that maybe she hasn't for a while. That's all. I know it hurts." She pats his leg again.

"You don't care at all, do you?"

"Of course I do, I'm your mother." She pauses, gives his leg a final squeeze. "Do you want pie? There's pumpkin pie."

"You're so frustrating sometimes," he says. "I could get in my car and go home right now if I really wanted to." As soon as he says it, he wonders how he didn't think of it earlier. What had he been thinking, coming all this way, leaving the apartment unattended? What if Alice decided to return? What if, knowing he wouldn't be there, she came and collected her things?

"Don't be dramatic," his mother says. With this she gets up and goes to the kitchen, leaving Elliot alone on the couch. A moment later she calls from the kitchen, "Do you want a big slice or a little slice?"

"Big," Elliot says. "And whipped cream."

He then goes to his room—his childhood room, with the twin bed and the ugly alien spaceship Roy painted above his window long ago, without Elliot's permission—and gets his bag in order. Soon, he will be back in the apartment with Alice's things—her necklaces, her toaster oven, her collection of miniature animal figurines. Where he will put the mallard, he still hasn't decided.

For now, he hurries to the bathroom to gather his toiletries. He flushes the toilet so that his mother will think he has simply gone to the bathroom, that this is why he is not still sitting on the couch, waiting patiently for her to return with his pie. Neither she nor Roy will think about the mallard until they run into Mr. McBride, perhaps while getting the mail or pumping gas at the QuikTrip. "Elliot came by to get some kind of duck thing," Mr. McBride will tell them. "Still don't understand how it got in my pool, but stranger things have happened."

# My Search for Red and Gray Wide-Striped Pajamas

PETER SELGIN

From *Drowning Lessons* (2008)

Since coming to New York two years ago, I've suffered from fainting spells. I'll be standing somewhere, doing nothing, *minding my own business*—at a street crossing or an intersection, somewhere where a decision has to be made. The first time it happened, I froze at the corner of Fifth and Forty-second, near the public library. I must have been blocking the crosswalk. People kept jostling me, cursing under their breaths. My back broke into a sweat. The moisture crept down my spine to gather at the waistband of my undershorts. My white shirt, the only dress shirt in my wardrobe, clung to my skin in ruddy patches as I stood in demented sunlight, paralyzed. Everything seemed to rush out of me then until nothing remained but a cold, clammy sense of my own uniqueness and a sound like a projector reeling. Then my knees went out from under me, and I toppled.

Strange, goggle-eyed faces lowered cell phones and peered down.

*You okay, mister?*

*Mister, you okay?*

Someone handed me a copy of the *News of the World*. "I believe you dropped this," the good Samaritan said.

At first I thought the fainting spells had something to do with my father, who'd died a few years before, since his face would always appear fleetingly among those looking down at me. My aunt and uncle took me to three doctors, one a specialist in inner-ear disorders, each of whom drew blood and reached no conclusions. Uncle Nick thinks I'm neurotic, that I should drink more ouzo and otherwise fortify myself. "You don't eat enough lamb shank; you don't eat enough spanakopita," he tells me, tugging down the lower lids of my eyes to see how anemic I am. "That or you need a kick in the ass," he says.

The evening after my first fainting incident, riding the subway train home with the *News of the World* spread open before me, I read, *"A passenger from the Titanic wreck has been discovered frozen solid inside an iceberg. Scientists and archaeologists are debating whether to thaw him."*

I thought of my dead father: to thaw or not to thaw?

I turned a page, read on.

*"A Haitian voodoo priestess claims that Hitler has been resurrected as a zombie and is raising an army of the undead to invade the United States. One eyewitness has reportedly spotted the Führer, a known vegetarian, sitting on a campstool in a graveyard, chewing on raw chicken livers."*

"A *purpose!*" says my uncle, slamming his fist down hard on the dining-room table—hard enough to rattle the plates in the china cabinet behind him. He knocks back a glass of ouzo. "That's what all humanity is after. To struggle for something well within your grasp—that's *wisdom!*"

Uncle Nick sits at the head of the long dining-room table, holding forth, as he himself would describe it. "To quote the great man Epictetus, *whosoever longs for or dreads things outside his control can be neither faithful nor free.*" Aunt Ourania, Nick's dark little ball of a Greek wife, watches in jittery silence as he chews, swallows, sips, considers. Nick fancies himself likewise Greek, though like my father he's only third generation. Ourania, my aunt, he met at a motivational forum that he presided over, this one for the Greek Restaurant Association of New York—one of dozens of such forums conducted by him each year in gray and mauve conference rooms across America.

Meanwhile my cousin, Marcia, his twenty-two-year-old daughter, eyes me with sullen contempt from the far side of a sage-encrusted lamb shank. Is she contemplating her lost virginity? She is; I smile. From the depths of one of Dante's lower regions, she repackages my smile into a sneer and ships it back to me.

"Am I right, Nephew?"

I'm getting that floating feeling again, like I'm in one of those sensory-deprivation chambers. The dining-room table, the floral wallpaper, the empty ouzo bottles lined up like infantry before the fireplace, Uncle Nick's lamb-and-ouzo-scented words—they all close in on me. Sundays are cruel.

"Am I *right?*"

Uncle Nick swats the back of my head, taps my untouched ouzo glass. "I don't drink," I explain to him for the hundredth time—as if it matters, as if anything matters to Uncle Nick but what *he* thinks.

He carves lamb, forks meat onto my plate. "I don't care if you're fat or thin, rich or poor, dumb or smart," he says. "It makes no earthly difference." The combined smells of lamb and anisette increase my Sunday nausea. "No difference whatsoever."

I await the aphorism, the one that invariably ties the knot on my uncle's dinner speeches. Uncle Nick has made a modest living, not to mention a name for himself, churning out aphorisms. He's written over two dozen—I hesitate to call them books—pamphlets? monographs? all with chrome yellow dust jackets and titles like *How to Lick This Old World and Everyone in It.* The pamphlets are packed with tidy Ben Franklinesque sayings. *"A penny saved is a penny scorned." "If you can't stand the heat, buy an air conditioner." "A fish out of water can't do much with a bi-*

*cycle.*" A person could spend many hours trying to decipher some of Uncle Nick's more elaborate aphorisms. Still, they've earned him a decent living, not to mention all those plaques and photographs lining the walls of his wood-paneled Astoria den: him shaking hands with the president and CEO of Marcal Toilet Tissue Corporation, for example.

"*A man without a purpose,*" Nick proclaims, "*is a chameleon on a scotch plaid.*"

By George, he's done it! Satisfied with this conclusion, Nick rewards himself with another glass of ouzo, places the empty in line with four others ranged before the fire grate next to his snakeskin cowboy boots. "*Stinyássas!*" He drains his glass, then eyes my full one with a brave man's disdain for cowards. "Got that, loverboy?"

Does my uncle know I've bedded his daughter? A prickle runs up my spine. Ever since I arrived in New York, Uncle Nick has been pimping his daughter to me as if I'm the last man on earth, and maybe I am. Or maybe he just wants to get rid of her, marry her off. Or maybe he sincerely thinks we'd be good for each other—incest and other small matters aside. Or maybe, just maybe, he just wants us to be *friends.*

Uncle Nick has my father's eyes, but none of my father's warm-heartedness. His daughter has the same eyes. When she and I make love, I close the blinds.

My search for red and gray wide-striped pajamas began this past Christmas and has since taken me from the disheveled, multicolored plastic bins of K-Mart, at Astor Place, to the vinegar-and-soap-scented oak cabinets of Brooks Brothers, at Madison and Forty-fourth. Uptown by subway, downtown by bus, crosstown on swollen, blistered, sweaty feet. Three months into my search I'm bruised but not beaten, tired yet hopeful, drawn but not defeated. Even, for brief shining moments, faintly optimistic.

Saturday—a day of dull, drizzly rain. I ride the no. 7 train from

Sunnyside, where, in the graveyard-encrusted, working-class muddle of Queens (zone of bars and cemeteries: a turf war between drunks and the dead), I rent a nine-by-ten room from a retired church organist named Filbert, who keeps a pipe organ in his vestibule and plays Bach to raise the dead.

But about Filbert I'll say as little as possible, having more important things on my mind, like the men's clothing store on Greenwich Avenue, in the Village. It came to me in a dream this morning, while dozing between snooze alarms.

"May I help you?" the clerk in the dream—his face its own caricature, poorly drawn—asked me.

"Yes," I answered. "I'm looking for a pair of red and gray wide-striped pajamas."

"Red and gray *wide* stripes?" said the clerk, raising his thin eyebrows, squeezing into the word "wide" a whole eastern city full of snideness.

"That's right," I said, slowly. "Red and gray wide stripes."

"Wait here," said the clerk.

And that's when I woke up.

I've seen paisleys, plaids, checkers, swirls; I've seen abstracts, geometrics, diagonals; I've seen winged horses, flying fish, golf clubs, chili peppers, hummingbirds, sunflowers, and tennis balls; I've seen bacon and eggs, doughnuts, coffee cups, stars and stripes, exotic fish and birds of paradise, trains, cars, ships, planes. I've seen smoking pipes, playing cards, woodwind and brass instruments, violas and violins, waterfowl, rainbows, puffy clouds. I've seen mandalas, spirals, stars, polka dots. I've seen pajamas of every color, every style, every pattern. I've even seen stripes: pink stripes, green stripes, red, white, and blue stripes, wide stripes and pinstripes—even red and gray stripes. But never, *ever* red and gray wide stripes.

The search goes on.

———

They're what he wore. My father. He wore them ragged, as a matter of fact, so ragged you could see the skin of his knees. Rayon? Silk? Plain cotton? I don't remember. But I do remember the faint smell of bourbon and unwashed vegetable bins burrowed deep into their fibers, musty and ripe. Though he died just over five years ago, it seems like so much longer, long before Astoria and Uncle Nick; long before Sunnyside and Filbert and his organ. Long before my obsession with red and gray wide-striped pajamas took hold of me and made me its crusader-slave. Something about the combination of those colors both grounds and disorients me, throws my world off balance while anchoring me to it.

They say that boredom arises from one's sense of detachment from all things, in which case a pair of red and gray wide-striped pajamas has become the least boring thing in the world, for me. For me those colors conjure a privileged, happy childhood. How many boys grow up with their very own private trolley car? My father built it from scratch in his spare time in our garage. Yellow with red pinstripes and varnished cane seats that flipped back and forth depending on which way it was going. The trolley ran on twin lawn-mower engines and had a brass bell I'd ring as we clacked along. We rode it up and down the wooded hill overlooking the brass-fastener and hat factories that dotted the landscape. My father wore his red and gray wide-striped pajamas. They were the closest thing he had to a conductor's uniform.

My father and I would watch the hat factories burn down. Some people wondered how he always knew when there'd be a fire; one man, a fellow employee at the Christmas-bulb-socket factory where he worked, even went as far as to accuse Dad of being an arsonist. But the fact is that when it came to predicting hat-factory infernos my father was possessed of a Promethean foresight. And insurance fraud was rampant.

We'd find the best vantage point up on our hill, then sit next to each other on trolley seats with dampened rags covering our mouths—since the hat-factory smoke carried noxious fumes from the mercury salts used as a block lubricant. More than once, the evening before the factories went up, he'd build a campfire, a tiny blaze to mirror the larger one at the bottom of the hill. Then, armed with marshmallows en brochette, as quiet as monks, we'd wait.

The factories burned gloriously, with marmalade flames augmenting the dusk, spitting sparks where they licked utility wires. Once, when the wind blew the right way, burning hats flew through the air. One nearly landed on my head. "Now *that's* something!" my father said.

Another time, just a few weeks before he died, for the very first time my father gave me some advice. "Son," he said while bobbing two marshmallows on a twig. "I've got two pieces of advice for you." He kept his bourbon bottle handy always and drank from it now. "Fifty-eight years alive on this earth, and I've only got two bits of advice to give to you, my son. The first bit is: *want everything, need nothing*. That may not sound like anything useful, but believe me, it's *very* important. The second piece of advice is . . ." He chewed his lip, looked around. "The second bit of advice . . ." His eyes went blurry and lost their focus; he scratched the short, rough hairs behind his neck. "Son," he said, "I'm sorry, but I forget what the second bit of advice was."

By way of consolation he handed me the bourbon bottle. For the first time I tasted, along with his tobacco-flavored saliva, the burning amber fluid that was as much a part of my father as his skin, and which tasted to me like the hat-factory fire. The whisky carved its own path through my lungs, into my stomach. With metal-stained fingers he pried a braised marshmallow—its formerly white flesh caramelized to a perfectly even ocher—from the end of his twig and fed it to my open mouth. We went on watching flames—those of the campfire and of the factory blazing—letting their tongues do our talking for us. When two firemen arrived to ask us what the hell we thought we were doing, my father smiled, slapped them on their sooty backs, and offered them marshmallows and bourbon.

I was sixteen when he died in the bathroom, straining and coughing on the bowl. He'd smoked like a burning hat factory all his life, until his pulmonary cells mutinied. I found him slumped against the cool tiles, blood drops flecking the front of the red and gray wide-striped pajamas, which hung from his shoulders as if from a wire hanger, he'd grown so thin. I sat on the floor near him, listening to the last chains rattle through his sacked lungs, then he was gone. I held him, the fingers of his hand in mine stained with powdered metal and nicotine. I smelled his earth-soaked mustiness, the tobacco of his hugs and kisses, the unwashed, vegetable-bin/bourbon odor of his flesh. His cancer soaked into my skin.

The trolley went up on cinder blocks in our swampy backyard. For a while I sanded and varnished the cane seats, polished the bell with Brasso, smeared moving parts with white grease, freshened yellow paint and red pinstripes. But the bell tarnished. Rust froze the driveshafts in their bearings; vines crept over the seats, strangling and finally splitting them apart. Two years ago, the day of my nineteenth birthday, carrying my father's ashes in a gray plastic box with a number on it, I arrived here, in New York, at the front door of my uncle's Astoria home.

Midafternoon. Greenwich Village. November. The air heavy under gray-bellied clouds. A sweet smell of honey-glazed peanuts tugs at my heart like leaf smoke. For a moment I'm at a loss: one of those moments when all existence slips out from under your shoes, when you forget to breathe, and heartbeats turn voluntary.

Then I remember my mission.

From outside the store looks pretty much as it did in my dream, but smaller, warmer, and infinitely sadder. The blue and white sign says "Minsky's Men's World." I peer through plate glass.

Slowly a precognition grows, swells, and settles in the spongy mass of my lungs. I feel outlandishly small: a barnacle on the back of a sperm whale. Suddenly the plate glass freezes into an iceberg, my body frozen inside it like a fly in amber. My heart decelerates. I can't breathe; I need to lie down. My father's whisky-moistened eyes shine through the frozen glass. I faint.

I know what Uncle Nick means when he says I need a kick in the ass. But it's not a kick in the ass that I need. It's what some people call ambition, and others call motivation, and others call God. Whatever—they're lucky to have a built-in "kicking machine" they can rely on, whereas people like me, we have to kick ourselves, or be kicked. When I hear the word "potential," my first impulse is to lie down somewhere soft and go to sleep. And though potential may *seem* like a fine thing, stored up for too long it eats away at the soul. You go through life thinking there are other choices, and so all days are rented and not wholly owned. Like buying subway tokens one at a time, or hiring a hotel room by the hour, hour after hour, day by day, year after year.

And as for commitment, to me commitment is a burning hat factory you can never escape alive. Nor does my uncle understand that during my worst periods of floating, fainting is all that tethers me to this world. It has *nothing* to do with ouzo or spinach pie. It's just me and this whole red and gray wide-striped dream that some people call life.

I look up, see faces looking down, their eyeballs swollen with concern.

*You okay, mister?*

(A fainting perk: they call you "mister.")

*Fine, fine, thank you.*

But I'm still floating, swimming in inner space. The lifeline has been cut, and I'm drifting free of the space capsule, which grows smaller. Now they've got me sitting up on the sidewalk against the window display of Minsky's Men's World. I turn, look inside, my eyes dead level with a silk plaid bathrobe. I think: *I'm the chameleon.*

"May I help you?"

The real salesclerk at Minsky's wasn't at all like the one in my dream. He had a soft, neatly feminine face, a *kind* face—nothing pointed or severe—almost listless in its lack of distinct features.

"Pajamas," I said, still woozy from my faint.

"We don't carry many," he said with a sorry look. "I'll show you what we've got."

He showed me the so-called pajama section, and right away my heart sank. There were no more than a dozen pair. All solids, no stripes. Not even piping.

"That's *all?*"

The salesclerk shrugged. He looked sincerely sorry.

But this is no time for hopelessness. Ahab had his whale, Shackleton his South Pole, Jason his Golden Fleece, the crusaders their Holy Grail. Off I march to Barney's, to Loehmann's, to Macy's, to Bloomingdale's, Saks, Lord & Taylor, Paul Stuart . . . Like a pig rooting truffles, I snort quickly through the discounted bins at Filene's, then head uptown, to jaunt along Madison Avenue in the sixties, among fur-coated, imperially slim housewives with tucked chins and powdered noses, and gather in the thrilling bad taste of the rich.

Sunday, that most tyrannical of days, a day dedicated to dates with my cousin Marcia, my beloved, Uncle Nick's sullen little lamb. For almost a year Uncle Nick has been bribing me to take her out with me, slipping me crisp twenties in the shadowy recesses of his plaque-lined den, whispering to me, "Show her a good time, eh, loverboy?" And I try, honest, I really try. But Marcia has no manners. She's constantly sulking, telling me off with that soggy face of hers. She knows what her father's up to: she's no Einstein, but she's not stupid either.

Alas, I have no folding money. Three evenings a week I wash dishes at one of several Greek restaurants owned by *her* uncle, my uncle's brother-in-law. I make barely enough to pay my bills. And so every Sunday, after lunch, Uncle Nick presses a fresh twenty into my reluctant palm.

But I refuse to spend his money on her. I keep all Uncle Nick's twenties neatly stacked on my dresser top, weighted down by the plastic urn holding my father's ashes, and treat my cousin as I see fit, with pocket change. At first I tried taking her with me on my pajama search, but Marcia would have none of it. "What the hell do you need pajamas for? Sleep in the raw!" She thinks the whole "quest thing" is loony. And maybe she's right. But I'll be damned if I'm going to stop on her account.

It's raining. We ride the no. 1 local downtown. I love riding the subway; I love the element of surprise each passenger brings into the car, like guests on a variety show, or show-and-tell. You can *smell* the damaged souls as they enter—a sharp, electronic odor of massed negative ions, a smell of anxiety and defeat. The lady seated across from us says over and over to herself, desperately, *"He was all I had!"* I hear my father's whiskey-logged voice, *"Want everything; need nothing,"* and want to correct her. I've no business giving people advice—I'm not sure anyone does. Still, I can't resist. And as I lean forward, Marcia's head, which she's been resting on my shoulder, stirs in protest. She opens her mouth to try to stop me, aware of my habit of confronting troubled strangers in public places. But this time Marcia is too late.

"No, ma'am, he *wasn't*," I say, reaching forward to grasp the subway soliloquist's hand.

The lady, whose cheeks are like powdered dough, looks surprised but doesn't pull away. "How do you know?" she asks.

"Because—I *know*." Marcia elbows me; I elbow her back. My cousin has deep brows and silky black hair and is exotic looking, for an Astoria girl.

"Who the fuck are *you*?" the lady wants to know.

"Steven—mind your own *bus*iness!"

"My name is Steven Papadapoulis. This is my cousin, Marcia." She elbows me again. "I'm taking her sightseeing." I elbow *her* again.

The woman stares at me. I raise her hand to my lips and kiss it, then fold it gently back into her lap, where I pat it like a small creature.

"What is *wrong* with you?" says Marcia as we climb out of the subway at South Ferry. Then, realizing where we're headed, she cries, *"Not the Staten Island Ferry again!"*

"What's the matter, don't you like the ferry?"

*"Fuck you!"*

"Tsk! Language."

"Can't we at least go to the Statue of Liberty?" she whines.

"What, and get trapped with all those tourists?"

She stops dead, gives me a devilish look, hand on out-thrust hip. "Or else take me to your place," she says. Her lips part hormonally; spermatozoa swim in her eyes.

Patience, I tell her with my flattened palm. Soon I'm marching three steps ahead of her into the crowded waiting room, an echoing cavern of spent faces. On the wall a lighted sign tells when the next ferry departs. The place smells of crowds and sticky orangeade. It's our third date here. Marcia grabs the tail of my windbreaker.

"Come on," I say. "Be a sport."

"You really, really hate me, don't you?" she sniffs. Our family runs to long, narrow heads, and she's got one.

"Hate you? What makes you think I hate you?"

The truth is, I like Marcia—more than I should. She's quite wonderful in bed and can be funny. I just don't want her getting wrong *ideas* about me, such as that I'm the type of guy who takes a girl out to dinner and the movies.

"It may surprise you to learn," I say, seating her on a long, chewing-gum-barnacled wooden bench beside me, "that there are in this world women who would all but die for a chance to ride the Staten Island Ferry in the rain with the likes of yours truly."

"You're right—it *would* surprise me," she says.

"You're sullen."

"And you're a creep."

"I'm also your cousin, and I have deep feelings for you."

"What the fuck is *that* supposed to mean?"

"It means—"

A bell rings. Grappled to each other by DNA, we shuffle up the gangplank.

"You were saying, creep?"

"Blood is thicker than water. Didn't your dad ever teach you that?"

"My father thinks I'm still a virgin."

"That makes two of us."

At seventy-five cents a round trip the Staten Island Ferry is still one of the best deals in town. And for one fare you can ride forever. Having grown up landlocked, with the hot breath of hat-factory smokestacks breathing down on me, I love everything to do with the ocean, including scavenger birds and iron corroded by salt. My father found his ocean in bottles and *drank* it. I won't make that mistake. Far better to be corroded from without, more natural. I watch the dirty waves slosh up against the pier coming and going. The *galumphs* of water against black pylons waterlog me with joy. Salt air inflates my lungs.

"Isn't it great?"

"You make me puke."

I plan our dates for late in the afternoon, in time to watch the sun spatter downtown with gold dust. Smoke-colored gulls follow orange and black tugs. The towers of downtown Manhattan pockmarked with twenty-four-karat gold. It's strange seeing the city looming so giant and silent, the towers like stalagmites and the sky a Hollywood rear-screen projector fake. So much removed beauty, silent, majestic, while at our feet banana peels and scum float in brown, murky waves, and in the waiting room behind us people swallow their daily dose of shouting headlines (I swear, some people live for gray suits and newsprint). Only the tourists pretend to see the skyline.

As for my cousin, she doesn't give a fig about this display. She huddles inside with the rest of the drained newspaper faces, her hands folded in her pugnacious lap, hating my guts while dreaming of the warmth between my sheets. I lean on the rail, feel the salted breeze in my hair, toss bits of pretzel to raucous gulls, glance at my cousin through rain-beaded glass, knock on it, point out the Statue of Liberty. Her sulk is as fixed as the skyline. I go to the concession stand, buy two oranges for fifty cents, toss her one.

"Eat up!"

"Up yours."

I sit beside her, peel my orange. "You know," I say, "it bothers me that you think I hate you. I think you have lots of good qualities." She gives me a fish eye. "Really. You're honest, fair . . . a bit on the flip side, but fair. You have a sense of humor, and integrity—a rare quality these days, or so I'm told. Plus you've got a very nice figure."

"I'm fat."

She's not; she's pudgy. But I like a little flesh. "The point, Marcia, is I think we have lots in common. I just wish you could understand just what these ferry rides mean to me; then you'd realize I'm trying to share something very important with you."

"Why does everything you say sound like a rehearsed piece of shit?"

I clutch myself, wounded. "What I'm trying to say, Marcia, is that . . . well . . . it's very possible that *I'm in love with you.*" Do I mean this? Could I mean it? Honestly I don't know. As if to plug up the hole from which that statement leaked, I plop an orange section into my mouth. Marcia looks at me. Her orange has fallen with a thud to the steel deck; I hand it to her. She beats her skull with it. I go back outside and finish peeling my orange in the drizzle. The peel floats out to sea. Then she's next to me.

"*What* did you say?"

She bends way over the rail to catch my eye. I face the water, take in flotsam and jetsam, finish segmenting my orange. The faint, oily smell of the bay corrupts its flavor.

"If you love me so fucking much, why don't you take me someplace decent—like the Rainbow Room?"

"This is fun," I say quietly.

"It was fun the *first* time."

"The first two times it was the *Samuel I. Newhouse*. This is the *American Legion*. It's a whole new ball game." I'm still not looking at her.

"It's *boring*! And *my ass is frozen*!" Boredom: when people refer to it, do most of them really have any idea what they're talking about, one of the most complicated emotions—a heady mixture of fear, loathing, and dread—a silent, poker-faced form of sheer terror?

She leans her plump breast into my arm. I feed her the last piece of orange, put an arm around her. She bites her lip. She has her father's eyes, my uncle's eyes, my father's eyes. The sunset turns bloody red against ash gray towers. My pulse stumbles, dies.

"Oh, God, Steven, no—*please don't faint*!"

From where I live, in Sunnyside, you can see the spire of the Empire State Building, but it may as well be on Jupiter. When not otherwise engaged, I'm here, in my rented room, with its foam mattress and metal trash pail stinking of yesterday's banana peel. Every so often, on weekdays when I'm not getting fed at Uncle Nick's or at the restaurant, I go out for dinner and to escape the funereal vibrations of my landlord's organ. There's a Chinese place a few blocks from here, where the boyish waiter always seats me facing the boulevard, where, under the elevated's girders clawing up into darkness, a red neon sign flashes

STEVEN'S

with the T and V in "STEVEN" turning blue every other flash. For the price of an order of chow mein, I can sit there all night watching my namesake flash in neon.

There's something very cosmic about eating alone in a Chinese restaurant in Sunnyside on a cold night. But mostly I stay holed up in my room in Filbert's apartment, at the mercy of a boredom so intense it turns the fruits in a bowl on his dining-room table gray as if seen through color-blind eyes. Thus I avoid the banality of having to go anywhere. It seems to me, has seemed to me for a while now, that many if not all of the ills of this world would be solved if only people could learn to sit quietly in their rooms. Where's there to go, anyway? What's to be done? Why all this hunger for activity? The earth spins: isn't that activity enough? Not that I mean to hold myself up as an example. It's just something that's occurred to me, as it occurs to me that my Christian name, punctured by a period, turns me into a saint of uniform disposition, an angel in equilibrium.

Lives are so disposable, moments like after-dinner mints melting in our mouths. It isn't so much a feeling that things don't matter, but rather a feeling that what we choose to *make* matter is arbitrary: a bright, vertiginous feeling, like sunstroke shining through gloom. This remarkable yet perturbing sense of arbitrariness goes everywhere with me, carrying with it the seeds of both possibility and impossibility, the need to do so many things, and likewise the urge to do nothing.

I bungle along Queens streets, dark with newspapers blowing. The lights of Manhattan shine upward, painting a fake aurora borealis in the night sky. A drunken sailor—or someone wearing what looks like a sailor suit—stumbles along ahead of me, clanging a section of metal pipe against the cast-iron fence that separates us both, at least for the time being, from the dead. My breath fogs the air. Within a block of my building it starts to rain; I hold my collar close. The wind makes a sound rushing through alleys, a drawn-out moan, a dreary sound. It seems to be telling me something, to want to grab me by the shoulders and shake me, as if I'm dreaming and it wants me to wake up, to snatch me from oblivion and call me a fool as the subway rattles off into darkness overhead.

Then I realize it's not the wind at all. It's Filbert's organ wafting down into the street.

Sunday morning, before lunch, Marcia and I make love on my foam mattress. We do it to the vibrations of Bach's Toccata and Fugue in D minor; we do it to the Tune of Conspiracy, to the Beat of Betrayal, to the Melody of Mutiny. Above the urn containing my father's ashes, Uncle Nick peers down at us, sipping ouzo from a glass as he watches the slow dance of his daughter's unvagination unfold under goose-pimpled flesh. Like the explosion that ten billion years ago sent all the stars and planets hurtling into space, our lovemaking is cataclysmic and chaotic, as if a critical mass had been reached, a density beyond that of all existing stars. In my fervor I forget about such things as guilt and where my skin ends and how long it takes Marcia's inverted nipples to pop. One of us is the chameleon, the other the scotch plaid. We disappear each in each.

"More ouzo, loverboy?"

We're woefully late for dinner. Uncle Nick keeps shedding his eye on me, a different look this time, like this time he knows for certain that I've deflowered his daughter, but whether this means victory to him or defeat I can't say for sure. Ourania seems to know it, too, but she merely looks thoughtful and sad. But then she looks that way always.

"You kids had a nice time last Sunday?" Uncle Nick asks.

"Oh, yes, very nice," I say.

"We rode the ferry," says Marcia through a lamb-stuffed smile.

"Again the ferry?"

"The *American Legion*," says Marcia.

Uncle Nick leans close and whispers, ouzo-breathed. "I give you good money and you take her on the *ferry*?"

"Next week we go to the Transit Museum," Marcia blurts. "Right, Steven?"

I smile.


Passing by Rockefeller Center. The heaven-topping tree is up. A crowd watches the colored lights as golden Prometheus burns, his torch shooting colored sparks that scurry up the dark facade of the RCA tower. I think of my father, who stole fire not from heaven but from burning hat factories. How I long to curl up in red and gray stripes, to sleep tucked into their ripe smell.

Snow falls as I cross Fifty-seventh. A cold gust blows. I fold up the collar of my windbreaker, wait for the ache to pass. The sky thickens to darkness.

"I'm looking for pajamas," I tell the salesclerk at Bergdorf's, a man with a nervous twitch to his upper lip and thick lines shooting up the middle of his forehead.

"What size?" He seems completely uninterested.

"My size. But it's the pattern and colors that concern me."

I follow the salesclerk's dispassionate back to a display case bursting with pajamas—diamonds, shields, polka dots—and, yes, stripes.

"Any wide ones?"

"Wide?"

"I'm looking for wide stripes. Red and gray, preferably."

With a desultory air the salesman opens drawers. From one he withdraws a stack of striped pajamas. Second from the bottom, I see them: a pair with red and gray wide stripes.

"It's a medium," says the clerk, unfolding them. "They run a bit large. These should fit you just fine."

I nod thoughtfully into my index finger, which I've pressed against my lips as if to suppress a painful outburst—something between a groan and the mewl of a cornered, pocket-sized creature—then take a step back, and then another, as the clerk, a toreador dangling a red and gray striped cape, fixes me with questioning eyes and the department store walls (decorated in wide vertical red and gray stripes) close in on me like the bars of a colorful jail cell. Question: how did they kill him? Answer: they gave him everything he wanted. *(He was all I had. No—not exactly.)* I think I'm going to die; I *know* I'm going to faint. Minutes later I'm sitting with a Dixie cup of cool water to my lips, surrounded by concerned faces, including that of the desultory clerk, who asks me do I still want the pajamas? should he ring them up for me? My mouth goes dry. I stammer.

"Well . . . actually . . . I really wanted . . . pink and blue," I say, merely to extricate myself. "You haven't got pink and blue, have you, by any chance?"

Spring. Together with my cousin I watched the magnolias in Central Park blow out again, flinging their snowy branches to snare the sky. The daffodils the gardeners had planted bloomed in sudden affray. By May's end I'd never felt better, only lighter, as if my bones had hollowed, like the bones of birds. I no longer floated; my lightness attached itself to earth. When the magnolia blossoms shivered, I shivered with them; when fat raindrops dimpled the glassy surface of the rowboat pond, my skin took their imprint, too. There was no obvious joy in any of this, mind you, only a great substantive indifference, as if the long, nearly total vacuity of the past year—my year of searching for red and gray wide-striped pajamas—had served its purpose, had scooped my longing for old comforts out like so much melon meat, had emptied me of something I didn't need *or* really want, and by emptying me had freed me—or at least delivered me from department stores.

I no longer suffer from fainting spells.

Standing on the stern of the *American Legion*, sifting my father's ashes into its wake, I watch the wind whip them into gray smears. I toss the plastic urn in; it bobs, floats. *O sweet gray banality of life! O bloody shank of day's end! O bourbon-and-ouzo-scented breath of night!* Under a red bay of sky Marcia wraps her plump arms around me.

Uncle Nick has asked me to go to work for him, setting up his symposiums, peddling his chrome yellow manifestos. A man needs a purpose, after all. *A man without a purpose is a chameleon on a scotch plaid.* In celebration we locked arms across his dining-room table, drained each other's ouzo glasses, then hurled them synchronously into the fire grate, where they shattered like snowballs. *Stinyássas!*

So I shall live on, lightening and lightening, until my body cells quaver in frequencies of every wavelength and spectrums of every hue.

Speaking of spectrums: next Sunday I've promised to take my cousin to the Rainbow Room.

Uncle Nick is pleased.

# The Uses of Memory

## DIANNE NELSON OBERHANSLY

From *A Brief History of Male Nudes in America* (1993)

Netta Cartwright believes these are the things that will bring her husband Franklin back from the dead: thick Velveeta sandwiches, fresh air, plenty of talk and music. She throws the windows open, though it is October in Boise and the smoke-filled breeze whips the lacy curtains, makes them dance in the near-cold. Netta works the radio dial the way other retired women learn to spin the Bingo basket up at St. Mark's on Thursdays—90 percent wrist, 10 percent luck. She turns up the radio's volume when something good comes in: Johnny Paycheck or "The Wabash Cannon-ball." She taps her foot and tries to find the music's rhythm and then tries to pass it on to Franklin.

"You hear that, honey?" she yells, her foot cracking thunder, louder than the radio now.

Carlene, Netta and Franklin's eldest daughter, watches her mother and shakes her head, amazement and disgust and weariness all rolling up into one big ball. "How can you be sixty-three and not know anything?" she asks Netta. Carlene is sorting through a bowl of butter mints, picking out the pinks and slowly eating them.

Netta is too busy to answer or to even listen. She must concentrate on the slippery rhythm, pick it up, then get it all the way down to her foot.

Just an arm's length away from the women, Franklin lies on a bed near the living room window, and in the strictest sense he isn't dead, of course, but he's close enough: low vitals, a complete loss of hair, a mouth that won't form a single word. The left side of his body is soft and slack, useless as a flat tire. Netta has been known to walk right over and smack that arm or give a half-soft karate chop to the withered leg, hoping for even the slightest reaction. She'd appreciate a blink or even a nod from Franklin—thank you—but he just lies there, silent, not even a half-light shining from his old, whiskered face.

Carlene finishes a mint and says to Netta, "There's got to be a special place in hell for you." She moves next to her father, or someone that used to be her father, and lightly strokes his arm: his knuckles, his knobby wrist, then the big, bare root of his elbow.

"Don't get him too comfortable, now," Netta says. "He's just about ready for his bath."

Carlene offers to take a turn cleaning him up, but Netta, as always, says no. To be honest, she doesn't trust Carlene with people. Dogs—yes. People—no. Netta considers her granddaughter Mandy a prime example of how Carlene can take a good person and screw her up, turn her inside out. During all the time that Mandy was growing up, she chewed her fingernails until they had to be iodined and taped; she ate her own long, brown hair; she would sit in front of the TV with her knees up in front of her and suck on them like a child trying to consume herself. Later, on Mandy's small body, the scaly patches of eczema bloomed.

Carlene won't admit to being a poor mother, but Netta thinks she has gotten the message, because after Mandy, Carlene doesn't have any more children; she turns to raising Australian Blue Heelers. They're a breed that cozies up to Carlene. They lick her face when she bends down to them. They bark and yelp for her when she crosses the yard. Her brown station wagon is scattered with dog kibble, and it doesn't even bother her; she just brushes the driver's seat clean and drives away.

When Netta comes back to the room carrying a big spaghetti pot filled with warm—bordering on hot—water, Carlene quickly steps aside like a pedestrian moving out of heavy traffic. Netta has generously added some of her Peaches and Cream bubble bath to the water, and a small eruption of sweet bubbles glides down the side of the pan and plops onto Franklin's sheet, but Franklin doesn't complain. He hasn't complained about anything in over four months, hasn't fed himself, hasn't been able to stand and take the short stroll down the hall to the bathroom, hasn't even been able to hold his own pruned-up pecker to pee since they put the catheter in.

Months ago, the doctors advised Netta to find a good nursing facility, but all their words were like Chinese to her. She brought him home from the hospital and started at the beginning with him. "Your name is Franklin. You're seventy-two years old. That's the TV the kids gave us a couple of Christmases ago. We can't get channel nine because the damn antenna's no good."

For once, Carlene and Netta agree on something: no hospitals, no old folks' home. Carlene's suggestion is to put Franklin in the living room, right by the window so that he can see out and—she doesn't tell her mother this part—so that he can gently make his escape from Boise and what must be to him a pretty dreary world.

Carlene believes these are the things that will push her father into the next best world: absolute quiet, smoldering pine incense, warmth and coaxing and a big window through which his soul can slip away. She pulls up a folding chair, sits next to his big bald head, and whispers to him: "Look out there and let go, Pop. It's time to let go."

The first time Netta overhears her whispering those things to Franklin she walks up and kicks Carlene's chair, would kick Carlene in that little, skinny, two-bit butt of hers, but she can't get her leg up high enough. "Don't you dare," she hisses at Carlene.

Carlene turns on her mother. "Well look at you, all dressed up like the damn Red Cross! Making him hang on so you won't have to be alone."

Carlene and Netta would gladly part company. They have managed to live as adults in the same city for the past twenty-two years, sidestepping each other except for Christmas and birthdays, but in their plan to bring Franklin home they suddenly need each other. Carlene comes over and spends the days with her father. Netta takes evenings and nights.

Both women are silent as Netta pulls the sheets back and prepares to wash Franklin. It's always a shock—that first, biting look at him: a scarecrow in T-shirt and socks; a pale, bony joke gone bad. Franklin, a licensed electrician for almost forty years, used to have a bumper sticker on his white Ford truck. *Electricians don't grow old. Their wiring just goes bad.* Carlene says that for her that's almost the worst part—the blank, dragged-out look on her father's face.

"It takes time to get well," Netta says, mostly to herself and to the walls. She looks for hope in the smallest of her husband's gestures: a hiccup, a sudden, uncontrolled blinking of the eye. She knows the stories of people who have come crashing up out of comas, big and sleepy as bears at the end of eternal winters.

She begins scrubbing Franklin's feet, starting on his soles, rubbing in much the same way as she cleans her kitchen linoleum. Carlene half expects to see her lather up a Brillo pad.

"Be a little gentle, will you?" Carlene tells her.

"He likes it," Netta says. "He likes the stimulation. It's good for him."

Carlene has to go out and sit in her station wagon to cool down—Netta makes her that mad. She leans her head tiredly against the driver's window. She closes her eyes and breathes in deeply the earthy, tranquilizing smell of her dogs.

Netta is preparing for Halloween, which is in four days. She puts her chubby hand, with four fingers up, in front of Franklin's face. "Four days," she says to him, loud and slowly. "One, two, three, four," she counts, making each finger bob. She gathers brown, crinkly leaves and randomly sprinkles them like fairy dust over the living room end tables. She sets a big, uncarved pumpkin on top of the TV so that the rabbit ears stick up behind it. She rolls Franklin temporarily away from the picture window while she decorates it with packaged cobwebs, then pushes him back in place.

She is surprised at how Franklin fits in with the holiday decor. Paper-skinned and mummy-like, he lies in front of the webbed window, already fitting in, contributing his best to Halloween. Netta can see that. She can see him struggling to come back, to move, to talk again so that they can have those crazy morning conversations that make him laugh and shake his head and threaten to go see if his old girlfriend, Danielle Berry, will take him in. Netta thinks, hell, if it would make him recover any faster, she'd double-time Danielle right over to his bedside, tie her there, feed both of them mashed potatoes and the baby-soft food of recovery.

Carlene can feel Halloween out there, the air thin and solemn, but unlike Netta she just can't get the heart for it. Nothing out of the ordinary decorates her living room. Drake and Faye, her two favorite Blue Heelers, snooze at the end of the Herculon couch, though they aren't really festive in any way, except for their braided brown and orange collars perhaps. Drake's eyes are closed but they twitch, indicating—somewhere—the murky dreams of a dog.

Even though Carlene and her husband Ham have been invited to a costume party, Carlene decides that she won't be anything this year. Last year she was a Viking, and Ham hung a potato six inches off his belt and told everyone he was a dictator. This year Ham has gone down to a local playhouse and rented a King Neptune outfit. For days he has carried his mock trident around the house, goosing Carlene with it, trying to get her in the mood.

"Can't you see I've got other things to think about?" she tells Ham, who, as Neptune, is only momentarily put off.

The fact is, she cannot get her father to let go, despite the incense she burns, despite the calming voice she uses to tell him that everything is okay here, that all of his work is finished, that he can stop holding on. She waits, of course, until Netta has left the house for the morning.

She rummages in Netta's haphazard filing drawer and finally fishes out what she's after. She carries a green vinyl packet marked Riverside Memorial Garden back to her father's bedside. She opens it to a page with a photograph of marble statuary, shows it to him, and reminds her father that everything has been taken care of. It takes Carlene a few minutes to find it on the down-to-scale map, but she finally pinpoints plot 124D, puts her finger on it, and shows her father. "Kinda on the hillside," she tells him, "looking down over the river. Remember? It's real nice. You helped pick it out a long time ago." Carlene hopes that this will be one more string cut for the old man who seems not her father, but only a man using her father's name.

She gets down at bed level and looks right into his face, but it's like peering into a cavern. He looks back at her with the blank, rheumy eyes of sheep or cows, and suddenly she wants it done, she wants to take a kitchen towel and shoo his soul right out the window. "Go on. Bye-bye. Vamoose." She imagines a white steamy haze scooting out the window, then rising higher and higher above the yard, a gauzy hand waving back at her. She knows that absolute relief could come for her in a moment that quick.

Midmorning, Carlene feeds her father applesauce, which is pure torture for her—feeding a man she once thought put the stars in the sky. He would lead her out into the darkness when she was young and they would lean against the house and look up. Holding his cigarette, he would extend his arm up into the blackness until the faraway, orangy end of his Viceroy seemed to burn a star into place. "There. Another one for you," he would say, a sudden twinkling appearing way out there, and even when she was older—a woman lying in Ham's arms, a mother fixing endless baby bottles—the stars, in some sense, were still from her father.

When Netta arrives home for lunch, she wrinkles up her nose, wants to know what that smell is. "Kinda like Pine Sol," she says, looking behind the couch, then lifting the throw pillows.

"It's nothing, Mom. Nothing," Carlene says, knowing that Netta in no way could understand how pine eases and lifts a person from this life.

Netta has enrolled in a morning crafts class at the Y, and Carlene asks her how it was.

"I left at the break," she tells Carlene. "Making grapes out of colored pipe cleaners is not a craft. Here," she says, bends and takes some books from her tote bag. "This is what I did."

She has checked books out of the library. *The All New Book of Muscle Recovery. Better in 30 Days. The Home Care Manual.* The lending period is three weeks, and Netta intends to memorize it all.

Carlene can feel the determined heat rising off her mother. She notices a thin line of perspiration on Netta's upper lip. Under the sleeves of her mother's cotton dress, there are the delicate beginnings of sweat rings. If Netta were not so dominating and petty, Carlene believes, she could feel halfway sorry for her.

All the little packages of saltines around the house, however, are there to remind her who her mother is. Netta, like some bag lady, shamelessly slips the little crackers into her purse whenever she goes to JB's or The Rib House, as if they are as complimentary as matchbooks. She says it's just automatic for her to take them; it's from the days when she had teething babies to always think about.

"Get over it, Mom. The last time you had a teething baby was more than forty years ago," Carlene tells Netta.

Carlene also notices how her mother slyly stashes away the last little piece of pie or cake or pizza, as if somehow she hasn't gotten her fair share. Weeks later Carlene finds these little treasures still unwrapped in the back of the refrigerator, mushy as jam and covered with soft, green fur.

"Honest to God," Carlene tells Ham on the night before Halloween when he surprises her with a six-pack of Old Milwaukee, "if I start squirreling things away like my mom, shoot me, please. You'll be doing everyone a favor." She grabs a pencil and uses it to open the flip-top can so she won't break her nail. She holds the beer up in a quick toast to Ham, then leans back and takes her first long, cold drink.

"Tell you what," he says. "I'm going to shoot you if you don't get a costume ready for tomorrow night."

Carlene's doorbell starts ringing at twilight the next evening. Goblins and rabbits, witches and ballerinas crowd her front porch, then drift noisily away when it is apparent that no one is going to answer. Carlene has exactly seven mini candy bars in a bowl, which means she has popped thirteen of them herself while sitting at the breakfast nook, feeling black and weightless, listening to her doorbell as it becomes one long, fluid ring.

Later, when Ham comes out of the bedroom dressed in a sea-blue off-the-shoulder robe with a cardboard crown barely balanced on his head and the gold trident flaking glitter everywhere, Carlene turns around on her stool, gawks at him, and finally claps. She knows that this is as good as Halloween will get for her.

Although Carlene is dressed in everyday jeans and a shirt when they leave for the party, Ham doesn't say a word, doesn't suggest disappointment in the least. In a tight spot Ham's discretion always comes through. He reaches down and puts his arm around her shoulder and as they walk toward the driveway they watch a tiny lion scurry down the street swinging an orange lantern, making bright arcs in the night.

On the way to the party, Ham suggests dropping by Carlene's parents' house since it is still early. Netta answers the door wearing an apron, the pockets stuffed to the top seams with Sugar Babies and Atomic Fire Balls. She throws her hands back and cannot stop laughing at Ham, who basks in her attention, strolling this way and that, thumping his trident on the wood floor.

Carlene walks over to her father in his bed. The polyspun cobwebs shimmer in the window next to him. His eyes are open, but she can't get him to look at her, and automatically her hand comes up, she snaps her fingers and softly swipes at his nose, a technique that never fails to get a dog's attention.

Carlene, for the life of her, can't explain whether she is watching a reverie or some tangled predicament. He is down to 117 pounds, his big, bare collarbone holding up the frailest of necks, and still he won't let go. All at once the anger that rises in her is so swift and complete that for a moment she can't get her breath. Her lips part and her shoulders lift two or three inches. She backs away from him, whoever he is, until she feels the chair behind her and sits down. She picks up a *Golf Digest* and fans herself and the air comes back to her in small, bitter waves.

Netta is feeding Franklin miniature marshmallows that night—a Halloween treat, she says—depositing them by two's and three's until his mouth is full. Franklin chews by rote, making a soft white soup which sticks in the corners of his mouth.

By the time Carlene and Ham leave, Carlene has her breath back and is brooding again, ready to wring Netta's neck. She sees that if nothing else works the old woman is bound to keep him alive with sugar.

There is a turkey scare two weeks before Thanksgiving. The news has reported a gross shortage of both fresh and frozen birds, which sends Netta into a tailspin. She hits five markets on her side of town, comes home with three frozen Butterball toms, six pounds of cranberries, enough yams for the block.

When she pulls into her driveway and stops the car, the memories start up, like a tune she can't get out of her head—Franklin bustling out the front door to help her carry in groceries. He'd be peeking in the sacks before he even had them into the kitchen, hoping for licorice or peaches or a dark, resinous bottle of Old Crow. Netta wants him back so bad she can taste it—a shallow sweetness in the back of her throat, a raw craving. She opens the trunk and carries in the groceries herself.

"Want one?" she asks Carlene when she is inside the house, pointing at a turkey.

"What are these?" Carlene is holding up a deck of flash cards. Turkeys and Thanksgiving are lost—a million miles away.

"Oh, watch this," Netta says excitedly, taking the cards from Carlene. She sidles up to Franklin's bed and shimmies a thick hip onto the mattress. She does a quick, fancy card shuffle—something she learned in Atlantic City, turns the pile face up, looks at the top card, then centers it in front of Franklin's face. "Tree," she says, "tree," bending her head forward with each hard *t*.

When there is no response from Franklin, Netta swivels around and says, "It may not seem like anything is happening, but the brain is a sponge, Carlene, and he's soaking up our every word, and when he's good and ready he'll start spitting it all back."

Netta moves to the next card. "Mouse," she says, at least three times, pointing to the picture, which simply infuriates Carlene.

Before Netta can get to the next card, Carlene stops her. "Okay, okay," she yells, "that's enough." Her arms are stiff at her sides. Her hands are balled into the tight fists that have started to dominate her life. "How can you do this?" she asks her mother. "How can you humiliate him? He is not getting better."

"Well, I'm glad to hear you have a medical degree now, Miss Smart-Ass," Netta shouts. She turns her back to Carlene and stops the argument flat, her usual tactic.

Before she really has time to think about what she is doing, Carlene glides past her mother and scoops up the thick, blocky, first-grade cards right out of Netta's hands. She walks to the front door and opens it, then pushes back the screen and throws the whole stack, Frisbee style. They catch the air and go down slowly. The rose card spirals. The hat card catches high in the privet. The zebra almost touches the ground and then is caught up again and carried to the neighbor's yard.

Netta puts her hands on her hips and walks to the door and both women stand there looking out at the white whirlwind of litter across the brown grass. Sorrow has hammered its way so far into their chests that a moment like this—a sudden mess, something that now has to be picked up off the lawn—is strangely welcome in their lives.

Carlene turns to her mother and says that, yes, she will take one of the turkeys.

Each evening, in the voice of a librarian that she once knew from Okinokee, Netta reads the newspaper to Franklin. She polishes the vowels, repeats any important names, and in general tries to make sense of the world to Franklin.

"Ice Palace Collapses" she reads to him, an article sadly detailing how the local Jaycees' icy Christmas wonderland melted due to a puzzling electrical short. "In only a few hours," she reads, "the life-sized ice reindeer were reduced to winter slush." She abbreviates the articles, tries to keep the news short and to the point for Franklin, who dozes often and unexpectedly. She is especially on the lookout for uplifting news—lottery winners, dogs that roam two thousand miles to find their owners, job openings down at the canning factory. She doesn't actually see a smile on Franklin's face, but for a moment his cheeks seem to draw up, he seems to want to smile, and certainly that counts for something.

Another thing that Netta is convinced he enjoys is the family pictures. From the attic, she has brought down several old albums and she is teaching him his family all over again. "You have two brothers, Franklin. Their names are Clarence and Reed. Clarence is in the nuthouse, I'm sorry to say, and Reed still drives for Greyhound Bus."

She points and turns the album pages slowly, lingering on some, getting teary-eyed over long-gone uncles and the way that all the couples loop their arms loosely, though the knot between them is tied deeply elsewhere. When she grows tired, she moves Franklin over and climbs up onto the bed with him. He has blankets up to his chin. He has lost his eyelashes and his eyes have receded back into the sockets, dark pools with no understanding. She lays her arm over him and thinks of peas in a pod, buttons in buttonholes, her crochet hook with the thread wound tightly around it.

That's how Carlene and Ham find them when they arrive at the house bringing the surprise three-foot spruce. Carlene walks over to the bed, appalled, her mother dwarfing her father as she has never seen before. And Netta's freckled arm pinning Franklin as sure as ground ropes.

When Netta wakes up, Carlene wants to give her hell, but she steadies and calms herself and gives Netta the Christmas tree she and Ham have brought instead. "See how it's nice and full all the way around," Carlene says, holding the top of the tree and spinning it so that a few dry needles go flying.

The tree sits there undecorated, untouched. Day after day Netta often looks over at it and Christmas has never seemed so small to her. The tree barely reaches to her waist, won't hold more than a handful of ornaments. It's not like the trees they used to have—bushy ten-footers, trunks thick as a thigh.

In the weeks before Christmas, in the stone-cold winds that sweep down from the north, Boise gets lively. Rum-filled carolers totter from house to house. Quiet holiday cocktail parties mushroom into entire block parties. Stray crepe paper and tinsel blow down the streets in the early mornings. The mood infects Netta and even Carlene. Netta gives herself a holiday goal: to get Franklin to sit up. She starts out small—five minutes at a time— the surgi-bed cranked up and Franklin secured with a soft rope of dish towels. His head droops miserably to one side or the other, but Netta knows she can't have everything all at once. When she has him up, she sets an empty coffee cup on his lap, stands back, and the results are impressive. To her, enough hope, an empty cup, and their lives are back again.

Carlene doubles her efforts on the days she spends with her father. She gives him short, hushed pep talks: "Go on. There's not a thing to be afraid of." She turns his head to the side so that he has to see out the window, so that he can't avoid the broad, welcoming sky. Cones of incense burn around him, the sweet smoke nudging him away.

What is usually a flurry to get the shopping done and the gifts wrapped becomes just Netta and Carlene moving frantically around the old man, cranking his bed up and down, bringing their separate messages to him: stay, go. Netta plies him with raw cookie dough and spoonfuls of half-cooked divinity, sings for him and dances—as well as she remembers how. Carlene brings him clear broth and melba toast and lays a warm cloth on his forehead.

It's finally Ham who decorates Netta's Christmas tree when he sees it won't get done otherwise. He goes for something novel—

he can see that this is no ordinary year, no run-of-the-mill Christmas. At a nearby Sprouse Reitz, he chooses plastic chili peppers and little white lights. He is slow and meticulous with the spruce, taking all of an afternoon to arrange it.

Ham gathers everyone that night for the tree's unveiling. He springs for pizza, and even before the tree is lighted Netta's house is full of the celebratory smell of pepperoni, rich and spicy. Drake has been allowed to come; he sits at Carlene's side and gulps the oily pepperonis that she tears off her pizza for him.

When they gather in the living room for the lighting ceremony, Netta has a surprise: she has managed to drag Franklin into a chair and prop him up with pillows. Most of his body is still uncooperative and any similarity he has to a man sitting in a chair is coincidental, but Netta doesn't care. She thinks that from where they have been it's a step forward.

Carlene has to bite her lip when she sees him. She decides not to interrupt Ham's program, but as soon as it is through, she intends to march Netta out to the kitchen and shake her out of the tree she's been living in all these months.

Ham turns off the overhead light. He feels his way back along the wall, bends and plugs in the tree. His work has paid off. The spruce looks larger, its boughs suddenly thick. The chilis hang in red, open-heart clusters and there, on the tree, become the essence of Christmas itself. The hundreds of tiny white lights pulse and glitter and shoot through the room.

For minutes, all of them are still and transfixed, caught in their private hopes and remembrances as they stare at the small, brilliant tree. Slowly, Carlene looks around and then Netta, and they see the old man with the white light from the tree shining right through him—his big head as clear as an aquarium, his eyes blinking as if on a timer. Drake gets up from the rug where he's been lying and barks twice at Franklin, not sure what he's looking at.

All at once Netta has to sit down—her legs are shaking, her chest heaving, and her first thought is, she hopes Carlene is happy. There's Franklin, empty and transparent as a bread wrapper, sitting up in his living room six days before Christmas. Just half a man, Netta knows, which, of course, is no man at all.

Carlene stands there and pulls her sweater tighter and tighter around her. She can see that the window has worked, that her father has been gone for at least weeks, maybe months, but that Netta has won her claim, too. Like a salty rind, Franklin's body has stayed to find its way through Valentine's and Easter and beyond to who knows when.

Ham messes with the top of the Christmas tree and rearranges a couple of lights. He turns to Netta and Carlene and wants to know who'll put on the star.

# Useful Gifts

## CAROLE L. GLICKFELD

From *Useful Gifts* (1989)

My mother believes in useful gifts, but when I saw the marionette hanging in Schiffman's Toys on Dyckman Street, I knew what I wanted for Chanukah. She was dangling in the middle of the window, wearing a pink net tutu over a pink satin slip. Her strings were fixed so that she was doing an arabesque, her arms reaching out in front and one leg stuck out in the air behind her, a little crooked. Her hair looked soft, like orangey red cotton, pulled back into a bun that dancers wear. Right off I named her Mitzi, like the girl in the movie I saw with Gene Kelly.

Mrs. Schiffman surprised me coming out of her store all of a sudden. Her arms were folded, but not quite, because they were too fat. "What are you looking at?" she said.

That's how come I dropped the quarter for the rye bread I was supposed to get.

"No s-e-e-d-s, sliced," my mother told me when I left the house.

---

Ruthie and her parents communicate in sign language, as is explained in the first story of the collection *Useful Gifts*. When they spell words out, a hyphen separates each letter. Words they denote with a single shortcut sign receive no special typographical treatment.

She also told me to be careful about the money. How did she know something would happen? The quarter rolled under a car.

Mrs. Schiffman went in her store and came back with a broom so I could push the quarter to where I could get it. I was sorry for thinking she was fat, but all I said was "Thanks a lot."

When I looked one last time at Mitzi, Mrs. Schiffman said, "Tell your mother it's thirteen ninety-five."

I didn't bother, because I knew it was hopeless. But I thought about Mitzi and even prayed to God, just in case. I told Him I'd never ask for anything ever again if I got what I wanted.

For Chanukah I got three cotton dresses for summer from the wholesale factory my father took me to. They were all alike but in different pastel colors. Then my mother took me to Miles, which has the machine that sees inside your shoes and makes your feet look green. I wanted the black patents with the T-straps, but my mother said if I was going to wear high heels when I grew up I had to get the brown oxfords. She got a pair of oxfords, too, in black, with a fat heel, not very high.

The day after, my friend Iris Opals, who lived across the court before they moved to downtown, invited me to celebrate Christmas morning with her family, so my mother and I had more shopping to do. We went to get Iris's present at the Five and Ten.

Right away I figured out what Iris needed: a set of jacks. We always played with mine, since she didn't have any. But my mother headed straight for children's clothes. "N-e-e-d socks," she said. "U-s-e-f-u-l wear out," she told me, meaning that socks wear out, so more socks would be useful to get.

My mother picked up a package of three pairs of socks from the counter in my size. Iris is a year ahead of me, but she's not as tall. The socks were white because white is my mother's favorite color. I swore that when I grew up I'd never have anything in white ever again, except my wedding dress, of course.

My mother was looking over the socks in case something was wrong when I tapped her on the arm. "Don't want," I signed. "Socks awful."

"One dollar, enough," she said.

"Not go," I told her, meaning that if we got the socks I wouldn't go to the Opals' for Christmas. For some reason she didn't look upset. She just put the package down and asked me, "Idea?"

I got her over to the toy counter and showed her the jacks. When she looked at the price on the back of the cardboard, I was sure she'd buy them. She took out some money, but all of a sudden she remembered the birthday present she had bought for my sister's classmate, Ellen Pruzan. Ellen lived in a fancy building across from Fort Tryon with air conditioners and a rug in the lobby. My sister said she'd rather die than take handkerchiefs to Ellen's party, so she got a stomachache and stayed home. The handkerchiefs were sitting in a kitchen drawer. "Left waste," my mother said, meaning the handkerchiefs should go to Iris. That's when I ran out of the store.

My mother came out after me, calling my name, except she can't say "Ruthie," so she said, "Ru-ta, Ru-ta," in that funny voice that deaf-mutes have. People always looked when she did that.

Next thing I knew, there was a man grabbing her arm. "Lady, you didn't pay for that," he yelled, about the package of jacks in her hand.

"She's deaf," I told him.

He yelled even louder. Now everyone was staring.

My mother tried to give him the dollar, but he wouldn't take it. "You'll have to come with me," he said, and we went back into the Five and Ten. He held onto my mother's arm till we got to the back room. All the time we waited there it smelled like pencils.

"S-t-e-a-m hot," my mother said, about the radiator. She made me take off my coat and she took off hers.

Then a man with a thin mustache came in and said he was the

manager and his name was Mr. Gary. Instead of sitting in a chair, he sat on the wood desk so that the corner stuck out between his legs. "She your mother?" he asked me.

"Yeah," I said. Then my mother nodded at him after I interpreted what he said.

"Ask her if she knows it's wrong to shoplift," Mr. Gary said.

"Know wrong take?" I asked her.

"Funny, many p-e-n," my mother said, about the pens sticking out over both his ears.

Mr. Gary was staring real hard, waiting for me to tell him.

"Can trouble," I said to my mother.

"Fault follow you." She looked at Mr. Gary and then pointed to me, waving her arms like I was running toward Dyckman. She made a sign as though she was going to spank me, but I knew she didn't mean it.

Mr. Gary got up and came over, so that he was standing between my mother and me. "She saying you did it?" he asked me. "Tell me the truth."

"It was an accident!" I told him. Except I yelled it.

"Kid's got moxie," the other man said. He meant some nerve. He laughed like I was a liar or something. I wanted to die.

When I looked at Mr. Gary again, he was running his finger over his mustache. He said they'd let my mother go this time if she paid for the jacks but next time they'd call the police.

"S-i-l-l-y," my mother said. She kept shaking her head.

On Christmas morning, when I woke up, I knew it had snowed during the night because I heard the sound of the shovel on the sidewalk. I didn't want to take the jacks to Iris's, but I was stuck. I wanted to forget the man's face who laughed, but it kept popping up in my mind. I figured that every time we played jacks from then on I would remember how I almost got my mother put in jail.

After breakfast I put on the new oxfords and the dress I got with my father at the wholesale factory the summer before for my birthday. The plaid was brown like the oxfords and there was a ribbon around the waist.

Since Iris lived just across the court, I didn't have to use my galoshes. The super already made a path. Her building was exactly the same as mine, but everything was backwards, like in the mirror. I counted the seventy-two steps up to the fifth floor and rang the bell. There was a sign on the door that said "Merry Christmas from THE OPALS."

"Merry Christmas!" Mrs. Opals said, half giggling when she opened the door. She smelled funny, not like White Shoulders, which my mother bought off Mr. Opals sometimes. He sold perfume and scarves on the side, my mother said, because he had to pay for all the lessons Iris and Ivy were always taking.

"What's that?" I asked Mrs. Opals, about the thick yellow stuff in the cup she was holding.

"Schnapps," she said. Then Mr. Opals came in with a bottle of liquor in his hand and poured some into the yellow stuff. It smelled like cough medicine. "Oh, you-u-u," she said.

As I was walking into their living room, I heard Mr. Opals behind me say, "Now I've got you!" I turned and saw him kissing Mrs. Opals right on the lips. My parents only did it on the cheek, but we never had mistletoe. It was like in the movies: their arms were around each other and their eyes were closed.

"You can put my present here," Iris said, pointing to a place under the tree where there was a lot of torn-up fancy paper and ribbons. The package of jacks was in paper my mother saved from the year before, and the green string came off a cake box, so it looked pretty bad.

The tree was very beautiful anyhow and took up the whole corner of the room, right up to the ceiling where there was an angel in foil. Red and green and gold balls dangled from the branches, along with candy canes and something called angel's hair, said Ivy, who is Iris's sister. Ivy might have been fibbing. She's only in the third grade in the parochial school where Iris goes.

Then Ione, who wasn't even two years old yet, came running in and stood next to Ivy, who was standing next to Iris. They were like the three bears in my baby book: small, medium, and large. They all had on blue velvet dresses with organdy collars, light blue knee socks and patent leather shoes with straps. I felt so ugly I could of died.

Iris and Ivy showed me all their presents. The best things were the red hatboxes for carrying stuff like leotards and makeup to their acting and modeling lessons. Across the top, their full names were written out in gold: Iris Dawne Opals and Ivy Deanne Opals. The "I" was for Mrs. Opals' first name, Irene, and the "D" was for Mr. Opals, whose name was Donald. I don't have a middle name, which is bad enough, but then my parents had to name me Ruth. I have two cousins and two classmates named Ruth besides Ruth Silberman in 42 Arden, which is between Iris's building and mine.

Iris showed me how to put my arm through the strap on the hatbox and walk back and forth like a model.

"Chin up," Mrs. Opals told me, before she asked what I'd gotten for the holidays.

I pretended like I didn't hear and walked over to see the figurines sitting on top of the radiator cover.

"Isn't the crèche gorgeous! Couldn't you simply die!" Ivy said.

Everyone was quiet after I asked what a crèche was. Then Ivy explained it had to do with religion. She was taking catechism, along with acting, dancing, and ice skating.

"Very nice," I said about the figurines, but they looked faded, like the plastic flowers we had in our living room, on account of my mother always washing them.

"You should have been with us at midnight mass," Iris said. "It was like a stage show at the Music Hall." Mr. Opals looked at her kind of funny but he didn't say anything. She showed me the different parts people played, even the boys in the chorus coming down the aisle and how the priest waved his arms around.

Mrs. Opals was smiling like she was in heaven. "You're a natural mimic," she said to Iris. "A son couldn't be nearly so talented,"
she said to Mr. Opals. Then he said, "That's my girl!"

Ivy must of gotten jealous because she put her toe shoes on
all of a sudden to show me how she could stand on *pointe* on
one leg. Her arabesque was like Mitzi's, because her leg wasn't
straight in back either, and then her blonde hair fell out of her
French twist, flopping down her shoulders like a horse's mane.
Mr. Opals caught the tree as it started to fall over when Ivy lost
her balance.

"Useless clumsy fool!" Mrs. Opals yelled at her, but Ivy acted
like she didn't mind. Her mother was always yelling at her because she wasn't as graceful as Iris.

I went into the kitchen with Ivy so she could show me her pir-
ouettes on the linoleum. When Ione crawled in behind her, Ivy's
foot whopped her in the arm. Ione screamed. Mrs. Opals couldn't
stop Ione from crying, which made Mr. Opals mad.

"Well, you're the one who didn't want Mrs. Zimmer to baby-
sit," Mrs. Opals said to him about my mother. Mr. Opals gave her
a look like he wanted to kill her.

Iris came in then. "I'm dying to open our presents," she said.
"You?"

"Yeah," I said, crossing my toes.

We went back to the living room. "You first," I told her.

Iris ripped off the paper. "Jacks!" she screamed. "How divine!"
She whispered in my ear that she'd said ten rosaries to get more
games for Christmas.

"No whispering," Mrs. Opals said. "And, please God, you're not
going to fritter away your time when you have more important
things to do." She turned to me and smiled real big, so I could
see a lot of the teeth she got capped because she used to model.
"Tell your mother, dear, she's thoughtful," she said. "I'm afraid,
though, Iris has to make the best use of her God-given talents."

Before I could help it, I told them the jacks were my idea. She and Mr. Opals looked at each other and he shrugged. "As ye sow," he said, which I knew was from the Bible, but I didn't know what he meant.

"Now you," Iris said.

I knew it was a book. I opened the paper without tearing it hardly. It was *Pollyanna*, which I already read from the library, but I said, "Thank you very much."

Suddenly Mrs. Opals started singing like a soprano. I thought Mr. Opals said something about a marionette but Mrs. Opals explained that *Naughty Marietta* was a play she was in once. The next thing I knew, Mr. Opals was blowing into a harmonica and we listened to Iris and Ivy sing Christmas carols. Then we all sang "Away in a Manger." I didn't sing the words about Jesus but just mouthed them, which Mr. Opals must of noticed because afterwards he said, "Jesus gave us the gift of His life and we must never forget that."

"Enjoy?" my mother asked me when I got home. She was real surprised by the present Mrs. Opals gave me to bring her. There were three big pictures in black and white of Iris, Ivy, and Ione in different modeling poses. Each one was autographed.

On the back of Iris's picture she'd written: "To Mrs. Zimmer With Love, Iris Dawne Opals."

Ivy wrote: "To Mrs. Zimmer, U R 2 Nice 2 B 4 Got 10, Love Your Friend, Ivy Deanne Opals."

Mrs. Opals wrote on the back of Ione's picture: "From the Opals Family with fond rememberance to dear Mrs. Zimmer and her lovely daughter Ruthi." She left off the "e" from my name and I looked up "rememberance" in the dictionary and found she spelled that wrong, too.

When I got back to the kitchen from looking up the word, my mother was still sitting there staring at the pictures she laid out on the table. "Not natural beautiful," she said. "Show-off, like actress." My mother was always saying that when Iris and Ivy were going to charm school. I still thought they were gorgeous, even without being made up. I wanted to look like them, take their lessons and be famous someday, which my mother said they were going to be.

Finally my mother put away the pictures in a dresser drawer. "What present?" she asked, about what to give Mrs. Opals back.

My mother made three pot holders for Mrs. Opals, which she took over when we went there on the Sunday before Christmas vacation ended. I was supposed to go skating with all the Opals, excepting Ione, who my mother was baby-sitting. But right off Mrs. Opals acted very strange. First she kept thanking my mother for the pot holders, telling her how beautiful they were, when she knew they were just made with loops on a loom. The blue and yellow didn't even match their kitchen. Then Mrs. Opals took a long time to tell me that Iris and Ivy were taking figure skating at Rockefeller Center, instead of Wollman Memorial, where I thought we were going.

It dawned on me that Mrs. Opals didn't want me with them because of what I was wearing. Ivy had on a pink outfit with a very short skirt, standing out like a ballerina's. Iris's was green and had sparkles and she wore matching gloves up to her elbows but without hands. I had on my brown corduroy pants and navy pea jacket. I didn't cry until after they left.

Not long after that my mother noticed Ione had a bad case of diarrhea. As soon as she changed the diaper, she had it again. "Must something eat," my mother said, meaning it must have been due to something Ione ate. She looked in the frigidaire, opening and smelling the milk bottle. "Sour," she told me. She couldn't find anything in the medicine cabinet to give her. Chernak's Drugs on our corner was closed, so she sent me to see if the big drugstore on Dyckman was open. That's when I saw the "Going Out of Business" sign at Schiffman's Toys, but Mitzi was still in the window.

When I got home I told my mother the drugstore was closed, so she said we were going to take Ione to the Jewish Memorial emergency room. It was so crowded we were there all afternoon. My mother brought along the milk bottle to show the doctor, which I thought was silly, but he smiled at her and tapped the side of his head, like he was telling her she was smart.

Mr. Opals must of found the note I left him on their kitchen table because he came running into the emergency room, yelling that he had to talk to a doctor in private. He got in with a doctor and they closed the door, but I heard them anyhow. Mr. Opals said, "My wife should never of left her in the hands of a deaf-and-dumb lady." Then the doctor said that if it hadn't been for my mother Ione would be critical. I didn't know exactly what that meant, but figured it meant very sick, maybe dead.

When Mr. Opals came out, he was quiet and he put his arm around my mother's shoulders. By that time Mrs. Opals was there, with her fur muff, which she kept waving around on one arm, when she talked. She kept saying to Mr. Opals, "Ask him, go ahead, ask him." Mr. Opals gave her one of his looks. "Well, I'll ask him myself then," she said. She asked the doctor if Ione could do some modeling the next day.

I didn't bother to tell my mother because I knew what she'd say. "First important baby" is what she always said when we passed by the baby carriages outside the bars on Nagle Avenue. My mother carried Ione in her blanket with the initials IDO on it all the way back to our stoop, then Mrs. Opals took her. She invited my mother and me for a ham dinner, but my mother mouthed, "No thank you."

Mr. Opals took money out to pay my mother, giving her five dollars extra, besides the two he owed her for four hours. My mother didn't want to take it, but he made her. "U-s-e-f-u-l, b-r-a-c-e-s," she said to me, meaning she was saving for the braces the dentist said I'd need in junior high. I went up with the Opals to get my skates and then went home for supper.

After we ate, my mother told me to telephone Mrs. Opals to see how Ione was.

"I was just about to call you. Ask your mother if she can baby-sit Ivy tomorrow after school. Iris has elocution and I have to take Ione to a modeling job. Cribs," Mrs. Opals said. "A national company."

"C-r-a-z-y," my mother said, about Mrs. Opals, but she said okay. Then Mrs. Opals asked if I wanted to talk to Iris. I didn't, but Iris got on the line anyhow to tell me about Linda Lindemann's party.

"You'll get invited," she said. Then there was a long quiet and she said, "Ruthie, can I ask you a favor? I want to give Linda the jacks."

I felt nauseous listening to Iris explain about auditioning for a play called "McDonald's Farm." She was trying out for the milk-maid part and for the goose, in case she didn't get the milk-maid. It was a smaller part. Her mother said she'd have to practice both every day. "Then, when I get a part," Iris said, "performing will take all my time, so I can't play jacks anyway."

"Okay," I told her.

"You're not angry?"

"Why should I be angry?" I said.

After I got off the phone my mother thought I looked sad on account of not going ice skating, but I told her I was thinking of what to get Linda Lindemann. Especially because Alan Gold-farb, who I had a crush on, would be at the party, but I didn't tell my mother that. Linda had practically everything, even a room of her own and a clown marionette. "Have many t-o-y-s," I told my mother.

For a few minutes my mother and I sat at the kitchen table without saying anything. Then she waved at me to get my attention. "Know," she said, looking real happy. "N-e-e-d hand-kerchief." She went over and pulled them out of the drawer. Of course, they were white.

Linda needs handkerchiefs like she needs more jacks, I thought. She already had two sets of jacks, one silver and one in mixed colors, red and green. I was sure Iris didn't know that, which made me feel a whole lot better.

The next week Mr. Opals came up to our apartment for the first time. He gave my mother two packages wrapped in paper that had tiny purple flowers. He kissed her, but it was on the cheek. "Thank you," he mouthed, and then she showed him how to blow a kiss with his hand to say "thank you" in sign language.

He told me Iris was going to be a milkmaid in the play and Ivy was going to be the goose because the other girl got sick. Then he asked me if there was something special I wanted. Even if Schiffman's wasn't already gone, which it was, Mitzi would of cost too much. So I said a hatbox.

He started to ask me what I was going to do with a hatbox, but he changed his mind. "It'll be a pleasure," he said. Before he left, I reminded him about the "e" on "Ruthie."

When he was gone, my mother opened the packages real carefully. She wanted to save the fancy wrapping. The little package had a necklace with a gold chain and the initial "H" for my mother's name, Hannah.

"How know?" she said, about Mr. Opals.

The other package had a big bottle of White Shoulders, which she opened and kept smelling. "Like flower," she said, putting a dot of it behind each ear and on her neck.

She stuck the bottle under my nose.

"S-t-i-n-k," I told her.

She smiled so that her dimples showed. "Not c-h-e-a-p, real perfume," she said.

"Waste money," I said.

She shook her head. "N-o, n-o. U-s-e-f-u-l," she said. "Keep long time."

# The Christmas Bus

## PETER LASALLE

From *Tell Borges If You See Him* (2007)

The shooting of the victim taken off the Transportes del Norte
bus there in the desert didn't get much attention. It might have
attracted more coverage in the Mexican papers if there hadn't
been the trouble in Chiapas the previous day. But Chiapas and
the latest flare-up of the endless fighting in the south had been
the big story—the government itself was blamed for the paramilitary thugs going into the village for the massacre. That filled the
papers, all of the television, and, of course, there was the tragedy
of it coming at Christmastime too.

Actually, because it was the day before Christmas this bus had
been added to the route. It was supposed to be a six-hour trip:
starting from the terminal in Monterrey; then over the wall of
chocolate mountains to Saltillo and going south and into the cac-
tus flats proper, all orange sand and spiked skeletons of aqua
Joshua trees; then on to stop at Zacatecas, and finally, to the terminal in Aguascalientes below that. The regularly scheduled bus
was a sleek stainless-steel monster with video monitors, which
inevitably and blaringly showed old Whoopi Goldberg or Steven

Seagal movies that nobody really cared about, anyway, dubbed in Spanish, but that bus was completely booked by noontime the day before. Which was fine with Teresa López. She was on her way to visit her son who was in the Mexican state prison in Zacatecas, and she considered it almost a stroke of good luck that even if this particular added bus was older and not in the best condition for *primera clase*, it didn't have those truly terrible TV screens suspended from the ceiling every four rows or so.

Teresa López was tired from her journey, all the way from Chicago. She hated that video noise and she was glad to be able to get some sleep.

The fact that he had been called in at the last minute to drive this bus pleased Hugo Padillo. He told himself just that as he wrestled the wheel of the ark, a 1972 GMC with riveted brown and buff sides and not very much power assist from the compressor for the steering and the brakes. But Hugo Padillo had driven enough of these old GMCs to know their quirks. Hugo Padillo also knew there was a better than good chance that the two girls would be there at the roadside restaurant/service concourse outside of the village of San Carlos. Granting he was an even fifty, Hugo Padillo prided himself on how full and black his head of pomaded hair remained, the mustache too. He fancied he looked as manly as a ranking military officer in the gray twill uniform (short-jacketed; green epaulettes) of the Transportes del Norte, a substantial man, and what did it matter if he wasn't back in his native Mexico City for Christmas? He would eventually be there for the Epiphany, El Día de los Reyes, a week or so later, and the Epiphany was when presents were given and all that mattered, really, to his complaining wife and four grown sons with their own children now. And for the moment there was something better to think about, yes, the two teenage girls and a couple of days with them in the Hotel Condesa in Zacatecas. The bus fumed its diesel exhaust into the brightening morning as he worked through the traffic and past the *colonias* of cinderblock shacks that spread on either side of the road leading out of Monterrey, to the main highway to Saltillo.

The bus terminal at Saltillo was jammed, with a festive mood, nevertheless, because the next day was indeed Christmas. The sun was strong now, and the bus growled in and out of the asphalt lot with its several bays. There was a row of stuccoed cheap-hotel buildings and cantinas, such bright pastels, across from the station. Along the side street leading back toward the highway, the vendors had set up their rickety stalls for coffee and *gorditas*, the grills smoking, and the ragged peanut sellers waited at the corners for just the right bus driver, one who for a few pesos would let you board and try to hawk your paper cones of nuts for a few dusty blocks, before hopping out again when a stop at another intersection allowed it. There was maybe something very beautiful about a particular scene in the morning sunshine—something about the way that on a cracked sidewalk a *campesino* in his best Stetson was drawing a small crowd with the bleating goats he had brought into the town to sell for the next day's feast. The creatures had glossy coats of assorted browns or black and white, and they were roped together, legs tied, so they lined up with their bellies flat on the pavement and snouts down, like so many little rugs; the *campesino* was feeding one loosened goat from his hand maybe some of those peanuts, and it could have been a happy puppy as it jumped up against his leg in the morning's freshness, frost still on the old pickup trucks parked in the shade. (Though in a few hours this baby goat, too, would be butchered, prepared for the Christmas table. In other words, maybe death was already very much in the day.) The traffic was bad on the road before the highway at the edge of town. The bus driver had already taken on extra people back at the Saltillo terminal, whole families who were now standing up and groping for balance in the aisle, and when he stopped a second time on this road to pick up another few people hauling suitcases and plastic tote bags bulging, a little rebellion of sorts began.

Rafael Hinojosa y Obregón didn't like any of this, not in the least.

First, he didn't like how the Transportes del Norte had added this junk of a bus and passed it off as *primera clase*. Second, he didn't like how this noisy oaf of a bus driver (he had been ordering people around during the loading of luggage back in Monterrey) was now taking on any passengers who managed to flag down the bus, entire families with screaming children and seemingly half of what they owned lugged up the worn-shiny steps and heaped high in the aisle. He knew the way this game worked, and if the ticket vendor in the Saltillo terminal had pocketed what he could by selling the extra tickets to those who boarded the already full bus there, Rafael Hinojosa y Obregón could plainly see that the bus driver here was taking in the palm of his own hand, held out under the giant white plastic wheel, whatever he could, certainly the bulk of it going into his pocket and never finding its way back to the Transportes del Norte till. Rafael Hinojosa y Obregón had married into a very old Zacatecas family whose money had originally been amassed in the city's famous silver mines. He had been in Monterrey for three days doing business with the banks on behalf of his father-in-law, who still controlled the family's wealth, now invested mostly in ranches. Rafael Hinojosa y Obregón sometimes found the *primera clase* bus more comfortable than driving his own Jaguar to Monterrey and back, but he had expected a good bus, with a good American movie to relax with, and not this rattling contraption *plus* a situation that was fast rendering it nothing short of a cattle car. He looked at his watch again to see that after being an hour late in leaving Monterrey, they had by this point lost almost another hour with the heavy traffic in and out of Saltillo. And now this ridiculous business of picking up every ragged ranch hand—or even more ragged Indian—with a family along the route. The bus squealed to a shivering stop still another time, and still another time it opened the doors for a new load. In his seat on the aisle, Rafael Hinojosa y Obregón, balding and slight in build, was jostled and jammed, and when the big, barrel-chested bus driver stood up to growlingly tell those standing to move back, for everybody else to make room, too, Rafael Hinojosa y Obregón could take no more.

"Señor! Señor, un momento, por favor!" he called.

"Señor?"

The bus driver responded with bushy eyebrows raised.

Rafael Hinojosa y Obregón told the bus driver that he was concerned. He didn't say he was entirely uncomfortable with the extra passengers. And he didn't say he would be entirely late in getting to Zacatecas this afternoon and doing what he had to do at his office, then rushing around to take care of some errands in time for *medianoche* mass and the big celebratory dinner later that night with his wife and two fine boys and all the relatives and in-laws at the house in town; they would go out to his father-in-law's ranch tomorrow, Christmas day. What he did tell the bus driver was that it was "muy peligroso" to have this many people on any bus, and this was how too many "accidentes trágicos" happened on the highways in buses. When he had finished delivering his little impromptu speech, there was silence on the bus, and Rafael Hinojosa y Obregón, smelling of Yardley's aftershave (he liked so many things British), watched as the beetle-browed bus driver first simply scowled at him, that gruffness shown earlier during the luggage loading. Rafael Hinojosa y Obregón wasn't sure if the brute was going to challenge him on this, another example of the rampant uppitiness from inferiors lately. But when the bus driver did finally respond, the man offered Rafael Hinojosa y Obregón what *might* be taken as an apology, if only to say, quite firmly, nevertheless, that he had no choice—he had been told by the company, Transportes del Norte, to pick up everybody on this particular run. He said this was a bus added to the regular schedule, and, after all, this was the day before Christmas when so many were traveling.

There soon was chatter and even some laughing from the other passengers. But Rafael Hinojosa y Obregón didn't know if the laughter was for the bus driver, nearly a parody of the no-nonsense ship captain wielding his utter authority for the duration of the "voyage," or if it was for him, Rafael Hinojosa y Obregón. So, to maybe win support, Rafael Hinojosa y Obregón leaned over to speak to the young man across the aisle—he wanted to make sure that somebody understood the point he was trying to make. He had heard this young man speaking very good English with a couple of *gringos* at the convenience shop at the Monterrey bus terminal. The *gringos* had serious hiking gear and were buying purified water, and Rafael Hinojosa y Obregón was looking at the newspapers there; in the convenience shop, the athletic young man had been smiling, nodding to everybody, even joking in English to the very cute girl behind the counter, saying to her that when it came to the *gringos*, "You better check these boys' green cards." It was a line she apparently understood, seeing that everybody in a large northern city like Monterrey seemed to have at least some English. She laughed, the *gringos* laughed too. Rafael Hinojosa y Obregón now told the young man that it was true, he had read of just such a terrible accident due to overcrowding on a bus occurring only a month before, somewhere near Guadalajara. The young man nodded, smiled his handsome dimpled grin.

Though the young man really wanted to tell this snooty rich businessman what surely everybody else wanted to tell him—as the driver had said, it is Christmas, man, and you certainly can put up with the crowding for a little while, a few hours, and think about the torture for the rest of us having to inhale that ridiculous flower water you seem to have taken a bath in. *Madre de Dios!*

This was Eduardo "The Cat" Martínez. Or, more exactly, that was the name his self-appointed manager, Deke from the gym in Lake Charles, Louisiana, came up with for him. Because a name was needed when it became certain that this boxer was going to be flown to the casino on the Indian reservation in Connecticut for an IBF preliminary light-middleweight event, which would be televised on HBO, no less. Eduardo Martínez was twenty-five. He had lived in Louisiana for seven years now, married to an American girl and working carpentry for Mr. Duval, and Mr. Duval was actually proud that his employee had a big fight at last and had to miss a few days with the crew, to go off to the Indian reservation in New England that weekend. Up there, it was a whole other world, all right; there was the sheer friendliness of the people at the airport in Providence in the state called Rhode Island, which he flew into, and there was the more exuberant sheer friendliness of everybody at the casino in Connecticut, which rose almost like a glittering Lost World there amid the fog-enshrouded forest of bright October trees. Eduardo "The Cat" Martínez lasted six rounds with the true contender, who, to be honest, didn't seem all that much faster or stronger than the kids Eduardo Martínez had boxed on the Louisiana/Texas circuit. And what did he care if he had heard at least two of the organizers up there speak of him as a "palooka" ("Where's the palooka?" from one, and "I guess he's the palooka," from another), because Eduardo Martínez had the tape now to show his grandparents in Aguascalientes. They had raised him. He hadn't seen them for several years now, and as the bus continued on in the glaring noontime sunshine, he told himself that his grandfather would appreciate that tape and surely somebody in their neighborhood was bound to have a VCR on which to watch it.

Eduardo Martínez with that dimpled smile that would make you think he was anything but a boxer, with a new baseball cap and good jeans and good Nike sneakers, all of which made him look more like a neat American fraternity boy than anything else, Eduardo Martínez had to admit that he got a kick out of that confrontation between the big-shot businessman and the trying-to-be-a-big-shot bus driver with his swaggering manliness—the whole thing was so much, and so typically, *Mexico*.

Where he was glad to be again, if only for a few days.

The worn tires of the Transportes del Norte bus sang along the satiny black asphalt of the empty two-lane. The day had warmed enough for some of the passengers in the packed compartment to have shoved open the windows a bit, the tinge of exhaust sweet and almost welcome in the fresh air.

And this was indeed the desert in earnest. If assorted litter and especially the shreds of old plastic bags dripped from the clawed mesquite bushes for miles along the highway outside a big city like Monterrey or even a smaller one like Saltillo, here deep in the desert plateau there was only the orange sand, and there were only the flats of still more stubby Joshua trees bursting their spiky aqua stars on top; there were only the jagged mountains far, far in the distance, the foothills of the Sierra Madre Occidental on one side and the Sierra Madre Oriental on the other, two walls of the universe—or at least two walls high enough to sandwich the essential *lostness* of the utter expanse of this particular kind of nowhere. The posts for the haphazard wire fencing that had been put up by the government beside the road were not real posts whatsoever, merely the black limbs of dead Joshuas—as squiggled as driftwood, dreamlike—and the sky itself was so big and so blue that it looked solid in its intensity. This high up, about a mile into the thinning oxygen, the mandatory vultures with their wide black wings and fleshy red heads (another suggestion of death waiting this day, more obvious than the little goats back at the Saltillo terminal about to be slaughtered?), the vultures at this altitude always appeared to glide more slowly, cruise and endlessly cruise in wider circles than they did anywhere else.

Having woken from her sleep, Teresa López from Chicago, on her way to Zacatecas to visit her son in the state prison there, looked at the desert outside.

She told herself that she had been wise to bring the electric blanket, because it would be cold at night in the guest house in Zacatecas. She told herself, too, that there actually had been a time when she thought that her son, Kiko, would turn into anything but a gofer for the *narcotrafficantes*. And there in Chicago as a kid didn't Kiko win the prize at the seventh-grade science fair? She could still see the crazy plaster-of-paris volcano he rigged up, a three-foot-high pyramid fed by a bicycle pump attached to a plastic bottle that he loaded with oozing red tomato juice for the eruption, a contraption he built by himself. Which was why Mr. Kells, a teacher and the final judge, said that he gave him the prize, and what Mr. Kells told her—he looked right at Teresa López with such big owl eyes behind horn-rimmed glasses—was that he admired that Kiko had built the thing *entirely* by himself, so it wasn't just a project done by a father, some complicated computer experiment or the like, as most of the projects were. Though hearing such from Mr. Kells did break Teresa López's heart: because *of course* Kiko made it himself, because *of course* she had raised him without a father, her sister helping out so she, Teresa López, could keep her good job as an LPN for so many years at the hospital of Loyola University. But she shouldn't blame herself, she knew, and it was the gang that had caused all the problems for Kiko the first time, when he was sent to the youth detention center in downstate Illinois for two years, well before this current sentence of four years after the arrest in Acapulco, the result of more work for the gang as well. The gang had been at the root of it all. On the other hand, Kiko was only thirty-three years old now, and in a sense he was lucky to be in a relatively comfortable prison in a rich city like Zacatecas, where all the inmates themselves always thanked their ultimate good fortune for that. He had promised Teresa López that he had certainly learned his lesson this time, he promised that when he returned to Chicago there wouldn't be any more trouble, because . . . because . . . *then Teresa López nodded off again, and in her dreaming she carried that shred of memory from a few moments before into a scene of her somehow coming upon her son with some of the other inmates in what passed as the prison lounge she knew so well in Zacatecas, and her son, Kiko, a grown man of thirty-three years old, was demonstrating for the other inmates there exactly how that science fair project of the volcano spouting tomato juice worked, and the tough men watched with interest and amazement, because Kiko . . . because* . . . and then she came out of that half-sleep, out of the dream. The bus swerved to the shoulder at a crossroads intersection, the few adobe houses golden in the day; one family that had been standing in the aisle got off, and then two more families got on. Teresa López offered to take the baby of the heavyset young Indian woman who had now been pushed back this far in the jammed bus, and the woman, smiling, was appreciative of the help, considering she had three other children to tend to and also a husband who seemed interested only in gazing out the window at the Joshua trees, as if it was work he had to do.

"Muy linda," Teresa López said to the woman about her baby.

"Sí," the woman answered her, still smiling.

Holding the baby for a while, Teresa López didn't know what to make of that dream. She rocked the baby some, cooed to it.

At the wheel of the bus, overtaking another fume-spewing diesel truck loaded high with stacked cinderblocks, tromping the accelerator hard, Hugo Padillo was probably as surprised as anybody else that the GMC packed the huffing punch to get him back on his side of the road again before another truck charged at him from the opposite direction. He was also satisfied that he had handled that situation with the *maricón* of a bald, perfume-smelling businessman well. Actually, Hugo Padillo, in a way, wished that he had *already* stopped at the roadside place outside of San Carlos to pick up the waiting girls, so they, too, could have seen it. He wished that he had *already* taken his time with a full hot meal there, which he planned to do, wished that he had *already* sat around with the girls for a long while, as he relaxed and made everybody on the bus—or, specifically, that businessman—wait until he was finally finished with the meal and was good and ready to resume the journey. Another driver, Pedro, had all but assured him just the previous day that the girls would be there, and Pedro had spent a lot of time with the pair, knew about them. Hugo Padillo had once run into Pedro with the two girls on Calle Amado Nervo in Monterrey, after Pedro himself had picked them up while working a route down from Chihuahua, coming into Saltillo and then Monterrey that way. Hugo Padillo pictured them from that day. There was the skinny one with her long hair curled and dyed reddish, little rectangular sunglasses showing purple lenses and a bum in satiny yellow slacks that you could cup in the palm of your hand, and there was the plumper one who was probably more to Hugo Padillo's taste, if truth be known, with short black hair cut in a single wing almost to her dark doll's eyes and a tiny rhinestone stud on one side of her button nose, a pink sweater nicely packing in her top-heaviness. They were prostitutes, but they were not common prostitutes. They liked bus drivers from the Transportes del Norte, Pedro said to him, though Pedro added emphatically that if Hugo Padillo was interested he better be willing to spend money on them. And Pedro had again told him exactly that only the day before, and Hugo Padillo had assured him he would spend money, not to worry about that. He said he would have a whole two days to kill in Zacatecas, after looping the bus back there from Aguascalientes and turning it over to another driver who would return the junk, probably empty, to the terminal yards in Monterrey, where it might sit for another six months before being put into service again.

"They will want to have a good time," Pedro had said.

"I will take them to the Hotel Condesa," Hugo Padillo told him. "And I will buy them drinks at that disco by the cathedral, La Mina."

"Cabrón!" Pedro gave him acknowledgment with the usual clenched fist thrust into the air. "Cabrón!" He repeated it, laughing.

"El más cabrón," Hugo Padillo answered him, the same clenched-fist signal offered in reply, "El más cabrón!"

The bus sped on. And Hugo Padillo wasn't going to allow for *any* doubt concerning the businessman; and while Hugo Padillo might have explained the crowding situation to the businessman, tried to keep things smooth, he now told himself once more that he had maintained his manliness throughout it all, had been firm. Why, hadn't that good-looking kid back there, the smiling one in the neat clothes of a *gringo*, told the businessman afterward, "Es verdad, hombre," saying to him, what else could a bus driver do but take on everybody who needed to arrive somewhere, somehow, this day before Christmas.

Then Hugo Padillo saw the man on the horse.

Actually, anybody who saw the rider from a distance like that, across the flats, would have been taken by both the frightening madness as well as the strangely mesmerizing essence of it—the substance of a dream not quite remembered but because of that more substantial, deeper, than anything subject to simple memory, the accepted routineness of things.

A family of *campesinos* wanted to be let off at the next half-hearted buildup of a few adobe houses, there at the upcoming intersection—a perfect right angle—of the straight highway and a straight, unpaved rural road. The speeding bus approached the intersection, and also approaching the intersection from far off, on the rural road, was a man atop a galloping horse. The man wore a filthy gold nylon winter jacket and a frayed straw ranch hand's sombrero, and the horse was a shaggily unkempt roan stallion, its hooves wildly drumming over the road and kicking up, true, somehow lovely clouds of dust that might have been magician's smoke, billowing. The man rode with complete abandon, bouncing high, and he reminded one of those old sepia lithographs that depicted Villa himself on the charge and recklessly conquering.

The enormous blue sky; the distant mountains that chocolate hue. It was very much like a dream.

*And the rider, his legs splayed in the stirrups for what was surely an odd, ancient gallop, moved across the flats and toward the two-lane highway, far off, then getting closer and closer.*

Everybody seemed to have a different story as to exactly what did happen to give to the local police, who showed an hour later. And a national officer, a *federale*, came after that to attempt to sort out everything.

It seemed that the rider, thoroughly *borracho*, had expected somebody to be arriving on the bus, had come there to meet a man or a woman— that part was never entirely clear. Right from the beginning he was yelling, off the horse, and then climbing up the steps of the bus, after the family of *campesinos*—with their bulky bags and boxes—had gotten off. Everybody on the bus did agree that the *hombre loco*, unshaven, was so rank with maguey that to light up a cigarette near him might be an invitation for a detonation, a booming explosion in itself. They agreed that he had pushed his way right onto the bus without the driver, Hugo Padillo, having the chance to block him. Because before Hugo Padillo could even get out of the seat, before he could wriggle from that cramped front compartment displaying its big religious card of the Virgen de Guadalupe, stars all about her and left by who knows what other former driver of the bus as a little makeshift altar, the drunk, raving man had slapped the pistol's handle flat on the pomaded hair atop Hugo Padillo's head, then proceeded to move down the aisle.

"Todos ustedes son mentirosos!" the man shouted, "You are all liars!" and possibly in his own momentary dementia he did believe that somebody in what amounted to this crowd was actually hiding whoever it was he was looking for, "Todos, todos, mentirosos!"

He waved the pistol crazily. He started picking out people to take off the bus. He pointed at the businessman Rafael Hinojosa y Obregón perhaps because Rafael Hinojosa y Obregón was visibly quivering and, needless to add, he did look much more prosperous than anybody else on that bus. He pointed to the mother Teresa López because she tried to talk with him, reason with him, in a motherly fashion, and possibly she did want to believe again that if somebody had shown even more love to her own son, Kiko, now in prison, he wouldn't have turned out as he had, and he, like this man, could have been saved at any moment along the way. Bleeding, standing now and the red running in a squiggle down his forehead, the driver Hugo Padillo had managed to regroup, had managed to attempt to impose some order on this mayhem and intercept the contingent coming back down the aisle—and at gunpoint he, too, was told to get off the bus. The man herded them outside. Meanwhile, as soon as Eduardo "The Cat" Martínez realized how dangerous this was (at first he had seen it more as comedy, the happy craziness of his beloved Mexico that he had been away from for so long), as soon as he assessed the horror of it, he shoved his way up the aisle and jumped down the bus's steps himself. Where the stubbled, leathery-necked, wild-eyed man in the filthy gold winter jacket and straw sombrero walked right up to him, placed the blue metal pipe of the pistol to his head, and ordered him, through very yellow teeth, to stand with the rest of them there in front of the luggage compartment door. The man raved and raved about lying in general, and how he was tired of it. And he got so carried away with the shouting that he obviously didn't see what everybody on the bus later agreed that they had clearly seen.

An old man, who lived in one of the sun-bleached adobe houses under that enormous blue sky, came slowly, cautiously, out of the lean-to garage attached to the house. (He had a little setup there for minor auto repairs, mostly fixing tire punctures, and he got maybe a dozen cars a week during the summer when it turned scorchingly hot and tires easily popped.) The skinny old man wore a salvaged, too-big Dallas Cowboys sweatshirt, and he had to admit, upon being questioned later, that while he had lived there just about all his life, he himself didn't know who the *pistolero* was, from what ranch he came or from what lost mountain village, to gallop up on a horse that day and expect somebody he knew to be on that bus the afternoon before Christmas. The old man stopped, very cautiously, when he saw the gun, and he said later that he wished he had never even noticed the commotion, never even abandoned work on a carburetor in that garage and come out to see what was happening at the bus. But such rewinding of time, looking back on the situation, really had nothing to do with a bus traveling and packed with people all going somewhere for Christmas, thinking only of that somewhere, the other place where they had to be. It was almost as if there was absolutely no time for death and they were, in a way, beyond it, because on the day before Christmas everything was more a matter of that future in which they would be soon enough. And how could Eduardo "The Cat" Martínez be the one who would be shot and instantly killed? He was so young and so fit from working hours and hours in the gym, and he had to show his grandparents the HBO tape of his fight in Connecticut. And possibly Rafael Hinojosa y Obregón was too rich to be killed, and what would his wife do, how would she explain it, if he wasn't there with the army of relatives and in-laws for the big feast after *media-noche* mass that night? As for Teresa López, it would seem that love alone should save her, with her concern and such hard work, as she had tried to give her son everything she could, to keep on trying to do it now, in this journeying so far from Chicago to visit him in Zacatecas. And even at thirty-three the poor boy needed her at the prison to visit him tomorrow (a prison that, as said, wasn't entirely uncomfortable, and the inmates had microwaves and tape decks and usually plenty of good food, all brought to them by relatives), and tomorrow she would make Kiko promise again, as she had told herself earlier, promise that he would return directly to Chicago after his release next year, he would take a job, any real work, even unloading crates on a shipping dock for minimum wage, and he would never, no, never, become involved with those worthless *pachucos* from the old gang; she couldn't be the one to die, because she had to be there in Zacatecas to help him, to assure him, to love him, or he would never have a chance. And the driver, Hugo Padillo? Death for him, it could be argued, was out of the question. For him to be shot, left lying in the gravel next to the bus in the middle of the desert, might be the most farfetched proposition of all. Hugo Padillo for the last day or so hadn't been in the present, the supposed here and now, and for all intents and purposes he just couldn't end life at this particular moment. Why, with the two teenage prostitutes waiting for him at the roadside restaurant only fifty kilometers down the highway, Hugo Padillo was already, somehow, in an oversize sagging bed in the Hotel Condesa in Zacatecas with the pair, the glow of lamplight on their flesh golden, let's say, the entwining limbs and the sweet fragrance of the girls' hair coconutty from the morning's shampoo. In other words, the whole situation wasn't simple, and if time was to be played with, the trick might be not to go back in it, as the old man who ran the makeshift auto-repair garage had later talked about wishing to do, but to jump forward from the entire absurd situation of this genuinely bad dream of a bus ride in a brown and buff GMC clunker, to make it merely a matter of slipping past this particular snag in the scenario that somehow had produced a madman with a pistol, drunk, which made no sense to begin with. And, again, you really couldn't pick one of these people whom the tragedy should befall, but it *would* befall one of them.

They could have been a little family. Sure, a family assembled for a snapshot, while the *pistolero* kept them lined up in front of him there. He stood, still talking his garbled nonsense and still waving the gun that flashed its haunting blue through the air. Others looked out the windows from inside the bus, noticing how the old man had frozen, was stopped and standing entirely still, and the drunk man apparently hadn't yet noticed that this old man had come out of the grimed blackness of his garage. It could be said that what eventually happened did happen because of the old man, who remained as motionless as a statue.

There came an almost warming moment when the businessman Rafael Hinojosa y Obregón implored the bus driver, bloody as he was, to try to take over the situation, what maybe the timid

Rafael Hinojosa y Obregón hoped this manly bus driver could actually do.

"Señor," Rafael Hinojosa y Obregón said to him, pleading, looking very small, surrendering any former haughtiness and acknowledging that a Transportes del Norte driver was truly the captain of his tire-rolling ship, "Señor, por favor."

"Amigo, por favor," the bus driver replied gently, an attempt to put him at ease, tell him that for the moment nothing could be done and he himself needed time to think of a plan. "Amigo, está ок," Hugo Padillo said.

Some more talk from the boxer Eduardo Martínez brought the cool metal of the pistol to his temple once again, and a warning to keep quiet, and then the drunk man backed up a few paces, to face his group a little farther off. Weary, Teresa López wept, probably not for herself but for so much ongoing sadness in the world, or for whatever could even make a world like this where something of this sort, so meaningless, could transpire. Which was when the *pistolero*, who certainly didn't have any set plan to proceed with himself, caught sight of the old man standing there behind him, apparently, and like a startled animal he just spun around to get a full view—then he spun back, to make sure he had his group covered. Somehow the pistol went off in the movement.

A small pop with an orange burst and the smell of sulfur; the bullet let loose for its clean drill into the skull.

At which point the drunk man, as surprised as anybody else at this unexpected turn of events, dropped the gun to the dust and dumbly stared at the body.

As has been said, the event didn't receive any publicity in the Republic whatsoever, either in the newspapers or on television, because the news was filled with that major tragedy, and its far-ranging political implications, the bloody confrontation involving the paramilitary group that had taken place in Chiapas a day earlier.

And also maybe because it was Christmas Eve at last, a tissuey, translucent moon already rising high over the jagged mountains on a night of incomparable holiness, no matter what anybody might try to tell you otherwise.

# What Do You Say?

MOLLY GILES

From *Rough Translations* (1985)

My daughter and I are having lunch at the counter of Loretta's
Coffee Shop. We have never been here before, but I can tell it's
going to be one of our favorite places. The hamburgers are good,
the decor looks as if it hasn't changed in forty years, and the cli-
entele—mainly high school students, construction workers, and
small-town merchants—doesn't seem to mind if my daughter,
who is four, kicks her stool or chews with her mouth full. Right
now she is humming to the Christmas carols we hear from the
radio behind the counter; I have asked her to keep her voice
down and as I am asking her again the glass door bangs open and
Mr. Brown comes in. The people at the tables glance up at the
bell and the gust of cold air, then go back to their sandwiches and
their newspapers. My daughter resumes her loud happy humming. But I continue to stare.

I have not seen Mr. Brown in almost ten years, not since I divorced his son. He is very changed. He is thin now, almost gaunt,
and uses a cane. His eyes are darkly shadowed in his large pale
face and his coarse white hair is windblown. The minute I recognize him I know I should stand up and say hello.

Yet I don't. I say nothing. Even though he is wearing a long
wool scarf I knit for him myself, I say nothing. Perhaps, I think,

he will notice me. But Mr. Brown, standing six feet away, returns my stare with such a brief, unlit stare of his own—a look so remote it is almost majestic—that I realize he doesn't know who I am. He closes the door and moves toward an empty seat at the far end of the counter.

The coffee shop is decorated for Christmas. Plastic boughs hang over the windows and plastic berries bob down from the overhead lights. My daughter, still singing, spoons whipped cream off the top of her cocoa. "Don't slurp," I say. My voice is louder than it usually is when I correct her in public. If my voice is loud enough Mr. Brown may hear me. He may stop and turn and say, "Diana?" But Mr. Brown continues toward his stool and my daughter continues to slurp. She is excited about Christmas, too excited for manners. "Keep your napkin in your lap," I remind her.

"It *is* in my lap," she protests.

"No it's not. It's on the floor."

I watch Mr. Brown climb onto his stool. His left leg appears to be crippled; he has to hoist it by the knee and swing it onto the footrest. He props the cane beside him and, in a move so familiar it takes my breath away, pinches the bridge of his nose with his fingers, pushing his glasses, for a moment, to the top of his forehead. As soon as he is settled I will go to him and touch his arm. Ben, I'll say, remember me? And then I'll wait, for I know I've changed. I am not the twenty-year-old girl who crashed his Lincoln into the garage door, baited him into arguments about Vietnam, helped him stock the bird feeder on the patio. My hair is short now and beginning to gray; I've put on weight, begun to wear glasses. I'm happier now. He will see I am happier— as I, now, see he is less happy than he used to be. Still, when I say, How are you?, I will keep my smile steady and expectant, as if his answer to my question will be the old one. "Beautiful," he used to say, beaming. "I feel beautiful, Beautiful, how about you?" I will not ask about his son, my ex-husband, who is going through another divorce, nor will I ask about his wife, Billie, who died two years ago of cancer. I will not ask about the weight he has lost, or his leg. I will introduce my daughter and spell the name of my present husband, and I will say, It's just so good to see you.

"If I be good," my daughter says, "will I get everything I want? Will I get a camera? Will I get a two-wheeler?"

"I don't think you're old enough for either of those."

"If I be *good*, I said."

I take another napkin from the dispenser before us and place it in her lap. There is a snowfall of napkins at the foot of her stool, and pools of cocoa and catsup dot her place at the counter. I open my purse and check my wallet to make sure I have enough money to leave the waitress a generous tip.

The waitress is young and pretty and wears huge glittery earrings in the shape of Christmas trees that swing when she speaks. She holds the menu in front of her breasts and smiles at Mr. Brown. "I hope you're hungry today," she says. "Bud made pea soup."

"Oh?" Mr. Brown looks at the waitress as if he's never heard of pea soup. His face, framed by the twinkling red and green lights around the mirror, looks both attentive and lost. Perhaps he's gone senile. His father was senile. "Shoot me if I get like that," Mr. Brown used to say. "Drive me into the desert and ditch me." The waitress reaches up and adjusts the mistletoe pinned in her hair.

"Pea soup is your favorite."

"Oh yes." He takes the menu the waitress hands him. He is wearing the garnet ring on his right hand—class of 1936, U.C. Berkeley—and the gold wedding ring on his left. His fingernails are broad and ridged and as clean as ever. I wonder how the waitress ever got the idea that pea soup was his favorite? Clam chowder, barbecued steak, baked beans, onion rings, shrimp salad, french bread, and black walnut ice cream—those were his favorites. He used to weigh two hundred and eighty pounds and sway around his swimming pool dressed in nothing but a towel, dancing to Herb Alpert and the Tijuana Brass with a glass of Scotch in one hand and a Marlboro in the other. Would this waitress, in her earrings and mistletoe, have liked him back then? He called himself the King of the Canyon, wanted the blacks sent to Africa, thought we ought to bomb Cuba, kept a samurai sword that he had bought on a business trip to Tokyo under his bed, and tried to have the fence around his property electrified to keep the hippies out.

"All ready for Christmas?" the girl asks brightly.

Mr. Brown clears his throat. "I don't do much for Christmas," he says.

"Just going to take it easy," the girl nods. "Well, that's the best way."

How many Christmases—seven? eight?—have I spent with Mr. Brown? Dreary days. Cigarette smoke rising through the sunshine of the house in the canyon, the turkey turning on the spit in the outdoor barbecue, Billie sipping a beer, barefoot, in her bathrobe and diamonds, doing the crossword. Their son—my husband—Benjy—spent Christmas smoking dope in the bathroom and jotting notes for his thesis, which he said was going to be about tribal rites among West Coast Republicans. I sat by the windows and knit. Mr. Brown watched TV. Mr. Brown's father, on loan for the day from the rest home, batted Billie's dogs back with large knuckled hands when they tried to lick him. Just before dinner we exchanged presents. Benjy and I gave Mr. Brown peanut brittle and subscriptions to the *New Republic*. Mr. Brown gave us money. Much too much money. He's trying to own us, I warned Benjy. We can't pay you back, I explained to Mr. Brown. But Mr. Brown said he didn't want to be paid back. He said he was saving us for something big. He was saving us for his old age. He thought he'd come live with us in a room in our house, and play with our children, and work in our garden. When we tried to explain that we didn't think we'd ever have a house or a child or a garden—when we tried to explain that our generation was different from his—freer, more spontaneous—when we tried to say: Don't count on us—he waved us away. He was the only one to cry at our wedding. He hugged us both and talked about "sacrifice" and "compromise" and "fidelity," his flushed face and hot eyes so frightening that Benjy and I gripped hands and giggled.

The waitress smiles at my daughter, who ducks her head and kicks her stool. "Smile back when someone smiles at you," I tell her in a whisper.

"Not if I don't have to," my daughter whispers back.

The waitress asks if I'd like more coffee. I hesitate. I ought to go to Mr. Brown and get it over with, and then I ought to leave. But Mr. Brown's shadowed, tired, disinterested gaze, meeting mine once again in the mirror, makes me feel relaxed and expansive. If I am invisible, I reason, I can stay here all day. I can watch and listen like a ghost, a good ghost, who intends no harm. I lean my elbows on the counter and push my cup toward the girl.

"Yes please," I say. "Thank you."

Mr. Brown accepts more coffee too, and I hear the click of his spoon as he stirs in sugar. We lift our cups to our lips at the exact same instant, and at the exact same instant sip. Sipping still, I look at the clock. It is a large brown clock that says "Hudson's Hardware." It must have been here forever, and as I look at it I feel that I have been here forever too. I have a vision of the restaurant as a railway car, slipping down some track off the edge of the world, with all of us—my daughter, Mr. Brown, the waitress, the other customers—sailing off into space on a voyage that has no beginning and no end. I don't find this unpleasant, and I am sorry when an aproned boy comes out of the kitchen, picks the radio off the shelf, and carries it out with him, taking the Christmas music away.

"Bud made pea soup." The waitress's voice, insistent, floats down the counter.

"I'm not very hungry today," Mr. Brown says. "I think I'll just have some toast. Maybe an egg."

"And how would you like your egg?"

Mr. Brown doesn't answer.

"The usual?" the girl persists.

"That would be fine," he says mildly.

"We can't stay here all day." I rouse myself and turn to my daughter. "We've got a lot to do. Are you almost through?"

"If I be good . . ." my daughter begins.

"Yes," I prompt.

"Will I get everything I want? All the time? Always?"

"No one gets everything they want." This is an old speech, one I've given again and again. My daughter listens, chewing, her thoughts on her camera. Good is usually rewarded, I assure her. Mischief usually is not. Most people get what they deserve. I wipe her chin, wondering how this applies to Mr. Brown. What did he do to deserve to end up here, in Loretta's Coffee Shop, old and ill and so alone? He was never a tolerant man. He repeated the same jokes over and over. He ate and drank and smoked to excess. But he used to stand with his arms around the garbage bags, staring up at the moon, and he used to take his glasses off and wipe his eyes when he laughed. He never cheated or lied and he never personally ordered napalm poured on babies, as Benjy claimed. Benjy detested him. But I never did. I liked the way he confronted things: head on. When he and Benjy argued it was like watching a dog fight a cat: he would lunge straight for the heart of the question, while Benjy, evasive, leapt from side to side, answering each question with another of his own. These fights usually happened during television commercials. Mr. Brown would switch the sound off with his remote control, lean back in his leather recliner, and ask Benjy to explain to him once again why he was studying anthropology in college instead of business education: did he expect it to help him in the real world? "What do you call the real world?" Benjy would ask. "I call the real world the real world," Mr. Brown would shout, "damnit!" Benjy would grin as if he had just scored a point, but I never understood the point. Benjy and I could have used some definitions of "real world"; we weren't convinced it existed. Mr. Brown was. He still is. He is facing the mirror unadorned and unsmiling. When he looks up at the clock he sees the time and does not try to escape the time with visions of railway cars sailing through space.

My daughter reminds me of her presence by spilling her cocoa all over the counter; I sop it up with handfuls of thin paper napkins. "It was a accident," she explains in her unhushed voice. "Everybody has accidents." The waitress brings a cloth and helps me clean up as Mr. Brown, unnoticing, raises a piece of toast and bites down. His dentures make the same old click. Benjy would snort at the sound of that click, snort helplessly, unhappily, trying to catch my eye. Sometimes I'd grin back at him; sometimes I wouldn't. It was so easy to see how Benjy, with his notebook and his giggle, drove his father crazy, and I saw too how Mr. Brown, massive and complacent, made Benjy want to smash him. I stayed out of it. But by the time I left—by the time Benjy and I agreed that "sacrifice" and "compromise" and "fidelity" were real words in a real world we hadn't yet entered—by the time the marriage ended, I had contempt for them both. Shall I go to Mr. Brown and tell him that? Shall I take all the old angers and shake them over his breakfast plate? It doesn't matter if you don't remember me, I will say. You never did know me well. You used to call me Beautiful because you couldn't always remember my name. I wasn't important to you. Benjy was important to you, but you didn't think Benjy was an important person. In the end, I didn't either. In the end I disliked your boy as much as you did; I found him young and lacking too. You won, I'll say to Mr. Brown.

Mr. Brown reaches in the breast pocket of his shirt and pulls out a packet of cigarettes—not Marlboros but something lighter, with less nicotine and tar. The waitress, earrings dangling, strikes a match for him. For a second, leaning forward, with both hands clasped around his lit cigarette, Mr. Brown looks like the King of the Canyon again, regal and at ease. Then he coughs. The cough takes me as much by surprise as it seems to take him. The force of it lurches him sideways. He might lose his balance and fall off the stool, and I slip from my own stool, ready to catch him. I see myself breaking his fall, cradling his head; I imagine myself pushing the stiff white unwashed hair back from the staring eyes. It's all right, I will say. I'm here. I've come back. Diana is here, ready to take care of you in your old age.

But Mr. Brown composes himself and does not fall. The long quivering afterwaves of his cough fade as I pay my bill, leave my tip. The waitress reaches over the cash register and hands a small cellophane-wrapped candy cane to my daughter.

"What do you say?" I ask as my daughter takes it.

She will not answer.

"What do you say?" I repeat.

"I have to go to the bathroom," she says at last.

"The bathroom?"

"There's a rest room down there." The waitress points past Mr. Brown and I see we have to pass directly behind him. As we near him, I pause. The scarf I knit is close enough to touch, and it is stained and unraveled. I could offer to fix it. I still have the yarn. It wasn't that long ago, the summer I knit it. I remember sitting under the oak trees, listening to the splash from the swimming pool as Mr. Brown dove in, the clink of ice cubes from Billie's gin-and-tonic, the thud of a basketball as Benjy threw it again and again against the side of the house. My head was empty that summer except for the ticktock of knit-and-purl, and as I shook the scarf out over my bare sunburned legs I thought how nice it would look when it was finished, and how pleased Mr. Brown would be to have something from me. My daughter pulls at one hand and even as I follow her I am imagining how my other hand will look on Mr. Brown's shoulder, how I will pivot him gently, and gently say, Hello.

# The Christmas House

## GAIL GALLOWAY ADAMS

### From *The Purchase of Order* (1988)


Jelly bears and Swedish fish surrounded by sugar cones, me-
ringue rounds, and two pounds of assorted candies—nonpareils,
candy canes, curls of ribbon—are on the kitchen table. Dean dips
blunt scissors into hot water and snips the spearmint leaves in
half. He is the only child of an only child who did not begin that
way. For Dean his mother is the only connection to those who
lived before. How did this come to be? she thinks, smiling and
winking at her five-year-old, his cheeks bulging with sneaked
sweets. How could a family that so loved the idea of family be dissolved? What had become of her imagined life as mother of three
with a husband who'd dress up as Santa Claus?

Measuring vanilla into the icing, she thinks about this season.
Is it one of loss or gain, giving or receiving, remembering or for-
getting, rejoicing or mourning? Dying children get Christmas in
July, people ache to be home that day, suicides rise and blues
abound and all the magazines have articles on stress. Why, then,
do I feel happy? she wonders. "Jingle Bells" begins another time
on the radio on this second holiday Anne and Dean have been
alone. Here, a few days before Christmas, she sits with her son,
following the directions for a gingerbread castle they are build-

ing. It can always be a happy season, she thinks, if there are rituals to observe.

Years ago the three Howard children—Anne, Dean, and Carla—lived in Berlin. That was 1954, in the American zone of that divided city, after the airlift, after the war. Major Howard had been with the first Americans to move into Germany after World War II, his family safe in Ohio awaiting orders to join him. When they debarked in Bremerhaven after a stormy November voyage, he was there to meet them, his face ruddy above olive-brown wool.

"You look so good," he said again and again, hugging them, squeezing their shoulders, pinching their cheeks. "You look so good." The sight of his children, fresh-faced with straight teeth, seemed a miracle to him—he'd seen what war could do to children. Now Anne, Dean, and Carla, safe with him and their mother in Germany, were watched over by a succession of women who received in exchange a room, meals, a meager salary, Mrs. Howard's old clothes, and the Majors sympathy.

He had no judgment save pity in matters of the heart and always brought home wildly unsuitable women to help his wife clean the floors, chase after children, and cook meals. Ingeborg Pitsch, who acts as a stop in Anne's Christmas memory, came between Ursula Geike and Heidi Boehn, one fired because of wrong connections in the East, which even then was closing down, the other because she was sluttish, always having cramps and hiding pastries under her bed, an action Mrs. Howard was convinced attracted rats.

Ingeborg Pitsch and Christmas are linked for Anne in the way that blue lights tacked in a star shape might trigger memory in another person. Before the war she was a philosophy student at Frei University, sent to a labor camp for political activism, and then to a factory near Darmstadt where she made machinery and parachutes and survived. She had little family left: a brother, Klaus, in the East zone and a distant cousin who lived in Dahlem. Destitute, broken in body and spirit, she registered with the American Post Command as a translator and/or housekeeper and met Major Howard during an interview where she discussed Pushkin in Russian and was hired as an *au pair*. Ingeborg wore almost always a gray suit, once Mrs. Howard's, with the short skirt fashionable before Dior's new look, pleated blouse yellowed down the tucked lines, heavy lisle stockings that made her legs look wooden, and navy tie shoes with ribbed soles. Her homely big-boned face with its sharp nose and sunken lashless eyes was rarely still. When she raked back her hair nervously you noticed all her knuckles were too big. Her fingertips, like the skin over her cheeks, twitched as though galvanized. She'd had two mental breakdowns since the war's end, so at the Howards', while overlooking the long walled garden, she grew healthy relearning her English against the sounds of American life as lived by the transplanted Howards of Vogelsangstrasse. Another rusty-faced woman in *putz* clothes, Frau Kleist, came three times weekly to clean and cook and fill the air with odors of cabbage and potatoes boiled too long. She left only her acrid scent behind in the bathrooms she scrubbed.

Each evening Ingeborg shyly emerged to help set the table, or hold Carla on her lap and fit the baby's hands to the keyboard and play and sing German lullabies in a soft hoarse voice. Sometimes she would knock softly at twelve-year-old Anne's door, and when given admittance would stand, hands clasped earnestly in front, sneaking glances at the *Photoplay* pictures of Janet Leigh and James Dean pinned to the wall, and try to talk to Anne about the cinema.

Once she was somewhat recovered, Ingeborg returned to her studies at the university, left the Howards, and rented a room in Dahlem. She came monthly to fetch Anne for walks down Lindenstrasse, S-Bahn rides, lunches of noodles with oxtail gravy and mineral water, and lectures on German culture, German

history, Schiller, Goethe, Brecht, and ballet. She never mentioned her lost family, friends, her labor, the holocaust, or her
lost history. She received a tutor's wage to shepherd a sullen girl,
and Anne, walking beside her resentfully, thought that Ingeborg
smelled like so many Germans, of heavy sweaters and suits never
cleaned that exuded sweat and grease, the musty odor of clothes
worn as blankets during cold nights. Anne disliked most Ingeborg's earnestness, the standing-back as she pushed Anne forward to mumble to a store clerk, *"Entschuldigung Sie mir, bitte.
Wieviel kostet es?"* Then make a false purchase, lesson done. She
secretly scorned Ingeborg's pride in her as a pupil, pride that
flushed a circle around Inge's mouth.

Once Anne went to the East zone with Ingeborg. First riding
the S-Bahn, then switching to the U-Bahn, they did not get off
when they were supposed to. Both trains were lettered with the
same red signs. There were announcements that said *Achtung*!
Anne was excited and afraid with the feeling that although people went into the East, no one wanted to stay there. It was too
cold, and poor, and everywhere were eyes. The canned goods and
American cigarettes the Howards gave Ingeborg helped her keep
her brother Klaus alive. Anne remembers they took him C ra-
tions left over from maneuvers, khaki cans with patties of con-
centrated cocoa, flat tin circles of jam.

When the last train stopped they got off, walking quickly.
Anne remembers nothing about Klaus except that he wore a
beige Shaker sweater that her mother had knitted for the Major,
but the sleeves were too long; Klaus had the cuffs folded back.
Was it a December day that she remembers as Inge's tears spotted the table, and smelling dust and emptiness in a bleak room
furnished only with a cot, a table, two chairs, and a calendar
bright with goose-girl scenes? The cheese they brought loosened
in its wax paper, seemed to grow during the long afternoon. Anne
leaned against the window, looking out at rubble, listening to Ingeborg and Klaus talking in low voices. Years later she asked her

father why Klaus hadn't left the East zone. How would anyone have known if he had just walked out of his apartment, stayed on the train into the West and not swung off to wave goodbye, already turned sideways to avoid Inge's weeping, hand clutching her bangs? Why didn't he simply stay with them to debark at Kurfürstendam to ride the double-decker bus down the wide linden-lined avenue that those who didn't know Berlin before the war thought beautiful? Why not end up with his sister, safe at the Howards' house to live on the third floor and eat sour bean salad and knockwurst and do chores?

"They always knew where you were." The Major's voice spoke, thin with age. "Once you were identified, they always knew." His hand pressing the remote control made the TV images jump.

Now Anne's parents live in a pink adobe house in Tampa and Mrs. Howard endlessly washes lettuce in the kitchen. Her father remembers little of the Berlin years, or pretends not to, but he knew that Klaus had lists, knew of lists; there was something to do with Inge's brother and hidden papers, hidden lives, that trapped him in the squares of bleak rubble, the landscape of broken brick, window frames propped on concrete blocks, the refuse of war still on the ground piled in pyres that was the East. On the West side such sites existed too and the children, American and German, clambered the twisted wire rope that marked them *verboten* to balance on slabs of downed tenements.

Anne's brother Dean was five when Ingeborg lived with them. He would dart from his room to where she stood and butt his head into her stomach, bending over and hitting gut-high, boring into her like the story Anne had read of a weasel who could only get out of a sack by eating through a boy's heart.

"*Ach, ach,*" Ingeborg would laugh, patting Dean's tabled back, twisting him from side to side, dancing in a strange, slow waltz. He could speak German better than any of them and often went with her to buy the evening's bread. "*Sechs brotchen, bitte,*" he'd pipe and bring back gummy bears as treats. The first time Anne saw them for sale in an American store she wanted to protest. To-night they are heaped on her table, stained glass shapes melting into each other.

Dean was another casualty of war. He joined the Marines af-ter his freshman college year. A square-faced boy with small, set-apart teeth, Dean was a ball player in high school, made good grades, and never caused his family any disappointment. Ma-jor Howard was angry that Dean didn't get his application in on time and ended up at teachers' college when time ran out, but Mrs. Howard didn't mind. She liked him to come home week-ends, to do his laundry. She liked to see the knickknacks shake with his bounds down the stairs. Anne had married by then, but remembers that first Christmas when Dean talked of his classes in code—Chem and Econ and Poly Sci; he was not engaged by any of them. The Christmas House that year was a log cabin con-structed from chocolate cookies and whipped cream.

During the spring semester he left school, became a Marine, and left for Vietnam to fulfill the dreams of life's adventures that they hadn't known he'd harbored. His letters were written to be read aloud, so intense with romantic description it seemed he wrote with a thesaurus at hand. Writing of that lush, green, alien atmosphere, he told of "air so humid it flattens your head." Sweat beaded his stubbled hair, wet his face, pooled in his collarbones, smeared the ink of his paragraphs. "My socks are never dry, Mom," he wrote, "so I pretend I'm wading in puddles like I used to do." December 17, 1968, Dean was blasted in the chest, blown back against a tree where he sat erect with his head hanging down; he died looking at the wound that killed him. He was sent home wrapped in layers of slick greenish-black rubber, sheathed like a tree's roots, balled and burlapped, to be lowered into the earth.

The hole that waits always seems too large for the tree. How can this small live fir, thriving so nicely in a pot of bright red foil, need so much room outside? Anne thinks. It does not seem possible that it will ever grow larger than waist high. She and her son Dean have decorated it with eight ornaments: straw stars, starched string rounds. Her brother's grave was so much larger than he was. There was never the possibility of filling the hole by hand, even if each mourner, each person who loved him, had heaved shovelsful of earth, carpets of flowers. A small tanklike bulldozer waited to push flat the soil over Dean's and so many other boys' graves.

His December death ended the Christmas season for her parents, who never recovered from the shock, the knowledge that as they chose wallets, books, and socks, packed divinity and fudge, and wrapped hermit's nest cookies in tissue paper, their son was on his way to dying. After Dean's death they never bought another Advent calendar. It was too hard to pull back the paper portals that counted down the days to his death. Harder still to open the days that followed, each one leading to a last door, which when swung wide revealed the promise of the world's only son, knowing that their boy was dead.

Dean, the third, scoops frosting from a can and adds green color drops. He was named after his dead uncle; it is his grandfather's name too. After the divorce Anne took back the last name Howard that she'd grown up with and put it on again. It fit like an old letter jacket, slightly shrunken, somewhat dated, still comfortable. Dean kept his father's last name, and she hopes that this might make her former husband care. He lives in California now and sends Dean wonderful gifts—link-lock castles, talking teddy bears—elaborately wrapped and mailed from a store. Dean and Anne form miniature popcorn balls to set atop sticks of trees that dot this sugary landscape. M&M's are forced into the sticky circles to become small Christmas ornaments. Dean selects carefully, red, yellow, green, rejecting the tan, the rust, the brown.

"Save those colors for the path, Mommy," he commands. Then wheedles, "Do the grass, Mommy, do the grass next." He is impatient to get to sprinkle light green coconut shreds in a sweet snow.

Anne piles M&M's as building blocks. She thinks, as she ices the flat side of the cardboard courtyard, of what is left to do before her parents come. Turkey thawing, all the side dishes of cranberry relish and creamed onions that her mother doesn't like to fix are done. The onion dressing and the pies, pumpkin and mince, await grandmother's touch. Dean can hardly wait to see his grandfather, whose hands are rough as a dry sponge, each finger with a space between that never closes since arthritis came. Rubbing the heel of his hand on the crown of Dean's head, he makes his cowlick stand straight up.

Carla, Anne's younger sister by fourteen years, was a war casualty too. Closer to her brother in age and temperament, she was his admirer, hater, and purest friend, for in addition to being good in school and sports he was good to his little sister. After his death Carla grew quiet, then quieter, finished college, became a teacher of third grade, and continued to wear her hair held off her forehead by a tortoise barrette. A woman who wears horn-rims, jogs in a purple sweat suit from Sears, Carla still lives at home and saves her money for an annual Christmas cruise. She will be in the Bahamas dancing, Anne hopes, under the Caribbean stars wearing a dress of pink pique. Anne recalls Carla's college graduation with all the girls wearing black robes ending in red Nikes; the boys with ponytails poking out of their mortarboards. Many held signs "End the War," while others refused to stand during the national anthem.

"Carla's going to the Bahamas with a school group," Anne's mother had written, "so you and Dean had better make the Christmas House."

Carla was a baby when Ingeborg Pitsch scooted behind her on stockinged knees down the corridors in the dark old house on Vogelsangstrasse. Carla sat as center ornament in a card table on wheels with a cutout in the middle, her fat baby feet propelling it along. Ingeborg followed, inched her way, limbo-weaving on her knees, arms outstretched, murmuring, *"Liebchen, liebe, Kommen sie hier, bleibt bie mir."* Carla scrabbled backward, then crowed with delight as the play chair tipped, threatened to topple.

This is the first Christmas House that Anne will build from scratch, the first that Dean is really old enough to help with or appreciate. Building this one, she remembers the first. Ingeborg, then living in a small flat, invited Anne for a Christmas House celebration, a German custom the Howards hadn't heard of, and one in which Anne was not interested. She was busy memorizing the lyrics to "A Little Love" and trying to find out what teenagers in America were doing. Worse, Ingeborg had invited another girl—a German—for Anne to meet. The Major, always enthusiastic about such cultural exchanges, accepted. Mrs. Howard, rolling Anne's hair, coiling strands like snail shells, sympathized with her daughter. She also did not like the way Germans smelled. She was suspicious of them, and her fears were deeper than slogan prejudice. Everywhere the Germans lied that they hadn't known what was happening to people in the camps, the Jews, so she distrusted them, even Ingeborg. Wasn't Ingeborg's brother still in the East? Didn't that mean something? But still she laid out Anne's clothes, wanting her daughter to look nice, bring credit to her family, her country.

Ingeborg's flat was one alcove and one room, small, dark, crowded with furniture, full of the smell of food sitting out, of books imperfectly dried and now mildewed, gray fluff in their creases. There was the cloying sweetness of marzipan, the incongruity of garlic sausage exploding with grease next to bittersweet chocolate brittle across a torte, a saucer of raspberry jam nearby. Anne felt no liking for the table, too heavily laden with strange food, or for the German girl Liesl with her heavy mottled legs, thick socks, and plump breasts flattened by a dirndl.

Everything that girl was, Anne did not want to be, splotch-cheeked with fuzzy French braids, alight with excitement at meeting a foreigner. Anne was aloof, a peroxided streak in her bangs, her lower lids lined with black. She nibbled the pfeffernussen, licked solemnly at the marzipan, her least favorite taste, and drank the lemonade. They talked in German, Anne's halting, then in English, Liesl's better. Ingeborg watched them intently, ticking her head from side to side, mouth twitching the words in correct pronunciation. Once she huddled them, and Anne smelled her, not rank but strong. Her nylon blouse showed that her slip strap had slipped to the vaccination hollow of her arm. She held the two girls close, pressing their cheeks hard against hers, as though they would break into trio harmony, the McGuire Sisters crooning "*Liebe, liebe.*"

The raspberry torte was dry, crunching to dust, the pudding thin, cheesed with gelatinous strands. The room grew hotter, close with doggy wafts from the German girls' wet wool socks. Noises from another room or the flat next door grew louder and Anne's head ached. Liesl never stopped smiling, cheeks staining redder, eyes glowing as night came. Ingeborg switched on a lamp, throwing over it a printed scarf that shadowed the room with leaves. Music swelled from the radio as she lit the Christmas House. Ringed around its icing yard were twisted silver trees with candles in their centers. The candles too were twisted spirals of white. One by one they sprung to flame, illuminating the candy house that she had built for them, all gingerbread ormolu, windows of melted sugar, spun thin, rolled flat, a roof rickracked with thick paste dripping down in icicles: a perfect chalet of patience and desire. The two girls ooh'ed and ah'ed. Anne couldn't help it. It was too beautiful to maintain her armored poise. They leaned to look, pushing their hands back and forth as if they would touch it. Ingeborg looked anxiously at them.

"*Der kuchen ist sehr schön,*" Anne praised.

"Is bootiful," said Liesel.

"Ah, good," said Ingeborg. "I am much pleased. *Sehr gut.* Now eat." She waved her hand as if to say, "Let the feast begin."

Both girls shook their heads no, oh no, they couldn't, how could they eat such a beautiful thing? It must be left, to be saved, to be seen, to be enjoyed.

Impatiently Ingeborg shook her head, said, "To eat, it is to eat. For this I made it. To see you, for you to see, then eat it."

Even as they protested again, she snapped off a shard of ice smelling of almonds and pressed it into Anne's hand, then broke off the door and lifted it to Liesl's lips. "Please, *bitte, alles essen, bitte*," she begged. "To eat—*esse zusammen* for me."

They stood shyly, eating tiny bits, plucking up a golden gatelock coin, a candy cane marking an eave, as Ingeborg, tilting her head from side to side, moving her jaws in encouraging chewing motions, watched them eat the beautiful Christmas House. As they ate, growing greedy, the girls began to giggle, sputtering pieces of cake, and Ingeborg was pleased, smiled widely, embraced them, happy at this breaking-down of barriers.

The last hour of that night was an exercise of smiles and blushes, crumbs spilled and liquid spilled, and parcels wrapped to take home; the exchange of addresses became embraces and the exchange of affections. Anne was bundled into her coat as Ingeborg tenderly wound a muffler around her neck. Liesl helped Anne with her gloves. Then they walked her to the bus stop, holding hands unselfconsciously, and snow softly fell, hazing the streetlamps, dimming the bus lights as it charged through the mists. Anne leaned across a seat to wave at the two standing under the light, their shoulders covering up with snow, bulky as epaulets.

Telling her family about the evening, handing Dean the present wrapped in tissue paper printed with pines, he asking "What is it? What's in it?" her parents wanting to know who was there, how it was, Anne to her horror and embarrassment burst into tears. She didn't know why she couldn't explain it. So she did not protest her mother's explanation of too long a day, too much strain being with people unlike oneself all day. Even as she sobbed against her father's chest, she knew her mother's reason were wrong. Dean ate the icing off a roof's edge and Carla ate a marzipan fruit which turned her lips orange.

The next year, back in the States, in a suburban Virginia high school, Anne was elected cheerleader, cut her hair shorter with bangs, and was told she looked like Molly Bee. That December, Major Howard brought home a Christmas House and thus began the Howard tradition of having a different house each year in a different style. That one was from the NCO Wives' Bake Sale.

"It looks like a quonset hut. Nothing like Ingeborg's," complained Anne.

"You decorate them, right?" asked her father. "Soldiers need Christmas Houses too."

Her mother made khaki icing and outlined the windows with silver dragées. "Your dad was in the Army Air Force, but never got to fly. And never got over his love for hangars, kid."

Dean set an Army helicopter model right in front of the house. He'd made a little sign: Rudolph the Red-Nosed Copter.

The year that Dean died in Vietnam they'd started the house right after Thanksgiving so he'd have a photograph of it finished. It was called "Snow Covered Lodge," its frosted roof thick with white pebbles of nonpareils.

Here in this kitchen Anne Howard and her son Dean are finally ready. All the castle parts are made, cooled, laid out along the plans; they must only be assembled. Dean holds up the first walls, their glued edges of icing stick and clinch. The third threatens to cave in. With the fourth it becomes a bungalow of hard brown bread. They're both intense and sticky. The table is littered with knives, spoons, spatulas, every implement to be used for decoration.

"Look, Mommy." Dean holds out a hand webbed with spun sugar, fingers encased in a sticky net. "I'm a duck."

She reaches for him, first licking her own fingers, then cleaning his hands with kissing licks.

"Leave some for me," he says. He solemnly sucks his two middle fingers as he did for comfort as a baby, then moves his mouth back and forth as though playing a harmonica as he eats icing off his wrist. "What do we do when it's done?" he asks.

"We look at it, admire it, say how did we do it—then after everyone's seen it we eat it."

"Eat it?" His voice is incredulous.

"That's the best part."

"We eat it," he says with a giggle.

"Gobble, gobble," she says, making him laugh.

This Christmas Castle was hard to put together, hardly the simple project, the easy evening Anne had thought and the magazine directions promised. Walls fell in, candies slid down icing to plop in the yard and get lost in the frosting drifts, tree cones toppled and died. Assembling a house took a touch she didn't seem to have. Her fingers stuck, pulled things apart even as the edges tried to hold. Finally, as she and Dean carefully, so carefully, cement the roof in place, she remembers Ingeborg's hands with their huge bruised-looking knuckles. In repose her hands were always cupped, the skin trembling with involuntary commands to fist up and protect the hidden lifeline in the palm. Ingeborg's hand looms up, candle lit. That glorious Christmas bungalow that she had built and then urged its destruction is somehow here on this table. And the two girls—so different—gingerbread pilling their lips, laughing as they crunched the open doors of Ingeborg's offering, are grown with their own children.

"Let me tell you a story, Dean."

"You're sure that we eat it?" Dean asks again.

"Absolutely," Anne says, "or what did we do it for?"

# CONTRIBUTORS

GAIL GALLOWAY ADAMS is a professor emeritus at West Virginia University, where she taught creative writing for more than twenty years. Adams served as fiction editor for *Arts and Letters: A Literary Journal* and for the *Potomac Review*. She has been a reader/judge for several short fiction awards series. She has recently taught at Kenyon College, West Virginia Wesleyan College, and the Wild Acres Writers Workshop. She also works privately as a short story and novel editorial consultant and lives on a small family ranch in central Texas.

DAVID CROUSE is the author of the short story collections *Copy Cats* (2005), winner of the Flannery O'Connor Award for Short Fiction, and *The Man Back There*, as well as numerous other short stories and essays. *The Man Back There* (2008) was awarded the Mary McCarthy Prize. David lives in Seattle, Washington, where he teaches in the University of Washington's MFA Program. His new collection of short fiction, *When I Was a Stranger*, is currently looking for a publisher.

MOLLY GILES, Flannery O'Connor Award winner in 1985 for *Rough Translations*, has subsequently published a novel, *Iron Shoes*, and three other award-winning short story collections, *Creek Walk*, *All the Wrong Places*, and *Bothered*. Retired from teaching at San Francisco State University and the University of Arkansas, she lives in Woodacre, California.

CAROLE L. GLICKFELD grew up in New York City, the setting of *Useful Gifts*, her award-winning collection of stories about a family with deaf parents and hearing children, and *Swimming toward the Ocean*, a novel that won the Washington State Book Award. She is the recipient of a Literary Fellowship from the National Endowment for the Arts and a Governor's Arts Award (Washington State) and was a fellow of both the Mac-Dowell Colony and the Bread Loaf Writers' Conference. Her stories, essays, and poems have appeared in numerous literary journals and anthologies. Now living in Seattle, where she has taught creative writing, she works on a consulting basis with aspiring writers on their manuscripts when she is not indulging her passion for travel.

JACQUELIN GORMAN, Flannery O'Connor Award winner in 2012 for *The Viewing Room*, teaches creative writing at Stevenson University in Baltimore, Maryland. She previously published a memoir, *The Seeing Glass* (1997), and is currently writing a collection of personal essays.

PETER LASALLE is the author of seven previous books, including novels and short story collections—most recently *Mariposa's Song* and *What I Found Out about Her*. His fiction and essays have been selected for several award anthologies, including *Best American Short Stories*, *Best American Mystery Stories*, *Best American Fantasy*, *Best American Travel Writing*, *Sports Best Short Stories*, *Best of the West*, and *Prize Stories: The O. Henry Awards*. He lives in Austin, Texas, where he is a member of the creative writing faculty at the University of Texas, and Narragansett, in his native Rhode Island.

KARIN LIN-GREENBERG story collection *Faulty Predictions* won the 2013 Flannery O'Connor Award and also won gold in the short story category of *Foreword Reviews'* 2014 INDIEFAB Book of the Year. Her stories have appeared in literary journals including the *Antioch Review*, *Epoch*, *Kenyon Review Online*, *North American Review*, and *Shenandoah*, and she was a finalist for the *Chicago Tribune*'s 2018 Nelson Algren Award. Her many writing honors include a MacDowell Colony fellowship and an appointment as Tennessee Williams Scholar at the Sewanee Writers' Conference. She lives in upstate New York and is an associate professor in the English Department at Siena College.

BECKY MANDELBAUM won the Flannery O'Connor Award in 2016 for her collection *Bad Kansas*, which was selected as a 2018 Kansas Notable Book and as a finalist for the 2018 High Plains Book Award for first book. Her first novel, *The Hurting Animals*, is forthcoming from Simon and Schuster. She currently lives in Washington's Skagit Valley.

ALYCE MILLER is the award-winning author of three collections of stories, a novel, and a book of nonfiction, as well as more than two hundred and fifty stories, poems, essays, and articles. An ex-Californian, she taught for twenty years in the English Department at Indiana University, Bloomington, and now lives in Washington, D.C.

DIANNE NELSON OBERHANSLY's latest book is *The Madonna of Starbucks*. Her Flannery O'Connor Award–winning collection *A Brief History of Male Nudes in America* was published in 1993. *Downwinders: An Atomic Tale*, which she cowrote with Curtis Oberhansly, was chosen as a Utah Book of the Year. Nelson Oberhansly's fiction has appeared widely in journals, including in the *Iowa Review, Ploughshares*, and the *New England Review*, and her poems have been published in *Paper Nautilus, Canary, Third Wednesday*, and elsewhere. She lives in rural Utah, where she is a hiker, a slow food enthusiast, and an arts supporter and educator.

PETER SELGIN is the author of *Drowning Lessons*, winner of the 2007 Flannery O'Connor Award for Short Fiction. He has written a novel, an essay collection, three books on the craft of writing, and several children's books. His memoir, *The Inventors*, won the 2017 Housatonic Book Award. He is an affiliate faculty member of Antioch University's low-residency MFA program in Los Angeles and an associate professor of English at Georgia College and State University in Milledgeville, Georgia.

HUGH SHEEHY teaches creative writing and literature at Ramapo College of New Jersey. He lives in Beacon, New York.

SANDRA THOMPSON has published a novel, *Wild Bananas*. She was a columnist, writer, and editor at the *St. Petersburg Times*, where she directed and edited a series that won the Pulitzer Prize. She lives in Tampa, Florida, and in New York.

ANNIVERSARY ANTHOLOGIES

TENTH ANNIVERSARY
*The Flannery O'Connor Award: Selected Stories,*
EDITED BY CHARLES EAST

FIFTEENTH ANNIVERSARY
*Listening to the Voices:*
*Stories from the Flannery O'Connor Award,*
EDITED BY CHARLES EAST

THIRTIETH ANNIVERSARY
*Stories from the Flannery O'Connor Award:*
*A 30th Anniversary Anthology: The Early Years,*
EDITED BY CHARLES EAST
*Stories from the Flannery O'Connor Award:*
*A 30th Anniversary Anthology: The Recent Years,*
EDITED BY NANCY ZAFRIS

THEMATIC ANTHOLOGIES

*Hold That Knowledge: Stories about Love*
*from the Flannery O'Connor Award for Short Fiction,*
EDITED BY ETHAN LAUGHMAN
*The Slow Release: Stories about Death*
*from the Flannery O'Connor Award for Short Fiction,*
EDITED BY ETHAN LAUGHMAN
*Rituals to Observe: Stories about Holidays*
*from the Flannery O'Connor Award for Short Fiction,*
EDITED BY ETHAN LAUGHMAN
*Spinning Away from the Center: Stories about*
*Homesickness and Homecoming*
*from the Flannery O'Connor Award for Short Fiction,*
EDITED BY ETHAN LAUGHMAN

CPSIA information can be obtained
at www.ICGtesting.com
Printed in the USA
LVHW111948221019
634997LV00003B/305/P

9 780820 356594